DMB

W9-AXW-233

THE LIGHT
IN THE WOODS

A POST HILL PRESS BOOK

The Light in the Woods
© 2017 by Jean Marie Pierson
All Rights Reserved

ISBN: 978-1-68261-401-3
ISBN (eBook): 978-1-68261-402-0

Cover Design by Phil Rose
Interior Design and Composition by Greg Johnson/Textbook Perfect

Post Hill Press
New York • Nashville
posthillpress.com

Published in the United States of America

THE LIGHT
IN THE WOODS

JEAN MARIE PIERSON

For Guy Francis

*… because you have hidden these things from the wise and learned,
and revealed them to little children.
Yes, Father, for this is what you were pleased to do.*

–Luke 10:21

CHAPTER 1

Grigonis House – Pittstown, New Jersey, last year

Sunlight flooded through the living room windows in the late afternoon, making squares and rectangles on the oval braided rugs where Ava sat playing with her grandfather's toy midget racer. He would have been sitting next to her, tracing its wheels around the rope track if he wasn't dying in the next room. Ava turned the car around the groves of the braided rug. Three of its wheels rocked and wobbled, while one did not move at all. The yellow metal racing car with the chipped red "8" was Ava's favorite, mostly because it was Pop-pop's favorite. Many Sundays ago, when he was well, they would spend the afternoons on that rug and race his collection of toy metal cars. The white sheer curtains would roll and billow in the open windows like starting flags and waves of the crowd. The spectators were always the same. They were family. Young and in black and white. Mostly people Ava never met. All long gone. A couple on their wedding day. A woman in a feather hat. A little girl with big glasses waving. A man and a young boy standing next to each other on a snowy day. All sat frozen in time around their woolen track in their cheap tinny picture frames. Some she imagined cheering her on and some cheering for

1

Pop-pop. The two would start their engines, with a powerful breath flapping through their rubbery lips. Ava would start out strong once the handkerchief dropped but Pop-pop's racer usually caught up to her by the third rope. At that point something inevitably happened to his engine and he would pull back, allowing the number 8 to easily pass him for a victory.

She knew better than to ask her mother if she could go into Pop-pop's bedroom to give him the car to fix. Her mom wouldn't let her disturb him for mere auto maintenance. But since her mom was in the kitchen folding clothes with Pop-pop's Polish hospice nurse, Ava thought he wouldn't mind if she stopped in for a quick visit.

Her little hand gently pushed the door open. You wouldn't know it was daytime as no sun made its way into the room. No billowy sheer curtains hung from curtain rods. Long swatches of velvet green fabric stood guard in front of the windows, blocking out all light. Machines beeped and hissed as her grandfather lay in bed, covered with blankets too hot and heavy for a late summer's afternoon.

Ava walked slowly over to his side of the bed and watched him sleep. His lungs made clicking sounds as his chest rose and fell. His face, normally smiling and cheerful, looked contorted in pain. His exhales sounded more like moans then breaths. She held the number 8 racer in one hand while she shook his shoulder gently with the other.

"Pop-pop? Can you get up?" she asked as she held the car up to his sealed shut eyes. "Pop-pop, you need to fix this."

But his pained expression didn't change as he continued to sleep. Ava kept shaking him until she heard her mother open the door.

"Ava!" her mother said in a loud whisper as she placed a stack of clean towels on the vanity. "Ava Grigonis, come here. Pop-pop's asleep."

Ava answered in a louder whisper, "I know but it's broken! How can I race if the wheels don't move?"

Ava's mother hustled to the other side of the room and quickly shooed her daughter out the door. Once outside the whispering stopped.

"Sweetie, you know Pop-pop is tired and is not feeling well. He needs his rest."

"I know but…"

"Please, honey," she breathed. Ava noticed her mother's face had more lines on it than it did at the beginning of the summer. "Not now. I've told you time and again to just let him rest."

"But what if…" Ava began to say as she clutched the racecar in front of her face in an attempt to hide her frown. Her green eyes peered and pleaded at her mom over the little hood. "What if…"

"What if, what?"

Ava's eyes turned in the direction of Pop-pop's door. Her seven-year-old expression appeared as pained as her grandfather's. "What if he doesn't wake up?"

Her mother lowered the car down from her face and stroked her cheek. She smiled sadly.

"He will wake up again. I promise." Her mother pursed her lips together and blinked twice. Ava had seen this face before. It was usually when her mom wasn't sure if she believed what was coming out of her mouth. As if she held the words tight enough inside her teeth it would make them true.

Her mother bent over and kissed Ava, resting her cheek on top of Ava's head for a time longer than Ava liked. Anything longer than a couple of seconds meant that the hug was more for her mother's comfort than her own. That scared her. She was relieved when Pop-pop's nurse, Berta, came into the room and broke her mother's embrace.

"Marion?" said Berta in a thick Polish accent. Her brow wrinkled with worry as she wiped a juice glass. Neither surprised Ava as the stern look of concern was Berta's permanent expression and her hands were always busy cleaning something. "Your father has visitors."

Ava's mother stood up and ran her hand along her forehead. She looked around the room confused. "Really? Are they family?"

"No. Say they are old friends of Raymond Kozak."

"That's odd. Everyone has already come by," her mother said as the three made their way towards the kitchen. Ava watched her mother shoot Berta a knowing look as Berta nodded in agreement. Two weeks earlier, family and friends paraded in to sit next to her sick grandfather in bed. They all acted the same. They walked into his room happy and left wiping their eyes. Ava couldn't understand why. Back then he could still talk and although most of what he said didn't make sense, he looked far better than he did now. Now, he was curled up in a fetal position with his eyes constantly closed, like every second alive on earth was agony. He no longer recognized Ava. He knew her mother only for fleeting moments before drifting away in some medicated sleep. He called out for people Ava didn't know. Names she remembered hearing around the dinner table and some names that sounded as if they were in another language. The disease that overtook his body rewound his brain and turned him back to being a kid. In his mind, it was the 1940s and he still lived in his childhood home on Jacob's Lane in a small town on the very tip of Long Island. He was not an elderly man spending his remaining days in his daughter's farmhouse in New Jersey. When he could talk, he would say things that would warm a heart. Like how he couldn't wait for to Christmas to come. How he knew Santa Claus personally. How Santa's reindeer kept an eye on him from the backyard, even in the summer. Ava loved when he would tell her his Christmas stories. But as he got sicker, he didn't just say these things to Ava, but to everyone who came to see him. Doctors, friends, even their priest. It got so bad that when he mentioned Christmas, her mother would cringe. But now the cancer wreaked such havoc on his body that he could no longer speak. They all ached to hear something come from his lips that wasn't a moan or a cry. Her mother's voice now raised an octave every time she walked into that dark room and spoke to him. Ava thought that this is what her mother must have sounded like when she was a little girl. That maybe she spoke this way in hopes of Pop-pop recognizing her. But it wouldn't work. Her voice sounded too sad. From outside the room, it sounded like a heartbroken child tending to a dying one.

"I thought it was odd too," said Berta as she puffed up her chest. "That's why I kept them outside."

"Oh, Berta, they could've come in," her mother said as she tried in vain to straighten up the kitchen, collecting medicine bottles, dropping them into the plastic pink hospital buckets. "I'm sure some elderly men wouldn't hurt us."

Berta pointed her hand towel at the door. "That is why they're outside. They are not old."

Ava walked to the window and peeked through the café curtains. On the stoop stood two men: one tall and lean wearing beige pants with his hands stuffed in his pockets and a clean linen shirt, the other, shorter man wearing dungaree overalls, a long-sleeved shirt and a tweed checked cap. Ava thought it odd as it was too hot to wear a hat, let alone long sleeves. Odder still, she saw no car in the driveway. For a house located in the middle of a field with only a long dirt road leading up to it, there was always a car. Her mother must not have been too concerned as she opened the door to greet the two men. The taller one's face seemed to light up when he saw her mother.

"Marion Kozak?" asked the man in beige. Ava crept out from behind her mother's pant leg and stood in front to get a better look at the men. She wasn't afraid. Her mother, however, put her arms around Ava's shoulders and held her close.

"Yes. Well, no. I was Marion Kozak. It's Marion Grigonis now," she said but the man's attention quickly turned to Ava. He bent over and faced her at eye level.

"And this must be Ava," he said with a smile.

Ava couldn't help but smile sweetly at the man. His eyes seemed warm and friendly like her grandfather's. She felt her mother's grip tighten.

"Yes, but you'll have to excuse me, sir. How do we know you?"

"I'm sorry," he said in a friendly tone. "My name is John. John Charles. Your father did work for my company for many years." He then took his right hand out of his pocket and held out a business card. Ava's expression changed in an instant from smiles to horror, as if the man was handing her mother a dead cat instead of a small piece of paper. Her mother reached for his hand and then stopped suddenly. Along with missing a few digits, his hand was completely disfigured. Ava had only seen hands this twisted in old people and not in a man that was no older than her mother. The short man in the cap behind him let out chuckle.

"It's alright," John Charles said. "They don't hurt."

Her mother took the card. She opened her eyes wider and moved the card to a place where she could read it without her glasses.

"INR," she read. Her studied expression dissolved into a smile. "I know this! I remember seeing checks on Dad's desk with this logo. For years, actually."

"Yes," John Charles said with a smile. "He's one of my go-to guys around the holidays. Never let me down. We just wanted to stop by and thank him for all his good work. We didn't want to miss a chance to say…" John Charles looked down at Ava quickly, then back up to her mother. "To say hello while we were in the area."

A loud whistle screeched from the kitchen, then stopped abruptly. Her mother looked back inside, then at the men.

"The kettle's boiled. Please, will you come in?"

Berta had already set enough cups on the counter for the men as they entered into the kitchen. John Charles introduced himself to Berta with a handshake. His gnarled hands didn't make her flinch like Ava or her mom. Nothing about the human body seemed to faze Berta. Ava thought she might go lightly on John Charles' hand, like when she would lift Pop-pop up to eat or take his pills. But she did not. She greeted the two men like everyone else: with a knuckle-breaking hand squeeze and one hard yank of the arm, as if she were shaking crumbs off a tablecloth. Ava winced but it didn't seem to bother John Charles. He just kept smiling.

"Dad is resting now," her mother said. "He might wake up soon. Please have a seat. I am so curious to hear about your company."

John Charles moved towards the table as the man with the cap looked down at the number 8 racer in Ava's hand.

"I remember those," he said as he took off his cap and stuffed it into his back pocket. "I used to play with these ages ago." For the first time she saw the man smile. He had a dimple like hers on his right cheek. Ava held it up so he could get a better look.

"It doesn't run," said Ava, defeated. "See?" She plopped on the floor in front of him and rolled it on the ground, illustrating the car's flaws. She rocked the only working wheels back and forth to show him the loud squeak. "The wheels are broken."

The man sat right down on the floor and crossed his legs tightly in front of him. Lowering his head, he closely examined the motion of the car. His expression looked more as if he were reading the racer than just observing its movements.

"I think your wheels are ok. It might just be the axles." He reached out to pick up the racer, then stopped suddenly. He asked with his hand suspended in the air, "May I?"

Ava looked at her mom, who nodded to her that it was fine.

"Sure, Mister," she said.

His rough and stained hands held the racer eye level to them both. A second smile stretched across his face as his thumb glided over the chipped red number "8". His concentration broke as he looked over the hood to Ava.

"Is this one your favorite?" he asked. Ava nodded her little head up and down affirmatively. He let out a quiet chuckle.

"Yeah," he answered as he spun the squeaky wheel. "It was mine too."

CHAPTER 2

Jacob's Lane – Southold, New York, 1944

She couldn't look at Ray as she pulled him through the woods. Ray had never seen his mother this angry. She hadn't even bothered to button her winter coat before she tore out of the door to get him. Her one hand clasped the front lapels together while her other hand gripped Ray under his armpit. He stumbled along the path to keep up with her as his left foot could barely touch the ground. His mother's fury gave her petite frame the strength of ten dads as she dragged him down the wooded path. He noticed the unpacked snow over the fallen leaves and twigs rose up and froze against her bare ankles. If she weren't so angry, Ray thought, she'd notice she was cold. He tried not to look at her face but couldn't help himself. Her glare cut a trail through thickets and trees that crowded around the path. No breath came from her mouth but the cold streams of air shot out her nostrils like an angry bull. It wasn't until they broke free from the cluster of trees and made it into the open clearing of their backyard when she seemed to find the words.

Ray's mother whirled him around and grabbed his other shoulder, squaring his contorted ten-year-old face up to her frozen hazel stare.

Her feminine fingers nearly punctured Ray's winter coat. Each word was punctuated by a slight shake. "Raymond. James. Kozak. How could you?"

"He's old enough," he said, ashamed that his voice was slightly trembling. Her anger frightened him.

"He's six years old, Raymond! Barely out of kindergarten. How would you have felt if…"

Her stare suddenly broke as she looked over his head. Ray looked over his shoulder to see Olive Mott, his fellow classmate and next-door neighbor. She stood quietly at the end of his driveway watching the scene unfold. Olive wiped the snow off one of her lenses with a thick mismatched mitten without taking the glasses off her face. Ray figured Olive came to see if his mother was actually going to murder him. After meeting his mother's glare, Olive nervously pushed her scarf over her nose and shuffled back through the snow towards her house. Although her head hung low, her chin stayed glued to her shoulder, in Ray's direction. Ray just pursed his lips as they exchanged a knowing, worried look. There was nothing anyone could do for him now.

His mother lowered her yell to a harsh whisper. "How bad would you have felt if someone did that to you when you were that age?"

Ray couldn't imagine it. He couldn't imagine anything making him feel bad before the war. He couldn't imagine anything bad happening when his father was home. But as he looked at his mother, breathless in anger, Raymond couldn't imagine there was a time when he believed in magic, Santa, or anything that rewarded those who were good.

❄ ❄ ❄

But Ray did believe. It was before the fifth grade. Before there were Axis and Allies. Before loose lips sank ships. Before salvage drives. Before when fathers were mechanics and not soldiers. Before a little man started a great big war, there was Santa Claus. And only two years ago, Raymond believed in Santa Claus with his whole heart. Every kid in Mrs. Hansen's third grade class in Southold Elementary School did if they knew what was good for them. So back then when the rumors started to fly around that Santa didn't really exist, Ray tried his hardest to ignore the talk. But the facts his buddies were lining up during gym class were hard to ignore.

"Every house in one night? Impossible, I tell ya. Impossible," said Ted as he sat next to Ray, waiting for the record to be changed in their square dancing lesson, his pudgy fingers refastening his Roy Rogers pin on his gym T-shirt.

"What about magic hooves and antlers?" Ray questioned.

"Magic antlers?" Ted scoffed. "What does that do?"

Ray fumbled with his thoughts and reasoning as much as Mrs. Hansen fumbled with the knobs and switches on the new record player. Neither seemed to be getting them anywhere.

"I don't know," Ray stammered. "Fly?"

"So he can fly. Big whoop. How can he go down every chimney in the world in one night?"

Olive sat in the bleacher by herself behind the boys, polishing her eyeglasses. She jumped to Ray's defense. "He doesn't hit every house," she said, matter-of-factly. "There were lots of kids who didn't get presents last year. Maybe that saves him time?"

Olive's inch-thick spectacles made her eyes the size of green golf balls. They also gave her an air of knowledge when she spoke about anything. When she stood silent, however, she looked slow, like her older brother. Her glasses and genealogy made her a constant target of her classmates. But since Ray lived next door to her and her four older siblings, he never said a word. Kids who lived on your block were treated like family. You couldn't pick on them because they were the ones you played with after school. Their toys were your toys. Their snacks were your snacks. And though Olive's family didn't have many toys or snacks, she was always up for any game, sport, or covert spy mission Ray could think up. Besides, Olive made a mean bunker from a fallen maple tree. She would always be swell in Ray's eyes.

"See?" said Ray, pointing to Olive.

Marty, who was recruited by Mrs. Hansen to help read the small numbers on the dials of the player, trudged back to the bleachers and plopped next to Ray. Ted broke his concentration with his pin and hit Marty on the shoulder.

"Whadda you think? Santa Claus real? You see any magic hoof prints on your roof last year?"

Marty rubbed his shoulder and surveyed the girls behind him on the bleachers, hoping he'd find one to dance with. "Magic smagic," he said in a hushed tone and leaned in. "I saw my old man put presents under the tree last year. Said he doing it for the big guy but I found the receipt for the train set in the car."

Ray's eyes bounced from Ted to Marty to Olive. This couldn't be true. There was only one person who could straighten this mess out. He believed in Santa. And he would never steer Ray wrong.

❄ ❄ ❄

Ray didn't wait for Olive when the school bell rang. He took off out of the classroom with his books tied together by an old leather belt and headed out towards Main Street. The only busy road that cut through the small farming town barked and buzzed with its everyday excitement. Cars raced home from the local grocers while kids scrambled into Kramer's Soda Shoppe to nab the corner stool. High schoolers perched on the wall in front of the library and smoked Pall Malls and Woodbines as the sky grew gray, giving the feeling that it was about to snow. Ray zigzagged through traffic trying to get to Mick's Garage where his father worked. Those who knew Ray gave a honk and asked him if he'd like a lift since most knew where he was headed. But Ray, too, focused and full of fear that the only person responsible for bringing a new toy each year wouldn't be arriving, just waved them off. Would Santa be angry and skip his house if Ray even doubted his existence? After all, times were tough for everybody. Last year five kids in his class only got oranges and underwear for Christmas. And though his mother would be happy with that, Ray couldn't stomach it.

The sound of a cowbell clanging marked Ray's entrance into the shop. He raced past Betty, the shop's receptionist. She was busy filing her nails with a coy smile as Bobby, one of the shop's grease monkeys, begged her to let him drive her home in his new Ford. She looked up from her red talons to see Ray hustle on by without a greeting.

"Hey ya, Big Ray. Where's the fire?"

Ray didn't answer as he made a straight line for the floor of the shop. All the mechanics hunched in and over their Hudsons, Packards, and Chevrolets in stained overalls gave a shout or a nod to Ray as he weaved around the cars. He didn't bother to say hello to the fellas, he just kept calling out for his dad. The shop's owner, Mick, emerged from the tiny back office wiping his blackened filthy hands with an even blacker, filthier rag. A tough, bald Lithuanian fellow roughly the size of a small horse, Mick walked with a limp which he got when he taught his daughter to drive. Rumor had it that even though she backed into him with a Studebaker he didn't break any of his bones. The car, however, lost its bumper.

"Looking for your Pops, Ray?" asked Mick with a cigarette dangling out of his chapped mouth. His voice sounded as if he ate the rest of the pack.

"He here, Mr. Mick?" asked Ray.

"Nah. Sent him home an hour ago. Said he had some urgent holiday 'business' he needed to tend to." Mick rocked back on his heels and widened his eyes on the word "business," which made Ray even more nervous. "Can I help you with something?"

Ray paused for a moment. "Well, my friend told me that...that..." he began to say until he thought the better of it. Ray remembered his mother said that more gossip got spread around that garage than any beauty parlor. And he was positive that if Santa skipped any houses, it would certainly be some of the men in Mick's garage. A few, like Bobby, had to be on the "naughty list" for sure. All the mechanics slowed their working and peeked over their engines at Ray.

"Well, what is it?" Mick asked. "Spit it out."

Ray thought fast and spoke even faster. "That the Brooklyn Dodgers will get beat by the Giants next year, for sure."

Ray's fib worked. This comment elicited a round of laughter from the men on floor as their focus returned to their respective engines. Mick managed to let out a hearty laugh while still holding the Lucky Strike between his lips. "Your friend has, what we like to call around here, a lug nut loose. Beat the Giants? Ha! That kid's talking crazy."

Ray let out a sigh of relief. Snow began to fall outside, which gave Ray his next excuse to run.

"I better get going. Mom will start to get worried if I'm not home soon." Ray turned on his heel and began a dash out of the garage.

"Hold on now! Your mom will be a lot more worried if she knew you were out in this weather. Bobby's heading home. Let him give you a ride."

Bobby looked up from Betty's sweater, confused.

"I wasn't heading home just yet, Mick," he said, deflated.

"Yes you were," Mick said slowly. "And don't hit anything. The Hamans thought the world of that dog."

Ray sat silent in the passenger seat of Bobby's Ford as Bobby muttered to himself and periodically hit his steering wheel with the palm of his hand. Ray could feel a calm settle over him as Bobby made the turn onto his street, Jacob's Lane. He kept an eye out for Olive but figured she must have already made it home before the snow. The stench of low tide began to creep into the car as they approached Goose Creek. Bobby began to accelerate once he got over the bridge in an attempt to outrun the smell of rotten seaweed and sulfur. Just as Ray was about to tell Bobby to slow down so that they wouldn't miss his driveway a deer bounded out of the woods and jumped in front the car.

"Holy shit!" cried Bobby as he slammed both feet on the brakes. The car hit a patch of icy leaves and spun in a full circle until it skidded to a stop. Neither Bobby nor Ray said a word. They just faced forward and stared out the windshield with their mouths open, both stunned as if their lives, and not a deer, just dashed in front of their eyes.

Bobby, still panting from fright, turned to Ray. "Don't tell Hal I said the word 'shit' in front of you, got it?"

Still holding his breath, Ray answered. "Got it."

Ray got out of the car and began to walk towards his house. As Ray walked away, Bobby rolled down the window and waved him back.

"Don't tell him I almost killed ya, neither."

Ray nodded as Bobby slowly backed his Ford up and drove away. As he watched the car disappear down the road he noticed Oscar Taglieber, the old clockmaker, standing in the street without a coat on, shaking his fist in Bobby's direction. Once the car passed, Oscar turned and yelled up the street to Ray.

"You alright?" Oscar bellowed. His low voice echoed down the street as if he were yelling to him from the end of a long tunnel. Ray nodded and called back.

"Yes, sir. I'm fine."

Oscar threw his arm up and let it down. His focus did not stay on Ray. He instead peered down at the snow as if he lost something or was following a trail. Whatever it was, it led him into the woods.

Ray watched Oscar shuffle off into the trees and disintegrate into the background.

Southold town had always been filled with deer. So much so that the mayor made every season deer season with no regulations on the animal's size, the time of year, or place to hunt. A person could shoot a doe with a bow and arrow during the July Fourth parade if they thought they could get a clear shot. This made most people happy as now they could add venison to their diet instead of eating cured pork and potatoes for days on end. But Oscar Taglieber chased most hunters off Ray's street. He chased most people off as well.

Ray didn't give Oscar a second thought. His attention went right back to the question at hand. Was Ted right? Were all the letters he had written to St. Nick in vain? Were they just a cheap attempt from his mother to get him to practice his cursive handwriting? He walked into his warm home and tossed his books on the couch. The silence of the gray snow falling outside was broken by the sound of the Lux Radio Theater and the smell of a pot roast cooking. Ray's mother stood in the kitchen and ironed as she listened to Barbara Stanwyck and Robert Young bicker over the ownership of their Madison Avenue mansion. The house rule of the small colonial on 5245 Jacob's Lane was to never talk to mother during the Lux Radio Theatre hour. Normally, she wouldn't even look up from her ironing during her radio program but this day she stopped long enough to give Ray a kiss and directions.

"Father's in the basement," she said before pounding her foot on the floor. A petite woman with soft features, she always kept her hair twisted and pinned back into a bun so that it never fell in her face. Ray got his black hair, hazel eyes, and love of pickled herring from his mother. Ray got his cowlicks, laugh, and love of tools from his dad.

Ray hustled downstairs into the musty, but organized basement. In the corner, under the light of a bare hanging bulb, stood Ray's dad, quickly packing up the contents of a large box on his workbench. Wood shavings littered the floor as the green scent of stripped elm and basswood mixed with the scent of the meat roasting upstairs. The light bounced off the rows of glistened shiny metal tools that lined the wall like soldiers waiting for their orders. After placing the box up on a high shelf, he turned to Ray.

"Hey, Big Ray. What did they teach you at school today?" his father asked before settling back down on his stool. Henry Lee Kozak's kind smile stretched lines across a young but weathered face. Although shorter than most men in the shop, Henry, or Hal, as everyone called him, was a giant in Ray's eyes. At least a giant in all ways a dad needed to be. He could fix anything, explain any of Ray's questions, and get the most irate man or dog to eat right out of his hand. Even the Kelly's mean German shepherd, Fluffles, that sometimes broke off his leash and ran barking and biting into their neighborhood. Ray pulled up a stool next to him and watched his father begin to clean off his wood-working tools.

"Dad?" Ray asked while his fingers fiddled with a file. "You believe in Santa, right?" His head faced the workbench while his eyes crawled up to read his father's expression.

Hal kept on shining the handle of the rasp as if the question didn't bother him. "Sure do. Why you ask?"

"Well, Ted said that it was impossible to do what Santa does in one night."

"Is it now?"

"Don't know," Ray gulped. "Is it?"

Ray's father put his rasp and rag on the table and slapped his knees. "Why yes, Raymond. It is impossible."

Ray's mouth dropped open. His worst fears were about to be realized. Without knowing it, he shook his head in disbelief. "You mean Ted's right?"

"Well, you asked me if I believe in Santa. I do. Do I believe he comes into our house every Christmas? That's something I'm not so sure about."

Seeing the disappointment in Ray's face, his father smiled and planted a stained leather hand firmly on Ray's shoulder.

"I think it's about time you know the truth about the big guy in the sleigh. You're eight..."

"Nine in eight months."

"Forgive me, almost nine. Practically a man. You'll be working at Mick's any day now. So I think you can handle what I'm about to tell you. After all, if anyone is going to tell you the truth, I think it should be your old man."

Hal rubbed his chin as he put on a stern, concerned expression. The kind Ray would see him give to older men and women who would come into the garage and explain why their new car won't start when they stick their keys into the cigarette lighter. He would never tell them they needed to find their glasses or that they might want to have their kids drive them to church. He would just scratch the white streak in his shaggy light brown hair, push his eyebrows together and go, "You don't say?"

"It's like this. Santa's a busy man. Busier than the storybooks and songs really let on."

"Too busy to give everyone presents?" Ray interjected.

"Now, hold on. I didn't say that. But he's too caught up in all his duties to be everywhere at once. So to make sure that everyone gets what's coming to them, he farms out his workload to a bunch of us so that no one goes without on Christmas."

"But I already wrote to him this year. Do I have to send it to someone else now?"

"No, you still need to let him know what you want. But the older you get, the more he relies on his team of people to help him out. Take this for instance." Hal walked over to his shelf and pulled down a small wooden chest. The unfinished oak lid was elegantly carved with the word HOP. Hal's fingers glided over the word then passed it to Ray, who then did the same.

"Who's HOP?"

"It's 'Hope.' Or at least it will be once I'm done. I was told that I needed to carve it for the big guy so that it could go to Mrs. Stelzer this Christmas. He figured she needs a special place to put letters and pictures of her son who's fighting over in the Pacific."

Ray's eyes got large. "You mean *Santa* asked you to make this?"

Hal's chest puffed up with pride. "It's a commissioned piece. You see, Mrs. Stelzer usually leaves every light on in her house when she goes to bed. She's scared of everything. Even her cat. So Santa thought it was best that I make it and give it to Mr. Stelzer to give to her on Christmas. You agree?"

Ray thought about it for a minute. House lights on all night would surely give Santa away to anyone who happened to walk by. And he would never want to scare an old lady, especially one whose brave son is fighting in a war. Ray put his index finger to his pursed lips and nodded in agreement.

"Makes good sense to me."

"Makes good sense to me, too," Hal said in agreement. "And maybe one day, if you work really hard, Santa will give you a job. Would you like that?"

Ray stood up and faced Hal, his eyes wild and wide at the thought. "You mean *I* could work for Santa?"

"Why not? I do."

Ray cocked his head to the side and crinkled his nose in confusion. "I thought you work for Mr. Mick?"

"Let's let Mick think I work for him. But we both know who's really the boss," he said, giving Ray a knowing, hard wink. The same hard wink he would give when he checked under the hood of that elderly customer's car. Hal would pull out a few plugs and wiggle a few wires and ask them to try and start the engine again. It would always turn over. He'd tell them to be careful on the wet roads and let them drive out without paying a bill. Said that learning how to fix their "unique" problem was payment enough. That's why everyone went to Hal. They trusted him. That's why Ray trusted him. His dad knew how to fix the things that people didn't know they broke in the first place.

❄ ❄ ❄

Everyone went to Hal when they were in trouble so it came as no surprise when Uncle Sam did as well. Although he didn't come himself, Ray learned that, like Santa Claus, he farms his work out to others. On a rainy summer afternoon, he came in the form of the postman. Hal had apparently been picked in some kind of lottery. This uncle Ray never met told his dad he was to enlist in the army and help Mrs. Stelzer's son fix this war. Everyone seemed to congratulate Hal and appear very proud. Everyone except his mother. Ray often found her crying when doing household chores. For a while, Ray thought his mother just hated dusting but after watching her wipe down her wedding photo five times and her eyes seven, he thought that maybe winning this lottery wasn't all that lucky after all.

Ray's parents didn't say much as they embraced on the train platform. When they stopped kissing Ray's mother buried her face in her lace handkerchief. Hal put his hands on his knees, bent over and looked at Ray at eye level.

"You take care of your mother, you hear? You're the man of the house now."

Ray sucked in some air and puffed out his chest. All he could do was nod as a tear crept over his eyelid. He couldn't open his mouth. He knew he needed to be as brave as his father and if he opened his mouth all the fear and sadness would come blowing out in a wail. His father's eyes sparkled gray as he smiled wide, as if his smile could stretch out the pucker and tears that were threatening to overtake Ray's face. Hal grabbed the back of Ray's neck so that he had to keep his chin up.

"I love you, Big Ray. And when I come home, we'll take those racers out for a heck of spin. A really Grand Prix. OK?"

Ray answered by throwing his arms around Hal. He never wanted his dad to leave but couldn't say it. That would be weak and now, as everyone kept saying, was a time for courage. The train that sat idling behind the three gave another whistle signaling that it was time for Ray to let go.

Hal gave kisses to Ray and his wife and then jumped on the train. As it pulled out of the station, Hal remained in the doorway so that he could see his family. Ray just stood clutching his mother's hand as she buried her face in the other. As the train pulled away his father fixed his tweed cap firmly on his head and yelled out to Ray.

"First to the oak!"

Ray broke free from his mother's grasp and took off down the platform. After school, when it was still light outside, the neighborhood kids would gather for a game of baseball on Ships Drive, the quiet road that cut through the woods behind the Kozak's house. Hal was always the impartial pitcher for all the kids. He made sure that the game always ended in a tie. He would pitch fast balls to Ray, lob easy ones over to little Tommy Goldsmith, never let Olive get tagged out and always conferred with Paley, Olive's slow older brother, on any calls that needed an expert opinion. After the game, Hal and Ray would walk through the woods towards their home until one of them yelled, "First to the oak!" This phrase caused them to tear off like hunted deer through the woods toward their backyard. Hal always whooped, laughed, and yelled after Ray as they leapt over logs and beat away brush. Hal made sure that Ray knew he was behind him, nipping at his heels. He would pick Ray up if he tripped or fell back if he got too close. But Hal never outran him. He never passed. Saying those words were like a shot from a starting gun. Hal had thrown down the gauntlet. The fire that burned in Ray's chest suddenly shot into his heels.

"I got ya beat, my boy!" Hal cried from the train. He smacked the side of the car as if it were the rump of a racehorse. "Come on ya old mule! Move it!"

Ray ran to the edge of the platform then launched himself over the railing. He hit the dirt path that ran alongside the train tracks with a thud and a cloud of dust. Ray followed next to the train, running as fast as his size seven Buster Browns could take him. All the while, Hal hooted and hollered from inside the car until the train picked up speed and passed Ray.

"Adventure awaits!" he heard his dad cry out. "Adventure awaits!"

Ray kept running until he thought his chest would tear open. When his feet finally slowed down he panted and stared at the 6:35 direct fly off in the distance. He could only see his father's arm waving his tweed cap from the train until it turned into a dot and then into nothing.

CHAPTER 3

Ships Drive – Southold, New York, 1944

Ray never had any intention to let the cat out of the bag. Tommy Goldsmith wasn't an enemy. In fact, Ray rather liked him. A chubby kid whose family owned the five and dime in town, Tommy always got the best toys for Christmas. Since he was an only child, he never had a problem sharing them with Olive and Ray. Ray was an only child as well and considered Tommy a little brother. He taught Tommy how to catch a pop fly and how to keep a kite up in the air. Ray figured it was his duty to teach Tommy certain life lessons. Unfortunately for Tommy, while walking home from school with Ray and Olive three weeks before Christmas, Ray decided his misery needed company.

"So is Santa still coming? Even with the war and all?" Tommy questioned Olive as the three trudged through the snow. Tommy struggled to keep his book bag from scraping the top of the drifts as Olive kept a watchful eye out for cars. Ray lagged a few feet behind with his fists clenched and stuffed in his coat pockets.

"War or no war, Santa will still make it here," Olive reassured Tommy. "Don't you worry about that." Olive looked back at Ray. His angry expression pointed down at the snow he kicked up. It was an expression he wore more and more since he got the news about his father nearly two months ago. Ray's normal smile appeared to be slowly dissolving into a steady frown. And the more everyone got excited about Christmas, the angrier Ray seemed.

"Good, 'cause I'm asking for a Mickey Owen catcher's mitt. It might be big and all but one day it'll fit right," Tommy said as they walked past Oscar Taglieber's small ranch house. Tommy and Olive gave a slight wave as they watched Oscar shovel his driveway. Oscar, dressed in stained overalls and large rubber boots, stopped shoveling briefly to nod at the three. Ray did not look up or care.

Tommy continued on as he waddled through the snow. "What are you asking Santa to bring you, Olive?"

"I'm asking for a telescope. A pirate telescope."

Tommy stopped and scratched his head. "Are pirates hard to find?"

Olive laughed. "I wouldn't be looking for pirates. I'd use it to look at the stars. And Paley would use it to look out for the enemy." Olive looked up at the snow-covered trees and sighed. Olive normally only received homemade gifts for Christmas. A scarf with her name on it. A doll with a fabric face, buttons for eyes, and a sewn-on smile. A tin of homemade Ginger Snaps. All were always well received. Ray didn't say anything but thought the odds of Olive getting a telescope would be the same as Olive getting an actual reindeer for Christmas. None.

The Mott's house was packed with people instead of things. With five kids, one grandmother, and one mom every member of the Mott house had a job. Mrs. Mott cleaned houses. Olive's three older sisters worked as waitresses. Olive's job was taking care of her older and only brother Paley. Which as jobs go, was not all that hard. At seventeen, he could dress and wash himself fine but didn't go to school with all the other kids. Instead, he spent every morning cleaning and sorting the tools at Mick's shop. Hal got this for him after Mr. Mott went to Doc's Tavern for something to drink and never came back. But every afternoon Paley's job would change from mechanic's helper to enemy lookout. He would stand in the front yard rocking back and forth, staring in the sky, looking for enemy aircraft using the plane spotter guide on a worn Pep cereal box. If the Germans or Japanese were going to fly their bombers over the east end of Long Island, Paley would spot them. Between Olive's love of star-gazing and Paley's hunt for enemy aircraft a telescope would be in constant use.

"Did you write Santa for it?"

"Sure did," Olive said. Ray looked up and saw her fingers crossed behind her back.

"What about you, Ray? What did you ask for?"

Ray didn't answer. Too lost in his anger, he grew heated by the hopeful talk of baseball mitts and letters to Santa.

"Nothing," he spat.

"Nothing?" Tommy shook his head in disbelief. "How could you ask for nothing?"

"I don't want anything, all right?"

Oblivious to Ray's anger, Tommy kept prodding. "Come on, Ray. You can't want *nothing*." Tommy lopped his head from side to side as he walked. "How about a Dodgers' cap or a train set? You don't have those."

"I don't want that stuff."

"But what's Santa going to leave you when he comes? He has to give you something." Tommy stopped in thought. "What about another one of those racecars?"

A racecar. That's all it took to break Ray. Last time he saw his father, he said he would set up a Grand Prix when he came home. He would have probably made Ray some new cars. But that would never happen. After The Worst Day, things like midget racecars, block baseball games, Christmas, and toys lost all their joy and shine. His dad and Mrs. Stelzer's son were going to win the war. Then he was going to come back home and teach him everything about cars. Then later, when Ray got older, he would teach him how to fix an engine on a Cadillac and then how to drive it. Now all of those things he'd have to learn from someone else. There was no more banging through the family room door and into the basement to listen to *Terry and the Pirates*. No more Captain Ryan. Dads could fix things. And Ray's dad knew how to fix everything. But everything in Ray's world was broken. There was no dad to make it better. And if his dad didn't exist anymore, there certainly wasn't a Santa Claus. And in Ray's mind the sooner that Tommy knew that, the better off he'd be.

"He's not going to get me anything, alright?" Ray yelled.

Tommy rubbed his hat in confusion. "But Ray, you've been good. He'll want to give you a present. You don't want to get stuck with a doll?"

Ray threw his hands up in the air and yelled so loud that snow fell off branches. "It doesn't matter! He's not coming! Not now. Not ever!"

Tommy's lips began to quiver. Ray never yelled in real anger before. Certainly not at Tommy. Tommy looked at Olive, whose jaw and math book both dropped.

"But…Mom said that if I'm good…" Tommy said quietly.

"Good? Who cares if you've been good? That's just something grown-ups made up. There's no such thing as Santa Claus."

"Take that back!" Olive barked. "That's not true, Tommy. Santa does exist."

"No he doesn't," Ray snapped back. "He never did."

Oscar Taglieber could hear Ray's yelling but only moved when he heard Tommy's wail. He let his shovel drop and ran as quickly as his old legs could take him.

Tommy wiped his nose on his sleeve as Olive tried to calm him down. Through his huffs he tried to argue with Ray. "But I got trains last year. Dad said he saw Santa put them there."

"That's a load of pucky, Tommy. Your parents put them there. Santa Claus is just a made-up story for babies. Are you a baby?"

"Stop it, Ray. Please…" Olive begged.

Ray leaned over and got close to Tommy's face. "Are you a baby?"

Tommy looked at Ray with his pursed lips and swollen eyes. He blinked each time Ray spat out a word. Olive stood motionless, too frightened of Ray to move.

"Are? You? A baby?"

"N…no?" Tommy whimpered.

"Then why are you crying like one!"

"Raymond," Oscar's voice, firm and low in timbre, calmly cut through the tension. He wrapped his large arm around Ray's chest and pulled him away from Tommy. "Raymond, that's enough."

"No, he ought to know there's no Santa."

By this time, Tommy's crying drew out the people from the neighboring houses. Soon, Tommy's mom came running to them, her arms flailing around as she squawked through the snow. Her rotund figure was perched precariously onto skinny legs, which punctured the foot-deep snow like ski poles when she walked. Her pipe curls too blond and too young for her age dangled below her fox fur-trimmed hat.

"Tommy-kins! What's going on?" she asked as she bent over and cupped Tommy's face.

Tommy looked at Ray and rubbed his eyes. Nervous vowels sputtered and fell out of his mouth. He wasn't sure what he was more afraid of: having his mother confirm Ray's beliefs on Santa or getting Ray into so much trouble that he'd lose his friend. "Santa's real. Right, Mom?"

"Of course he is, my Sweetness," Mrs. Goldsmith answered as she petted Tommy's apple plump cheeks. The question, however, began to dawn on her and she slowly rose up and cocked her curls to the side. She stared down at Ray, who stood breathless with Oscar's arm still wrapped across his shoulders. "Isn't that right, Raymond?" she leered.

Ray swore that underneath the snow Mrs. Goldsmith was tapping her foot as she waited for his answer. It seemed like a year before Ray let out his breath.

"I was taught that lying is a sin, Mrs. Goldsmith."

Mrs. Goldsmith's nostrils flared open as wide as her eyes and she rose on her toes in disgust.

"Your mother will hear about this!" she yelled, raising her pointed finger up over her hat. She grabbed Tommy's arm and whirled him around in the direction of their house. Tommy looked back at Ray, who stood with a clenched jaw and furrowed brow staring at the snow.

As the three stood in the center of the street, Olive quietly picked up her book. In a hushed tone and without looking up, she spoke.

"You should tell Tommy you were wrong. Before your mom comes."

"Why?" Ray whined. "He's not real. Why does he get to live in a fantasy world?"

"That wasn't a kind thing to do to a child," Oscar said. "For some, Santa's very real."

"Well, he's not. And it doesn't matter how good we are. It doesn't matter what we do. No one's coming. Nobody cares. Nobody watches. And the sooner he stops believing and hoping for this junk that's never going…"

"Raymond!" his mother's cry echoed through the neighborhood. In Ray's fury he didn't notice his mother marching through the woods. What took Oscar an arm to control only took his mother one hand as she grabbed Ray up by his armpit and pulled him down the path she carved in the snow.

CHAPTER 4

The Kozak Kitchen – Southold, New York, 1944

The ladle smacked the bottom of Ray's bowl with each scoop. Since it was only the two of them, Ray considered his mother's silence a far worse punishment than her yelling. Her anger, however, needed a voice and that was the metal ladle dishing out the stew she made for dinner. Instead of hollering she let the hard "ting" that the serving spoon made on the bottom of the bowl convey her displeasure.

"Pray now," she ordered. Ray lowered his eyes but couldn't get the spirit to bow to anyone. His mother, however, clasped her hands together so tight her knuckles turned white.

"Dear Lord, thank You for the food we are about to eat. Bless this house and all who dwell in it. We ask for Your love, protection, and guidance for ourselves and for our country, through Jesus Christ our Lord, Amen."

Ray grunted out an "Amen" and hunched over his soup. Protection, Ray thought. What protection? Who protected his father? What patron saint looked after his dad and the rest of those men who died with him in that building? Were angels not strong enough to lift the bricks off of them? Could they not fly faster than the planes dropping bombs? Ray wondered time and again what his father was thinking on The Worst Day.

The report from the field said that Henry Lee Kozak and seven members of his squad rescued a group of schoolchildren from a building that was on the verge of collapsing due to heavy enemy fire. In the final attempt to get the children out, the men headed back into the building as it took a hit from the air. The building collapsed with all eight still inside. Every child, however, made it out alive.

Ray stabbed his stew as he wondered if any one of those kids reminded his dad of himself and the gang from the neighborhood. They must have. Why would he run back into a falling building to save the enemy? Or maybe, you needed to be a certain age to be the enemy. Maybe ten? Thirteen? People said his dad died a hero. But every time someone mentioned that word "hero" Ray felt horrible in two ways. The first because he didn't want him to be a hero. He wanted him to be a mechanic. A designated pitcher. A sprinter in the woods. Someone to stay up with him on Christmas Eve and read *The Night Before Christmas*. The second made him feel even worse. He wished those German children were old enough to be the enemy. Maybe then his dad and the other men wouldn't have gone inside to rescue them. Maybe they would have watched the building fall into a pile of rubble from a safe distance, thinking those people were too old to be saved.

His mother stopped eating and took a breath. She placed her elbows on the table and folded her calloused, cut hands in front of her chin. After a long pause she asked, "Why would you tell him there was no Santa? Why would you take that away from him?"

Ray kept his head down and mumbled into in his bowl. "He doesn't need Santa. He still has his dad."

"What does that have to do with anything? Did that matter to you?"

Ray kept quiet and shook his head. She was right. A hundred days before it would not have mattered. Dad and Santa were both larger than life. Both existed. Now, neither did.

"What would your father think of what you're doing now? What would he say about all this?"

Ray could feel tears drip down his cheeks, off his chin, and onto the potatoes floating in his soup. He wanted to know what his father would think. But he didn't. And he wouldn't. For the rest of his life he would have to guess what his father thought from what he could remember of him. Ray looked up from his bowl at his mother, meek as a dog when it came home after a feeble attempt to run away. Ray's mother extended her thin arm over the pot and grabbed his soggy chin. With no smile, she furrowed her brow, tilted her head forward, and with her cold green stare dug into Ray's eyes.

"We will find a way out of this," his mother said over the soup.

And by the looks of her hands it appeared as if she had already started digging.

CHAPTER 5

Dart's Christmas Tree Farm – Southold, New York, 1944

One would have thought they were giving away trees at Dart's Christmas tree farm. Children buzzed and scurried through the rows of Douglas, Fraser, and balsam firs and blue spruces yelling and pointing out their top choices to their parents. Fathers lumbered along, holding their saws, and mothers gripped cups of hot tea, vetoing each child's choice of tree after spotting a gaping hole on the side or noticing needles sprinkle over the ground after a slight shake. Ray and his mother quietly walked up and down the rows. Ray held the saw, taking over the job his dad had last Christmas. His mother promised that if he came with her she would let him cut down the tree. It would be a small tree. Nothing that Ray couldn't handle.

After examining a row of Douglas firs, she noticed a small tree sitting at the end of a row, almost in the woods. She circled and shook the tree the same way Hal would circle a car and kick the tires. She tilted her head and nodded.

"Looks like it could work. What do you think?" she asked.

"Looks small," Ray said, wondering if his mother was trying to shrink Christmas.

"Oh, I don't know. I think maybe we'll have enough room for a star this year. Wouldn't that be a nice change?" Usually, Ray's dad cut a tree down so large that he would have to chop the top off just so it would fit through the front door. Its shape resembled a trapezoid rather than a triangle. They never had room for a star. Ray figured that this Christmas his mother might need one.

"If you think so," Ray said as he knelt down and crawled on his belly towards the trunk. It didn't matter to him what size the tree was. It didn't even matter if they put up a tree. But it made the house smell nice and his mother happy. He would give her at least that.

As Ray bellied up to the trunk he noticed Mick's size 14 boots next to his mother's rubber galoshes.

"Let me help him with this, Estelle," he said. Ray saw Mick's knee drop into the snow with such force that it shook the ground.

"Thank you, Mick, but Ray can handle this."

"It's not a problem, really, Estelle..."

"No, Raymond is the man of the house. He can handle it. Can't you, Raymond?" she called down to him.

Ray knew that Mick didn't even need a saw to take the tree down. He could probably break it off its stump with his bare hands. But Ray wanted to do this. He didn't need Mick. He didn't need anyone. He just needed his saw. Mick took over his father's job at the shop. If anyone was going to take over his father's job running the house, it would be him.

"Got it, Mom," he called out. With that Mick's knee rose out of the snow.

"If you need anything, Estelle, I'm over there. Just wave."

"Thank you, Mick, but I'm sure we'll be just fine."

Ray pulled the saw up to the tree and began to rub its teeth against the fir's bark. The sharp green smell oozed off the trunk. He tried harder to cut but the saw seemed like it hit cement and refused to cut any further. In his anger he pushed the blade back and forth and realized that no matter how hard he tried, it wouldn't budge. His hand, sticky from sap, felt like it was glued to the trunk. His arm grew tired and he laid his saw down in distress.

"Everything ok down there?" she asked.

"Just resting," Ray answered as he rested his head on his burning arm. He stared out aimlessly at the trunks of the trees that left the straight lines of the Christmas tree farm and ran amuck in the woods. It was then he noticed the four hooves of a deer. He kept waiting for the animal to move as deer usually do not like to stop and hang around people. Then the deer's head lowered and appeared to be looking Ray right in the eyes. Ray's head jolted up at the sight of its face.

"Are you sure you don't want some help with this?" his mother asked.

Ray didn't answer. His eyes were locked on a six-point buck that seemed to be staring right back at him and wondering the same thing.

"Ggg…got it," Ray sputtered as he lay frozen in the snow. The deer didn't move from its stance. Its legs buckled slightly at its joints as its proud head hung low, as if it were noticing the beauty of a geranium right before devouring it. Under Ray's breath he muttered, "Shoo… shoo," hoping the animal would prance back into the woods. But it didn't. The body of the animal was the color of wet sand until it reached its neck, where a white patch crept from up around its throat to the area behind its snout. His ears rimmed in black and with white centers blended into a soft shade of ash on its face. His antlers, sprinkled with a slight crisp of snow, looked like branches sprouting from his head. But what caught Ray's breath was the deer's forehead. He couldn't tell if the deer got into trouble with a paintbrush, lightning bolt, or a snowball as it looked like a bright white star in the middle of its forehead, with a lighter streak fading up its head and disappearing behind its antlers. By the way the deer's eyes examined Ray and the warm breath turning into puffs from its nose, Ray didn't want to sit there too long to figure it out.

His uneasiness gave him a quick adrenalin jolt, causing his arm to saw easily through the uncut layer of trunk. From above he heard his mother cheer as the tree slowly eased its way to the ground.

"Hooray! I knew you could do it!" she cried as she leaned over to give Ray a hand up. Ray patted off the snow on his pants as he looked behind him for the deer. Instead, he only saw the prints the buck made in the snow.

The two dragged the tree through the yard to the old farmhouse. Her happiness at Ray's accomplishment couldn't be contained as she wished everyone a Merry Christmas twice upon entering and exiting the building. As they pulled the tree over to the car, Oscar Taglieber walked over to the two holding a large ball of twine. Ray's mother greeted him with a double dose of Merry Christmas.

"Mr. Taglieber, Merry Christmas, Merry Christmas," she chanted. "My Raymond here cut down his first tree."

Oscar leaned back on his heels and pushed his thumbs in his pockets. "You don't say? That's impressive with those Douglas firs. Hard as rocks, those trunks."

Ray gave a slight smile but his attention drew back into the woods. Ray's mother, slightly embarrassed by her son's distraction, turned to Oscar.

"Well, we could use your help getting this onto the roof. Would you mind giving us a hand?"

"Not in the least," he answered.

The tree went on top of the car easy enough. As Ray steadied the trunk, Oscar wrapped the twine around the fir and through the car windows. Realizing he forgot the saw, Ray abandoned the group and ran back to the edge of the woods. The saw was still there, like a party hat left the day after a New Year's celebration. Sawdust and scattered needles circling a castrated trunk were the only traces remaining of their once living Christmas tree. Ray picked up the saw and began to clean its handle when he heard the snaps of the branches. He spun around and noticed the same deer, this time standing tall, his neck elongated, stretching upwards to show off the span of its antlers. Ray froze as he looked into its glassy marble black eyes. He had never seen a deer this close up before and never one so brazen as to not appear to be afraid of a person.

"Scram," Ray said as he waved his arm in the air. The deer twitched its snout but did not move. Ray walked closer to the deer, only twenty feet away, and pointed the saw at him.

"Beat it, will ya?!" Ray yelled. This time the deer lowered its head slowly then jerked it back up. The deer didn't seem to be afraid of him. Ray grew angry as he felt that he did the duty of a man by cutting down a tree. A deer should at least run at his sight. Ray ran closer to the deer and began screaming out.

"Go on! Get out of here!"

The deer jilted its body around in the direction of the woods but kept its head pointed back, looking at Ray. Ray instantly focused on the deer's face, in particular, that white birthmark. Maybe the deer was branded or electrocuted and not afraid of a kid. Maybe this deer had seen worse than a child wielding a hacksaw. But what army would take him if he couldn't fight off a wounded animal? How could he take care of his mother if he couldn't shoo a deer away? He put the saw on the ground and took a large step forward. With arms waving wildly in the air, Ray hollered out at the animal.

"Ahhhhh!"

The buck turned around in a circle but wouldn't move past its stance in the snow. Just as Ray was about to throw his saw in the air, he heard a sharp high-pitched whistle followed by a light-hearted command.

"Hup, hup!" ordered Oscar as he crunched his way through the snow towards Raymond. Ray watched the buck snap to attention, turn, and spring back into the woods. The two stood silently as they watched the upturned white tail rise and fall with each leap, eventually fading into the fog of the woods.

"I couldn't get him to move," Ray uttered, dumbstruck.

Oscar, a man who was never prone to smiling, tilted his head back and let out a hearty laugh. "That's ok, Raymond," he said, patting him on the shoulder. "Sometimes, I can't get them to move either."

❄ ❄ ❄

A small cloud of dust flew off the star onto the breath of Ray's mother.

"Haven't seen you in a while," she said quietly to herself. She stood on a small stool as she shined a small tiny star that was meant to top a Christmas tree. It was a wedding gift from Ray's aunt in Chicago. The star was engraved with his parents' monogram and read, "Our First Christmas 1932." The five tips grew black and tarnished from the years of being kept in its box but the heart of the star still held its shine.

"I think you should face it towards the window," said Olive as she carefully draped each strand of tinsel on the tree. "This way people outside can see it too."

"That's a good point, Olive," she said as she stood tiptoe on the stool. "What do you think, Ray? Towards the window or towards the couch?"

Ray sat on the floor amongst opened boxes of ornaments trying to untangle last year's garland. "Doesn't matter to me. Why do we need a stupid star anyway?"

"Don't call this star stupid, Raymond," his mother warned. "It represents the Star of Bethlehem."

Ray scratched his head. "But stars are in the sky, not a tree."

Olive laid down her tinsel, made two circles with her hands, and looked through them as if she were looking through a telescope. With one closed eye she peered through the holes in her hands as if she were practicing for the real thing.

"It's supposed to look like it's above the tree in the sky. Like it's somewhere way off in the distance," she said, squinting up at the star. "Our teacher said that some think that the Star of Bethlehem may have actually been a comet."

"You don't say," Ray's mother said as she angled the star towards Olive.

Ray shrugged his shoulders in disinterest and returned to the tangled mass that sat in his lap. His mother looked down at Ray and drummed her fingers on the metal star in thought.

"I'm happy we ran into Mr. Taglieber at Dart's," his mother said as she fastened the star on the top branch. "Do you know what he makes this time of year? Toys. Can you believe it? A company hires him to make toys for kids who write to Santa Claus. Like Santa himself."

Ray did not register what his mother said. He snapped the garland in half as he tried to pull a knot apart.

"He even looks like Santa Claus," Olive said as she held up shiny strands of tinsel to the light for inspection. "With his white beard and big belly and all."

Ray's mother nodded in agreement. "You know, it never occurred to me but you're right, Olive. He would make a good store Santa."

Ray wasn't listening to the talk of his silver-haired, portly neighbor. Christmas and all its words just made him feel bad. The word Santa made him feel guilty about Tommy. Gifts did not matter. There was nothing he wanted. Trimming the tree used to be fun. Now Christmas felt like the garland that sat in his lap: a knotted mess of last year's cheer. "I don't get it," Ray said. "How did they know where to go?"

"Who?" asked his mother.

"The wise men? I mean, how did a star get them to Jesus?"

Ray's mother cocked her head to the side. "I don't know," she wondered aloud. "I guess when you're looking for direction and you see a light that bright in the sky, you follow it."

CHAPTER 6

Taglieber House – Southold, New York, 1944

"Was it because I said the star was stupid?" Ray asked as he lagged behind his mother. She marched at least five feet in front of Ray as they headed up Jacob's Lane. Ray had no idea where they could be going. His mother already dragged him to the Goldsmith's house to apologize to Tommy. He would never forget Mrs. Goldsmith's scorn as her rotund figure teetered on the edge of her loveseat like a boulder on the edge of cliff. Her legs were crossed and her hands stacked on her knees as she took in Ray's humiliation. The only person who didn't want Ray to be standing in the Goldsmith's living room to recite an apology more than Ray was Tommy. When Mrs. Goldsmith asked Tommy if he found the apology acceptable, Tommy jumped up, grabbed Ray's arm, pulled him out of the room and said, "Ray, I got two mitts! I'll be Mickey Owens."

Ray followed along and racked his brain to think of anyone else he might have indirectly wronged. His stomach sank when his mother turned onto Oscar Taglieber's driveway.

"Mom!" Ray cried. She whirled around and stared Ray down.

"Do not say a word. I'm doing all the talking. Understand?"

"But Ma..."

"Not. A. Word," his mother ordered, her voice barely a whisper, conveyed as much strength as a full-blown scream. She straightened her feathered cap and Ray's head sank as they made their way to his front door. Ray watched from behind as his mother's worn hands banged on Oscar's front door. She didn't wear gloves anymore. Being a corset maker made her once strong and smooth hands look as if she spent her days holding angry kittens. Oscar's shadow grew slowly as he appeared in the doorway. He only opened the creaky storm door an inch as his breath took shape in the cold air.

"Estelle," he said matter-of-factly. "Raymond."

His mother's stern look transformed in an instant to a sweet plastered smile. Her voice even raised an octave. "Hello Mr. Taglieber. I was wondering if Raymond and I could have a moment of your time?"

Oscar turned around and looked back uncomfortably into the dark house. He shifted nervously in his black boots. "I would ask you to come in but the place is covered with sharp tools. I wouldn't want you to touch something and get..."

Holding up her hand to the glass on the door as if to tell him stop, the polite smile she put on vanished from her face. She flipped her hand around to show him the other side, a side covered in punctures, scraps, and scars like frost on a window pane. "I can assure you there is no more damage you could do. May I please have a word?"

He looked down and let out a long exhale. His breathe turned into a white mist which dissolved into a flag of surrender.

Ray and his mother followed Oscar as he lumbered down the hall. His heavy gate creaked the boards as her heels hammered the Kozak's presence from behind. As they walked, Ray noticed each room they passed seemed frozen in time, as if a lady stepped out for a cup of tea but couldn't find her way back. Dust covered all the dainty features that were once lovingly and particularly placed in the room. A doily was draped on every piece of tiny furniture. The delicate lace parlor shades hung on every window. Porcelain figurines of dancers curtsied to each other from the edges of the end tables. The house reminded him of a museum until they made the turn into the living room. Ray figured it had to be called the living room since it was the only part of the ranch house that seemed to have been actually lived in. But instead of a room designated for company or entertaining, it was filled with tools. Handsaws and hammers, wrenches and rags, screws and screwdrivers, nails and nuts, snips and solvents and everything in between littered each surface. It smelled like paint, oil, and wood, much like Mick's shop if a tornado had picked it up and dropped it in the middle of a lumberyard. The once precious couches were covered in various stains and tears. The chairs were no longer used for holding people but rather as legs for makeshift workbenches. But the most shocking part of the room was, by far, the walls. Every inch of each wall held a clock. Numbers fat and slim, swirling 8s, military 2s, faces with only dots or dashes or jewels, and roman numerals in every style one could dream up covered the walls. From father to cuckoo, not one looked like the other. Each clock looked as if it were made in a different country and by a different maker. The only thing they had in common was the position of their respective minute hands.

Oscar searched over the table he constructed from an old door resting on a radiator and handed each of them two clean towels. Finding anything clean on that table was a miracle in this living room workshop.

"You'll need these in about two minutes."

"Oh, thank you, it will only take me as much." Ray's mother, not knowing what to do with the towel, laid it on a chair and sat on it to protect her dress.

"Raymond here," she said with a smile, "and I were wondering if you might need some help," she swallowed as she nodded to the room.

"You mentioned at the farm that you make toys for the children who write to Santa. I take it you must be very busy."

"Well," Oscar said as he patted his forehead with a dirty rag. "I seem to get along just fine. There is quite a bit of work. We try not to scale back, even with all that's going on. War and all."

"I understand, Mr. Taglieber, but my Raymond. He is so eager." She cleared her throat as if it weren't in her to stretch the truth so far into a lie. "I am so eager to keep him busy around the holidays."

"Well," Oscar said as he rubbed his knees nervously. "That's awfully kind of you to offer his help."

"Ray is very handy with tools," she said. Ray looked down at his mother's hands and noticed she was wringing the other towel into rope. "His father taught him a great deal on how to handle himself around a shop. Ray spent every moment of his free time around some kind of saw or jack."

Her eyes faded off over the hammers and picks scattered over the tables. Ray could tell the surroundings reminded her of his dad's workbench in the basement. He remembered them talking about how his workshop in the basement had been a battle the first year they moved into the house on Jacob's Lane. Ray's mother came from a clean Polish family who couldn't help but put everything in its place. Each time his mother would walk through the basement, she would separate and place Hal's tools in size order, making it impossible for Hal to find anything when he came back to his bench. Understanding his wife and her fastidious nature, Hal drew an outline of each tool on the wall with a hook, so if his Estelle felt the need to make order in the orderless world of a man's workshop, she would find that each tool had a home. When he went off to the shop, she would gingerly put each one back in its assigned space. Except once. The only time she did not put any of Hal's tools back was the day he left for basic training. For the first time, Hal would know his hammer was where he last left it. Now his mother asked Ray to fetch things from the basement. His dad's delicate line drawings looked like a police outline of deceased instruments. Ray didn't know that Hal's workbench became her world. The little lives Hal loved couldn't find a place after he left. Nothing seemed to be able to find its way home, no matter how clear the directions were.

"It would only be a few hours after school. Before I came home from work," she continued.

Oscar shook his head as if he didn't want to hear himself agree to it. "I can't pay him," Oscar said. Then his eyes glanced up at the wall. He took two towels out of the back pocket of his gray dungarees and put them over his ears. "And it's four o'clock."

And with that, every clock on his wall came alive. A chorus of brass bells and silver whistles, metal tubes smacked by rubber mallets, oak-carved birds singing, spinning dollies and gears whizzing rang in the air. Ray and his mother stared up at the walls in amazement. His mother let out a girlish laugh as one hundred clocks belted in joy that it was one, two, five or ten o'clock somewhere in the world. Then, after ten seconds of clamor and chiming, they all stopped as if an orchestra conductor sliced his wand and silenced them on cue. The room became silent as each clock turned back into another face on the wall. Each numerical face looked down at the three seated in the living room and waited patiently for their next big moment to arrive. Ray's mother dropped the rags from her ears but the smile remained on her face.

"No, Mr. Taglieber. That won't be necessary."

After a few moments, Ray, his mother, and Oscar made their way to the door. Oscar shuffled quickly behind the two as he seemed eager to be left alone with his clocks. Oscar stayed in the doorway as he watched the two walk out in the snow.

His mother stopped and dusted her cap as Ray kept walking. Ray figured that if he couldn't talk he could put some distance between him and the ticking walls. After he walked a few yards ahead he stopped and the let the future sink in. His afternoon playtime was gone. Now his few remaining hours of daylight would be spent in that odd house helping that odd man. Not with Olive or Tommy or in the woods playing *Terry and the Pirates*. He remained a safe distance away and kicked at the rocks that sat under the snow. Even from the end of the driveway he could hear his mother and Oscar talk about him.

"It has been hard for Raymond," he heard Oscar say quietly.

"It is hard for everyone, Mr. Taglieber," she said, cleaning her feather. "Telling that boy there was no Santa was the first sin I've ever seen my son commit. I believe it is the only sin one can commit at his age."

Oscar scratched his beard. "A sin, you reckon?"

"He took the magic out of someone's life, Mr. Taglieber," she said as her eyes and voice drifted higher into the darkening sky. "Christmas day, the most joyful day, will be less joyful for that child because of my son's actions. I can't think of anything that is more sin, can you?" Her thin eyes appeared like dark wells with no floor. Oscar took in a deep breath and looked over at a deer that appeared in a far corner of the wood.

"No, ma'am. Right now, I can't."

Ray followed his mother's gaze and watched the deer take a few tentative steps towards them before turning and bounding back into the woods. She shook her head, put on her hat, and straightened the brim as if she was affixing a helmet to her head before going into battle. The pools retreated and the fire came back into her eyes. Her jaw clenched as she turned to face Oscar.

"My son's magic was taken from him. But that gives him no right to take it from someone else. He is not the enemy. Under my roof he will not act like one."

Ray watched his mother nod to Oscar and march back up the lane. She didn't look at Ray as she passed him. Her chin tucked in her collar, her fists clenched inside her coat pockets. The falling snow melted before it could even touch her cap.

CHAPTER 7

Ray's Room – Southold, New York, 1944

As Ray lay in bed, contemplating his new afterschool life with Oscar Taglieber, his eyes drifted up the walls. His did not hold a hundred clocks. Instead, they held a hundred shadows made from the light of the moon. The only nice thing about winter nights was the moonlight. The maple and oaks that covered the Kozak's lawn acted like a canopy. Some trees were so high that Ray couldn't even see the tops. In the summer and fall the leaves blocked most of the moonlight away from the windows. Only the shush of the leaves and an occasional shadow would make its way onto Ray's walls. But in the winter, the moonlight could be blinding. During a full moon, Ray would have to draw the shades to block out all the light.

His bedroom, a small room tucked away in the corner of the second floor, had two windows. One faced the backyard and Ship's Drive, the street that ran through the acre of woods behind his house. On a winter night he could see clear through the trees and past their homemade forts to the quiet lamppost lights dotting the lonely road. The other window faced Olive's house. The Mott house was almost identical to Ray's except it held triple the number of occupants.

Olive's room faced Ray's, which is why Ray kept a flashlight and a can of rocks under his bed. He would flick a rock or shine a flashlight into Olive's window when he couldn't sleep. Even though Olive shared a room with her grandmother, their options to communicate were not limited. Her grandmother slept on the opposite side of the room and was selectively deaf, choosing to listen only to Olive's mother and only conversations that centered on Olive's lost father. The nightly business of a ten-year-old would not be something she would bother to hear. Unless the window blew open and Ray struck her in the head with a rock, her grandmother would never know or care.

Ray stared up at the shadows of branches that crisscrossed around his room. He imagined they were barbed wire and pictured his dad cutting through them on his way into enemy country. He pictured the eight men covered in mud, crawling over the cold earth on their elbows with their rifles crossing their chest. He used to wonder if his father looked at the stars and thought of him if he got scared. For Ray, his dad was no further away in heaven than he was in Germany. Only the hope of a reunion was now gone. The reunion, which he used to measure in hours and weeks, would now be measured in a lifetime.

He sat up in bed and waited for the lamppost lights to go out. First would be the Jernick's post. Ten minutes later would be Van Dusen's. Finally, the Goldsmith's at the end of the block. As he stared across the woods he noticed a deer gently walking and poking its way through the brush. Ray crawled up the window and rubbed his eyes. It was a buck. Ray couldn't believe his luck. Two bucks in one week. No one ever saw bucks. Only does and fawns. He rapped on the glass slowly to see if the buck could hear him from so far away but the deer kept pushing its snout through the branches on the ground. Ray cracked open the window. The sound of the creaking window seam caught the deer's attention. Its head jerked up and twisted over in the direction of the sound.

"Come on now. Run," Ray uttered to himself. He loved to watch the deer take off and leap through the woods. It always amazed him to see an animal that big move so fast through the woods. It was the only thing that could outrun him and his dad through these parts. The only thing that knew this area better. Instead of taking off, the buck started to move toward the house. Each leg deliberately and cautiously placed itself in front of the other. Ray opened the window higher. A burst of cold air burned his wrists. The sound stopped the buck for only a moment before it kept its pace towards the house. Ray whispered as loud as he could.

"Go! Get!" His breath turned into white puffs and floated upward. The deer stopped momentarily and looked up in Ray's direction but kept its deliberate pace towards Ray's window. Fright crept up Ray's spine the same way it did at the Christmas tree farm. Why were these bucks not afraid? Every time he saw a deer, it fled at the sight or sound of a human. Now another was walking towards him. He ran across the room and grabbed the flashlight from under his bed. He shined the light out of the window and down at the deer. The deer stopped and pushed its head further back. Ray pressed his nose up the screen to get a better look at the buck. As soon as Ray could focus on the buck's face his heart flew into his neck. He blinked hard three times.

There it was. That star on its forehead. It was the same buck.

The beam of the flashlight suddenly went all over the room as it smacked the floor. Ray scrambled to pick it up and shut it off. Soon the soft creak of footsteps came from the hall as his mother's voice squeezed through the crack in the door.

"You ok in there?"

"Fine, Mom," Ray said softly as he sat under the window, clutching the flashlight to his chest.

"Ok. Get to bed now." He could sense her lips leaving the door's edge. "Good night and God bless you," she said as she headed down the hall to her room. The nerves left her voice. Ray knew if he heard those words he would not see his mother again until the morning.

Ray took a deep breath and slowly turned up towards the window. He looked down to see the deer standing closer than before. The animal stood tall right under this window displaying its rack with pride. Ray wouldn't sleep knowing this buck was standing there and guarding his room. Throwing a rock at the buck might make things worse. Ray searched his mind on what he could do to chase it away. Then he remembered Oscar. Oscar got it to move. In a fright Ray pressed his lips up to the screen and puffed out the only words he hoped might work.

"Hup! Hup!"

The buck turned itself towards the Mott's house and bolted across the backyards as if it were being chased. Ray smiled wide as he closed the window. It worked, he thought. It really worked. The buck listened to him. Ray remained at the window until his breath covered the glass and there was nothing left to be seen.

CHAPTER 8

Grigonis House – Pittstown, New Jersey, last year

"How do you take your tea?" Berta asked John Charles as she poured boiling water into a line of mismatched coffee mugs.

"Just plain for me, thank you," said John Charles as he sat at the table with his hands resting on his lap. Nothing about him looked out of place or awkward. It was as if he had taken his seat at this table every Monday afternoon for the past one hundred years. The other man in front of Ava looked completely lost in the act of trying to fix the toy racer. He produced a tool from the back pocket of his overalls and already removed the undercarriage of the car from the body. Ava held the number 8's frame as the man worked silently on. Each part he removed he handed to Ava for safekeeping.

"And you there?" Berta barked at the man whose concentration was firmly fixed on the underbelly of the car's chassis. He didn't even look up at Berta. "What you take?"

"Nothing for me, ma'am."

Berta brought the two cups over to Ava's mother and John Charles. He nodded his thanks as he just sat with his hands safely out of sight, with no motion of touching his cup.

"After all these years, someone from INR is here," Ava's mother said as she held the hot mug up to her mouth. She shook her head in disbelief as she blew on the water. "I'm sorry but I'm just so... surprised."

"Why is that?" asked John Charles. He tilted his head and gave her a pretend scowl. "Did you think we didn't exist?"

She let out a chuckle. "No, no. I always believed." She gave a quick look at Ava and then leaned in. Her voice dropped in tone and volume. "Dad would sometimes let me read the letters."

John Charles let out a full-blown laugh. "Well, I can assure you, what they ask for now is quite different. We don't make many toys by hand. Now we do everything through computers." He lifted his lumps of bone and knuckles and did his best to imitate the act of typing on a keyboard. Ava thought, no wonder he needed help. No one would have presents under their Christmas tree if the typing were left to that man. "But in a way, it makes it easier."

Berta, who stood by the sink, turned around quickly. "Wait a moment. Is this the man with the letters?" Berta pointed her mug at John Charles. "The one Raymond speaks of?" Her accent thickened the more excited she became. "I thought he made it up. He..." Berta circled her one free hand in the air as if she were trying to whip up a breeze. "You know. Tell fairy tales."

"I can assure you it's no fairy tale. We sent Raymond letters for a number of years," John Charles said as he finally reached for his tea. His fingers would not allow him to grasp the handle. He scooped up the mug carefully in both hands and held it to his chin. "Before everyone wanted something electronic."

Ava's mother cleared her throat and shot John Charles a look. Her eyes then pointed to Ava. John Charles put his mug down and looked over at Ava affectionately. "I'm sorry, Ava. You do believe in Santa, don't you?"

The man fixing the car broke his attention from the metal racer and looked up at Ava, waiting for her to answer.

"Yes," Ava answered.

"And do you know your grandfather worked for him?"

"Yes," Ava said tentatively as she looked up at the adults. All of them looked at her as if they were waiting to hear her lead them in evening grace or recite the Pledge of Allegiance. "Pop-pop says Santa and him would make gifts for kids at Christmas time."

"He sure did. We heard it all the time," her mother said as she rubbed her forehead. "I mean *all the time.*" Her eyes widen and she let out an exasperated breath. Berta nodded in agreement as she took a sip of tea. Ava did not mind her grandfather's constant talk about Christmas. She couldn't believe how amazing and lucky her Pop-pop had been to be handpicked by Santa himself. But her mother said that all the talking about Santa Claus turned Christmas into a four-letter word. Ava wondered what that four-letter word was. She prayed it wasn't the word "over."

"But yes, honey," her mother continued. "Santa sent Pop-pop his letters through this man's company."

"No," Ava said while shaking her head. She stood up and put one hand on her hip as she pressed her index finger to her lips in thought. "He knew the *real* Santa. Pop-pop said he made toys with him when he was a little boy. In his house full of clocks."

"Oh, yes. You're talking about when he was young, like you," John Charles said. "When he worked alongside Oscar Taglieber."

Ava's mother looked taken aback. "Wow, how did you know that name? That's going back quite a few years."

"He's a legend," John Charles said. "Oh, he is not the first Santa Claus but the general consensus at INR was that he was one of the greatest Santas that ever lived. He brought a lot of joy into children's lives," John Charles said with a smile. He looked down at the man who was in the middle of taking off one of the wheels on the racer with his small Swiss Army knife. The man did not look up but nodded in agreement. John Charles finally took a sip of his tea. "Yes, he did. Lots and lots of joy."

CHAPTER 9

Oscar's House – Southold, New York, 1944

Ray couldn't have been more miserable as he walked up Oscar Taglieber's driveway. On the orders of his mother, every single day up until Christmas he was to go to Mr. Taglieber's weird workshop and spend at least two hours assisting him in making whatever it was he needed to make. She said it would help, only he did not know who or how. After the many fruitless negotiations with his mother, Ray couldn't make her budge. Ray thought of every excuse. From doing more chores, to protecting Olive and Tommy from the stray dogs that roamed the neighborhood, to the fact that even Oscar himself didn't seem to want Ray around, nothing would change her mind. Nothing ever did.

Ray did not lift his heels from the ground. The entire two-mile walk from the school to Oscar's was one long shuffle. His footprints resembled wagon tracks in the snow. He hoped Olive and Tommy would catch up to him if he lingered long enough on the road but every time he stopped and turned around they were nowhere to be seen. Then an idea popped into his head. Maybe, if he knocked softly enough, Oscar wouldn't hear him. Then he could run home and still have some daylight left to play with Olive, Tommy, and Paley. After all, how could he help Mr. Taglieber if he wouldn't let him in the house? Hope began to bubble up until he turned the corner into Oscar Taglieber's driveway and saw him sitting in the front bay window wearing crazy looking goggles. Oscar looked up and spotted Ray through the window. He pushed the gear away from his face and gave him a less than enthusiastic nod. Great, Ray thought. I guess this makes two of us.

Ray heard the footsteps before he even knocked at the front door. From the sound of Oscar's gait it seemed as if he had a problem with lifting his feet up as well. Ray felt like an hour had passed before the door opened and Oscar appeared.

"Hello, Raymond, glad you could make it," Oscar said with a voice which sounded anything but glad. Ray followed him in and took the long walk down the dimly lit hallway towards the living room. Ray looked back at the sad little dusty rooms he passed the first time he entered the house with his mother. Ray asked his mother if Oscar had a wife and kids. Apparently, he did. A wife and a little boy. Both passed away from some fever long before Ray was even born. That's the one who must have decorated these rooms, Ray thought. She must have liked doilies and dancers. She must have been pretty.

"Don't mind the mess," Oscar said nervously as they entered the living room. Nothing had changed from the last time Ray was there. The hundred or so clocks stared down at him as he took in the sights and smells of space. Looking at the room was like looking through a stereoscope with two totally different photographs layered on top of each other. One, a gracious living room with a gold mirror over the fireplace, tasseled tie-backs on the curtains, a throw pillow embroidered with the word "love," and fancy rugs on the floor. The other, a man's shop with a tool for every job a person could think up and a screw, nail, washer, or bolt to match. Wood boards hovered over chairs creating flat surfaces in mid-air; each acted like a "dead end" sign for potential visitors. Ray fought the urge to shut one eye at a time, thinking the room would magically change from one version to the other. He also wondered if this is what his house would look like if his dad were alive and his mother had died.

Ray suddenly remembered what he needed to say to the old man upon entering his house. His mother made him recite it five times over breakfast to make sure he got it right. Ray looked up at the ceiling and spat out in staccato his greeting.

"Oh, umm, thank you, Mr. Taglieber, for letting me in into your home and helping you with your work. It is very kind of you to…"

Oscar lowered head and raised his hand. "Please, call me Oscar, Raymond. You are working for free. When I start paying you, then you can call me Mr. Taglieber," he said as he wobbled his round frame to a table made from a barn shutter to pick up some paper. Ray couldn't imagine addressing a man by his first name, especially one as old as Oscar. Ray couldn't tell his age. Oscar was whatever age old is. Fifty-five, one hundred, eighty-four? He couldn't tell. He looked more like a grandfather than a dad. There would be no pitching a baseball game or running through woods with Oscar. His fastest speed appeared to be a wobble. His thick wavy hair and beard were both white as flour with no other traces of color or gray. Ray thought Olive and his mother were right. He would make a good department store Santa if the store didn't mind that Santa didn't smile or like kids.

"So you are probably wondering why the toys," Oscar said as he put on his reading glasses.

"Mom said you are Santa."

Oscar let out an unhappy chuckle. "No, no, no. I'm not Santa." He looked at Raymond over his spectacles. "Just to be clear. You don't… you know…" he said as he circled the air with the paper, attempting to speak the remaining of the sentence with his hands. "…believe?"

"In Santa?" Ray said, finishing Oscar's thought. "No. I meant what I said to Tommy."

A look of relief came over Oscar's face. "Good. Just wanted to make sure before I showed you this." Oscar put the stack of papers he held in front of Raymond, each lined and filled with children's handwriting. Some with pictures, some written in colored ink, but all started with the same two words: "Dear Santa." Ray flipped through them with wide eyes, as if he were secretly reading a teacher's grade ledger. Dolls, gloves, trains, ages, Bobby, Jacob, Sue, Matthew, Mary Jane, kittens, dogs, love, believe, were all words that jumped off the page and into Raymond's memory. He looked up at Oscar in amazement.

"Wow," Ray said slowly. "How did you get these?"

"I get them every year. Schools, hospitals, post offices send their letters to Santa to this company INR Industries. They then farm them out to some of us to fulfill certain orders. I take care of all the toys made of metal. You'd think since everyone is tossing their belt buckles in scrap metal drives kids wouldn't be asking for trains and cars, but oh no. The requests keep coming in. And a zeppelin made out of wood? Well, you might as well put a dictionary under the Christmas tree."

Raymond cocked his head as Oscar spoke. "It's like you work for Santa, sorta?" Raymond said.

Oscar scratched his beard in thought. "Why yes, one could see it that way."

Ran looked down at one of the letters and ran his hand over the name. The corners of his lips tighten. "My dad told me he worked for Santa once."

"Absolutely he did!" Oscar said as he flung his arms in the air. "Hal Kozak's no liar. Helped me out many, many a time. Any part made of wood I gave to Hal," Oscar said as he made his way back to the workbench and donned the crazy goggles. "Little kids all over Suffolk

County would have toy boats that looked like bars of soap if wasn't for your father."

Ray smiled inside. It was nice hearing someone talk about his dad this way, to hear someone speak about his father and not lower their voice or droop their face. Everyone seemed too nervous to speak about his dad in front of him except his mother, Olive and, on the rare occasion that he spoke, Paley. Every mention of his dad began with, "I remember" and ended with "God rest his soul."

Oscar pushed the crazy goggles up to his forehead, which made his white hair stand up like lightning bolts on top of his scalp. "First things first." Oscar creaked down onto a stool and slapped his knees. "My stool," he said as he pointed in the direction of the stool that hid under his wide bottom. He pointed over to the other end of the long table. "Your stool."

Ray saw a small, clean, wooden stool fifteen feet away from Oscar. Both of them faced the bay window. Ray sat at the stool, looked out over the front yard and immediately saw Olive and Tommy slowly walk down the road. They certainly saw Ray before Ray saw them. Olive lifted her hand no higher than her waist to signal a subtle hello, her half-smile meant to not draw attention to the greeting. Tommy, however, raised his hand over his head and waved it back and forth as if he were washing a window. He could hear Tommy yell his greeting through the bay's pane. Ray smirked the other half of Olive's smile back at the two and held his hand up like he was showing them the number "five." The whole neighborhood could see them in the window. Ray felt himself blush.

"This is the best spot for light in the afternoon. Now, have a look-see at the tools in front of you. Recognize them?"

Ray's attention broke away from Olive and Tommy as he looked at the lineup of small instruments in front of him. Ray peered down and tried to focus on the tools. He recognized nothing. These objects seemed to be from another world. They almost didn't look like tools at all. More like silver and brass gadgets and utensils used to fix a flying saucer. He picked up something that looked more like a needle from a doctor's office than a tool. He gulped. "No, sir. Never saw a tool like this in my entire life?"

"Your entire life, you say?" Oscar said. "Good. Don't touch them." Oscar rolled his stool over to Ray and took the needle-like tool out of his hand. "This is used for making pocket watches. If you said you knew what this was, I'd think you were weird or fibbing. Neither trait will help you in life." He put the tool right back in its place. "Don't touch these guys. If you have the urge to know, I'll tell you. I will put the tools you will need here." He pointed to an empty spot to the right of the mysterious instruments. "This space is your domain. Your tools will go here and I won't touch them. Good?"

"Good," answered Ray, relieved. For a moment, he thought his mother oversold Ray's ability.

"Now to the letters. You see these red circles?" Oscar grabbed one from the top of the stack. His chubby sausage finger pointed in the center of a red circle. "This is what we have to make." On this particular letter, Stanley, age 4, wanted a puppy, a football, and an airplane. Someone had circled the word "airplane" with a big red marker. "We only have to do what's circled in red. Nothing more. We're not in the business of making dolls or puppies." Oscar scratched his sideburns in thought. "Well, we can't really make a puppy. We'd have to just find one at a junkyard or steal one from the pound, I guess. But no, we'll do none of that."

"But what about the other things on their list?" Ray asked, pointing to the lonely uncircled items on the letter. "What happens to those?"

"Well, that's why God invented parents," Oscar said. "Or they'll just have to understand that you can't get everything you want in this life." Oscar leaned back and with one push, propelled himself back to his original place at the end of the bench. "But they'll get the airplane. And if they are not a spoiled ninny that will be enough."

Ray looked at Oscar in amazement. If ever there was a Santa Claus then this guy was, without a doubt, not him.

CHAPTER 10

Goose Creek Bridge – Southold, New York, 1944

"A hundred? Really?" Olive questioned as they walked over the bridge towards their homes. Olive and Ray resumed walking home from school together even though Mrs. Goldsmith offered to drive Olive home with Tommy. Apparently, the apology did not get Ray back into Mrs. Goldsmith's good graces or her Pierce Arrow. Ray wasn't at all sure why Olive turned down Mrs. Goldsmith's offer. It wasn't even winter yet but there was already snow on the ground. *The Farmer's Almanac* predicted December 1944 to be one of the harshest ever on the North Fork. A ride home in the Goldsmith's warm, comfortable car would be preferable to trudging through the snow with grumpy Ray. But it made him smile nonetheless when he saw her waiting for him by the tennis courts after school.

Ray lifted his chin in conviction. "A hundred. Really," he answered. Ray had only worked with Oscar for three days but he felt like he could tell Olive three years' worth of stories. Between the clocks blasting off every hour to the crazy tools laying around the workshop to the crazy things kids ask for in their letters to Santa, Oscar's place had turned into a treasure trove of neighborhood fables. "Not one alike. But I swear to Christopher Columbus they all stop chiming at the exact same time."

"Why so many?" Olive asked. "Why a hundred?"

"I don't know. They must be for sale. Or maybe it reminds him to do things." Ray chuckled as he thought aloud. "Maybe he's says, 'It's one o'clock! Time to chase the kids off the street.' "

"Or, 'It's time to smile!'" Olive added.

"It's two o'clock! Time to pick my nose!" Ray demonstrated this by putting a gloved finger up his nostril. Olive dissolved into a fit of giggles.

"Time to laugh at jokes," she said.

"Or scratch my rear end!" Ray turned around and scrunched up his face at Olive as he scratched the back pockets of his pants. She stopped walking as she put her mittens up to her mouth to cover her laughter. Ray enjoyed goofing off in front of his captive audience. He threw his arms in the air and swatted down. "It's time to let one rip…"

Suddenly, Olive's eyes turned from slits to large balls of terror. Her laughter stopped but her hands stayed close to her face. She whispered from behind her mittens.

"Ray. Behind you."

Ray heard the low growl before he even turned his head around. Twenty feet up the road crouched Fluffles, the Kelly's dog. A mix from among a German shepherd, a wolf and a demon, there wasn't one kid on Jacob's Lane who wasn't bit, or chased until they fainted, by that dog. Fluffles used to run free to terrorize the neighborhood until the Goldsmiths moved onto the block. Then Fluffles spent his afternoons chained to a post in the Kelly's backyard, left to barking and chasing weaker animals that came in his circle. But from the silver links that dangled from its neck, Fluffles wanted to hunt bigger game.

"Don't…run…yet…" Ray said as he stood in front of Olive. He put his hands out to try and calm the beast. "Easy, Fluffles. We don't want to…"

A stream of loud barking erupted from its dripping jowls. Fluffles didn't seem to care what Ray wanted. Baring its teeth, Fluffles slowly moved towards Ray and Olive. A hum of fear came from Olive as she peeked under Ray's armpit at the dog. Steam crept out of the dog's mouth as it snarled at the two. Ray stared at the dog but spoke to Olive.

"When I say go, run up that old hunting stand we just passed, ok?" He could feel Olive nodding in agreement behind him. As its paws inched closer, Ray whispered, "Go!"

Olive's presence vanished behind him as he heard her run towards the woods. Fluffles lurched to the left in an attempt to chase Olive until Ray's math textbook hit him in the face. The dog shook it off and bolted after Ray, who had turned to run to the deer stand. Ray's feet flew with fear over the books Olive dropped in the snow. The barking had stopped but the chilling sound of Fluffles' panting and the broken chain smacking the pavement grew louder behind Ray. He would never outrun that dog, Ray thought. Even if he got to the hunting stand the dog would certainly take a bite out of his leg. Just as his feet left the pavement towards the woods he heard another set of feet smacking the pavement. Only it wasn't a person or another dog. It sounded like a small horse. Then, for a split second, all sound stopped. It was as if someone turned off the radio in the middle of the show and then put it back on during another program. The running, the panting, the chain rattling stopped and was replaced by a loud, high-pitched yelp. Ray looked over his shoulder and saw Fluffles sprawled out on his side, then scramble to his feet. The dog sneezed in disgust and rocked its head side to side. Ray stopped and turned to see what car might have hit the dog when his mouth dropped open.

There, between Fluffles and himself, stood a buck. Its head hung low and back legs hunched, as if it were going to charge at the dog like a bull. Fluffles let out a queasy growl until the buck slapped its front hooves on the pavement. Its rack pointed at the dog like six branches whittled into wooden blades. And with that the mutt let out a small bark in defeat and trotted up Ships Drive, away from the victor. The buck raised it head high in pride but kept its attention in the direction of the dog. Ray stood in shock and stared at the back of the buck's head, focusing on the sharp antlers that it must have used to toss the dog. The buck only stood a foot taller than Ray but its antlers gave the animal an impressive height. If the buck wanted to gore Ray to death with those bony daggers, it would be easy. Ray couldn't move, speak or breathe. All he could do was pray he wasn't next on the receiving end of those horns. It wasn't until the dog was safely out of sight when the stag's head whipped around in Ray's direction. Then Ray let out another gasp.

It wasn't a buck. It was *his* buck. The buck with a star on its face.

"Olive!" Ray cried. He needed someone to see this. To know that this buck existed. That it wasn't in his head. Fear left his body and the overwhelming urge to show Olive took its place. But as soon as his cry hit the air the buck turned its body around and bounded into the woods, its white tail high in the air in victory as it leapt over fallen trees and brush.

Ray ran after it and yelled out the only words that seemed appropriate. "Thank you!"

"Who are you thanking?" Olive said as she raced over to the books strewn across the snow. "And what happened to Fluffles? Did you hurt him?" Olive asked as she wiped the dirt off the cover of her history book.

"Did you see that? Did you see the buck with the star on its head?" Ray asked, pointing into the woods. His eyes fixed onto a nonexistent point in the distance.

"No," Olive said as she picked up Ray's math book. Her balance wobbled as she continued to jog with an armful of books. "But we better get to Oscar's quick. Before Fluffles comes back. If Mrs. Goldsmith and a chain can't stop that dog, nothing will."

Ray ran behind Olive, confused and amazed by what he just witnessed. "Olive, are you sure you didn't see that deer?"

"I didn't but I believe you," Olive said as she turned the corner onto Oscar's driveway. She ran up to the door, dropped all the books on the ground and banged on the door until Oscar appeared behind it. He looked even crazier than usual. Wearing a welder's cap and high water waders, Oscar looked as if he spent the day soldering lobster pots in the bay.

"What? Where? When?" Oscar said as he opened the door. He looked down and saw Olive. "Who?"

"I'm Olive Mott," she said to the ground as she feverishly picked up the scattered schoolbooks. "May I please come in?"

"Umm…uhhhh?" Oscar didn't seem to know what to make of the request. He didn't have much time as Fluffles' distant bark made Ray and Olive jump up in fright and run past him into the house. Ray led Olive into the living room, leaving Oscar to lumber along behind. "What in the Sam Hill is going on here?"

Olive turned to Oscar and said just one word, empathically. "Fluffles."

"Oh." Oscar raised his hand in the air. "Say no more. If that mangy mongrel broke off his run the outside is not safe for man nor beast," he said as he waddled past the two to take his place on his stool. "You can stay here until it's time for Ray to go home."

Olive stood in the center of the room and stared up at all the clocks. "Wow, Mister. Those are a lot of clocks," Olive said, dumbstruck.

"Well, I guess those…are," Oscar sputtered as he put on his work apron.

"Why so many? Are they for sale?" she asked.

Oscar pushed the welder's mask down on his face. The answer came out in an echo from behind the shield. "No. They are not for sale."

"Why not?"

Oscar appeared uncomfortable with the line of questioning. Ray put on his apron and tried not to look at Oscar. It made him uncomfortable that Oscar felt so squeamish about the question but like Olive, he wanted to know the same thing. Oscar uttered some noises under the metal veil in a search for the right answer but gave up in frustration. He pushed the mask back up in defeat.

"I don't know," he said sternly. "I am a clockmaker. I have a wall. I need to know what time it is. You're a smart girl. You do the math."

The answer satisfied Olive but Ray didn't buy it. Ray walked to his seat and looked at the assembly line of zeppelins and airplanes that lined the long bench. Oscar made the exteriors of the two forms during the day. Ray's job was to put together the axles and wheels to fit underneath the bodies. By the time Ray got to Oscar's place a toy air force was lined up and ready to be fitted with its parts. Ray felt like a smaller version of his dad, which is why he started to like going to Oscar's after school. Only it was so quiet, except for the constant clicking from the walls. He wanted to talk to Oscar but he usually grunted at the tools and hid behind some kind of odd goggle or mask. He never felt like he could ask him anything, at least not as directly as Olive.

"Can I have a job too?" asked Olive. Ray and Oscar turned around and looked at Olive with their eyebrows raised. "I can help you," she continued timidly. "You know, with this." She pointed to the colorful letters from Santa strung up like sheets on a clothesline over the workbench. Oscar looked blindly around the room and patted his overalls as if searching for his wallet. Finally, he picked up a blowtorch.

"Can you weld?" Oscar asked, holding up the small blowtorch.

"No." Olive's answer was barely audible.

"How much do you know about tools?" Oscar searched the area of the bench reserved for his clockmaking instruments. Finally, he hoisted something up that looked like a sundial with two spinning arms. "What's this?"

Olive's chin sank down. "Don't know."

Oscar huffed as he rifled around the workbench and picked up another tool made of wood with a hole on one end and point on the other.

"Well, how about this one? Can you tell me what this does?"

Olive shook her head dejected. "No, sir. I don't know what that is."

"I didn't think so," Oscar huffed. Ray's head sank too. If he didn't know what any of those were then how could Olive? She would have an easier time if he asked her to read Latin. Oscar reached down aimlessly and picked up another tool. "What about this?"

Olive's head lifted up and a smile sprung on her face. "That's a paintbrush!"

Oscar did a double take to the small brush he held in his hand. "Why…huh…what do you know, I guess it is a paintbrush. Look at that. Shoot." He shook off his indignation. "Well, do you know how to use it?"

"Yes, sir. I paint very well," Olive said smiling. "I paint model planes with my brother Paley all the time."

Ray nodded in agreement. "Olive's draws the best in our class."

"Does she now?" Oscar said while scratching his beard. He looked madder than a spider caught in its own web. He picked up a plane that looked as if it were dunked in a pot of mustard. "Can you do better than that?"

Olive walked over to and examined the plane in Oscar's hand. "I think I can do a better "G" than that."

"G? G!" Oscar yelled. Ray couldn't tell if he was serious. "That's a number 6! You sure those glasses you're wearing work?"

Olive's smile turned into a full-blown laugh. She put her hands to her mouth to push it back. Ray tried to cough back his laugh but found Oscar's rage hilarious.

"G, my guts," Oscar mumbled as he motioned Olive to the other side of the room. "If you can do a better number "6" I'd like to see you try. Let's set up you here." Oscar cleared off a table which was made from an old board resting on the arms of a fancy dining room chair. "This is your space, Miss Missy. If you see Ray coming over here and messing with your business, you have my permission to paint a 'G' on his forehead. Let me get you an apron." Oscar waddled out of the room as Olive turned to Ray and quietly clapped her hands in excitement.

Ray leaned forward and whispered. "Told you he was…" He finished the sentence by circling his finger around his ear.

Olive whispered back. "I like him. He's funny."

"He's as cuckoo as his clocks."

Oscar came back to the room with small tins of paint in one arm and a long apron draped over the other. "Here you go. It's a bit big but you'll grow into it."

"Thank you, Mr. Taglieber," Olive said as she put on apron and a sweet smile. The apron draped down to her feet. "It fits perfect."

"Thank Fluffles," he muttered as he put the paint down and headed back to his seat. "And don't call me Mr. Taglieber. What can she call me, Raymond?"

Ray sat down and spun around towards the window. "Oscar."

"And when can she call me Mr. Taglieber?"

"When you pay her."

"My guts! That's a smart man, right there," Oscar yelled as he smacked the workbench. All the little zeppelins and airplanes jumped and shifted, like an earthquake erupted under their little airstrip. "Now then, tell me. How did you manage to outrun Fluffles?"

"Ray hit him with a book," Olive said proudly. "And he ran away."

"Well done," said Oscar. "I hope you used a biology book. I was horrible in biology."

"No," Ray said as he studied the axle. "I mean, yes. I threw a book at the dog but there was a...a," Ray's voice faded out. He couldn't decide whether to tell Oscar about the deer. After all, he was the only other person who knew about that particular buck. He also saw it that day at the Christmas tree farm. He might understand. Or think he was nuts. "I think it was my math textbook."

Oscar stopped working and looked over at Ray with his eyebrows raised. He sat with his hands on his knees as if he were waiting for Ray to continue. Ray saw Oscar's look but kept his head down, faking concentration on the wheels. After a moment Oscar just exhaled, shrugged his shoulders and said, "A math book works fine in a pinch, I guess."

❄ ❄ ❄

Ray said next to nothing for the rest of the evening. Each of the three sat at their respective stations and worked quietly until the clocks on the wall cried out that it was four o'clock and time for Olive and Ray to leave. Their walk home turned into a run for fear of Fluffles returning and picking up where his bark left off. They only stopped the pace when they saw Paley rocking back and forth in the front yard.

"Hey ya, Paley," Olive said as she patted his back. Paley stood at least a foot taller than Ray and looked like a giant next to Olive. Paley wouldn't look down or stop his rocking. His body chugged along like a pendulum on a grandfather clock, always moving to a constant pulse but never leaving where it sat. His concentration held tight to the sky as his hands gripped the cereal box. His face contorted in concentration as if he were trying to read the evening clouds. Olive kept on with her cheery tone. "See anything today?"

He shook his head back and forth while still staring up at the empty white sky. Today, Ray scanned around the three for any sign of the dog. He wouldn't let his eyes travel upward. Sometimes Ray joined Paley in his search for enemy planes. He would sit in the leaves and stare up over the treetops for hours, looking for ominous black dots to appear against a blue and white backdrop. Tonight, however, the enemy felt closer to the ground.

"That's a good thing, right?" Ray asked, looking past Paley into the woods. The underbrush of the woods sat motionless in the background and growing darker by the second. He didn't know if Fluffles would be a match for Paley but he had no intention of finding out. There were no dads around to fight off the dog and Oscar's place was far out of screaming distance. "Paley, you guys should go inside. I think Fluffles might still be out."

"It's getting dark anyway," Olive chimed in as she grabbed Paley's forearm and led him towards the house. "Ray will look out for planes in his room, right, Ray?"

"Yeah," Ray said, keeping his eyes on the woods. "I'll keep my eyes peeled for planes."

Paley's concentration broke from the air. He stopped moving and turned towards Ray. His one hand released the cardboard box and pointed to the woods. "And soldiers," Paley said with all the conviction of a general. "Look for soldiers."

"I'll look for soldiers too," Ray insisted, half paying attention. "I promise."

Paley nodded his head in agreement and left with Olive towards their home, where Mrs. Mott stood with the front door open, welcoming the two in for dinner. As soon as Ray saw the two safely step on their front porch, he ran as a fast as he could towards his own house. The house where a single light in the kitchen illuminated the whole first floor and where he knew his mother would be standing in front of a steaming stove, dropping peeled potatoes into a boiling pot. Before Ray could even reach the front door a chill ran up his spine as he remembered how his father explained war. He said that a war doesn't happen in just one place to one person. It starts as evil. And evil is bad feelings that gets in a person's heart and comes out their hands. Enough evil feelings get into enough hearts and enough hands, then it makes a war.

His dad was right. Ray could feel it. Something bad was in the air. That's why his dad needed to go over and help stop it. Even under Paley's watch, even though tanks and guns and bombs exploded an ocean away, Ray felt helpless. Maybe the wind picked it up from the battlefields of France and Germany and swept it over the ocean to the shores of his town. And like any big storm, maybe the animals were the first ones to sense that trouble was on its way. Maybe that buck knew that trouble was already here.

❋ ❋ ❋

Ray kept his promise to Paley. After they said their evening prayers and his mother kissed him good night, Ray looked out his window and scoured the landscape for activity. No sightings to report. No soldiers, no Fluffles and no buck. Ray crawled back into his bed again with thoughts of his buck heavy on his mind. He told his mother about the incident with Fluffles over soup but barely mentioned the experience with the deer. Ray's mother peppered him with so many questions about Oscar, Olive, and Fluffles during dinner that Ray couldn't tell her what happened with the deer even if he wanted. He instead brought the topic up sideways with questions like, "Do deer hit other animals?" "Do bucks ever attack people?" and "Do deer hate dogs?" hoping she would change course in her line of questioning. His mother's response was the same for all three. "I guess. If they're scared enough."

But that buck didn't seem scared. But maybe it was. Ray couldn't tell. His dad had a streak of grey hair on top of his head. He said it came from where he cut his head as a kid. Maybe the deer had gotten into a fight. Or maybe grazed by a hunter's bullet. Maybe the buck knew no fear. Maybe the animal that gave it that white mark had the strength of twenty Fluffles. A bear claw maybe? Maybe a wound? Maybe a birth mark? Maybe magic?

Raymond did not believe in magic anymore. Not after The Worst Day. But he knew his father did. More than any episode of *Terry and the Pirates*, more than *The Night Before Christmas* on Christmas Eve or any tale from Mick's shop that Ray could eavesdrop on, Ray loved to hear his father retell the story of the day when he was a little boy and candy magically appeared out of thin air. The day when everything good that ever happened in his life started. He called it his Most Magical Day. A day that made him believe that if you look hard enough you can find miracles hiding in the most unlikely places and in the most unusual of people.

CHAPTER 11

The Most Magical Day – Southold, New York, 1919

It started like every other day in the spring of 1919. An eight-year-old Hal Kozak walking eight feet behind his two older brothers, Tim and Christopher. His little head buried under an oversized cap one of his brothers stole from a five and ten a few towns away. On this day, they were heading to Shiller's Penny Candy Store to read the next installment of "Detective No" in *Adventure* magazine. Although there were only three, the Kozak boys banged into Shiller's Penny Candy like they were an army of twenty. Christopher pushed open the door so hard that the bell hit the high tin ceiling, causing the customers to cringe. The storeowner let out a loud growl as he sat behind the counter and glared at the boys, adding up the amount of gum and *Adventure* magazines that would most likely be leaving the premises without being paid for.

Kozak is Polish for criminal. Or at least that's what one would think in the town of Southold back in 1919. None of the boys went to school after the age of ten and all, except Hal, were considered *persona non grata* in every store that sold items small enough to fit into a coat pocket. The brothers were often spotted walking in a line from pool hall to pool hall and were rarely, if ever, seen with their father. Tim and Christopher spent most of their time and money hustling men at pool while Hal spent his time playing with ashtrays under the bar tables and trying not to be noticed. The only time Hal would take an interest in anything Tim and Christopher did was when they would work on an old jalopy. Then he would stick his little hand into whatever small space in the engine Tim or Christopher asked him to. Machines made sense to Hal. One wheel made another part move. If you could learn these things, then the engine works. It was all cause and effect to him. Hustling and stealing did not make sense. It required too much running and hiding for what you wound up getting. It seemed like a large price to pay for the way people looked at you. Hal didn't like that people were happy when he and his brothers left a store. Shop owners typically waved people in and opened doors for customers. Not close them and turn the locks over when they passed by.

Hal loved his brothers, although he did not look up to them. Protectors do not always need to be heroes. Hugs and hand-holding never came from Tim and Christopher. They showed love in harder ways. Like the last night he ate dinner alone with his father. His father's drinking didn't get better after his mother left the house but the aim of his drunken fists did. One night while Christopher and Tim were out at the Broken Down Valise Pub, Hal felt sick and couldn't finish his supper. For some reason beyond Hal's young mind his father flew into a rage and threw his dinner plate at Hal's head. When his brothers walked into the house they found Hal crouched in the corner trying to stop the blood spilling out from a cut on his forehead, with their father eating at the table and reading the local paper as if nothing had happened. After that night, Tim and Christopher made sure Hal never spent a moment alone with their father. They also made sure their father could never use his right arm again.

"You aiming to buy anything, boys?" hollered Mr. Shiller from behind the counter.

Christopher let out a sly chuckle and blew air through his teeth. "Nah, just looking, Fatso," he said as they headed towards the pulp and dime novel section of the store, pushing kids out of the way who didn't immediately scurry at the sight of them. The two lanky teens perched on the shelves with their feet up and rifled through the colored magazines as if they were relaxing in their bunks.

Mr. Shiller's eyes narrowed as he grabbed the counter's edge, shifting his three hundred-pound frame back and forth on the stool. If he weren't so fat he could get out from behind the counter and chase away the Kozak boys. But he couldn't. All his rage allowed him to do was watch the crime and yell. "I got my eyes peeled on you fellows."

"And some bananas too, I'm sure," Tim chimed in with a laugh. The two kept to their reading and ignored the threats. Hal made his way past the front counter, avoiding the glare of Mr. Shiller. Mr. Shiller couldn't be bothered with Hal. He just sat there steamed, mad enough to melt all the caramels that lined the counter.

Hal put his hands in his pant pockets and shuffled the thin material through his tiny fingers, hoping to turn it into penny for some candy. Hal looked around the store at all the kids running to open big jars of the pink, brown, and red confections. Each one would reach in and emerge with tiny fistfuls of gold. The only one in the mob not interested in the candy was a girl roughly the same age as he, corralling smaller kids. Her shiny black hair and round face looked pretty against her purple coat. She was too busy directing their hands into bags or getting them to stop crying to find anything for herself. Her bright hazel eyes glanced up at Hal for only a moment, causing Hal to jump. He didn't know that he stopped to look at her and could feel the heat rush to his cheeks. He pushed the rim of his dirty cap down and made his way back through the aisles.

Hal walked down the rows, passing the Orange Slices, pepper-mints, Tootsie Rolls, and colorful Necco Wafers to the big glass jar that held his favorite chocolate candies. He only ate them a couple of times in his short life when his mother gave them to him for his birthday but he never forgot the taste. Since he had no pennies he propped his feet up on the shelf, opened the lid, stuck his head as far as it would go into the jar and inhaled the scent as deeply as he could. The rich chocolate smell luxuriated in the back of his nose and throat. He thought if he breathed it in hard enough then one would materi-alize on his tongue. But the more he huffed, the more he couldn't get the taste of cigarette smoke from the pub out of his nostrils.

He stepped down and stared in the jar filled with the individu-ally wrapped chocolate treats. There were so many. He reached his arm in and pulled one out. Then a thought came to him. Mr. Shiller's attention was on his brothers. All the other kids were busy running about the store buying bags of candy. Would anyone even know if one candy disappeared? Would it even matter to Mr. Shiller? Hal held the wrapped treat up in thought. Kozak is Polish for criminal, after all.

Then another thought popped into his mind. What if he got caught? What if his father found out? It wasn't the thought of his father's punishment that was frightening. He knew all too well the weight of his father's hand on him. It was the thought of his brothers' hands on his father. A punishment for Hal meant an even larger one for his dad. A small row of chocolates would translate into a row of bruises that would take a much longer time to fade than the taste of sweets on his lips. The chocolate treat no longer tasted so good. He returned the candy to the jar with its mates and slowly closed the lid. When Hal turned around he noticed the little girl in the purple coat standing at the end of the next aisle. She looked at him curiously. Hal just smiled and turned towards a jar of gumballs tracing the tiny circles on the outside of the glass.

"Excuse me." A man in a fine linen suit walked between Hal and the girl and reached towards a box of Hershey bars on a higher shelf. He placed his hand on the counter for balance as he grabbed two bars. After he reached them he showed them to Hal. "Can't go home without one of these," he said with pride as a kind smile stretched across this face.

As he walked away Hal noticed a glimmer from the counter. In the spot where the man's hand just was sat a shiny new dime. He picked it up and rubbed it between his index and thumb. It looked as if it just came from the mint. Hal ran through the aisles looking for the man and found him at the register trying to make idle chat with Mr. Shiller, who was pressing buttons on the register and staring at his brothers. Hal ran over to the man. He held the dime in the air as if he was trying not to get it dirty.

"Excuse me, Mister," Hal said as he tapped the man on the arm and held the coin over his head. "You dropped this."

Mr. Shiller's gaze finally broke from his brothers as he stared at Hal in horror. The man looked confused. "That's kind of you, my boy, but I don't think it's mine."

"I know it is. You left it by those Hershey bars. It's next to the ones I like," Hal insisted.

The man reached in his pocket and pulled out a small handful of coins. He moved the coins around his palm with his other index finger while his lips counted and examined the change. His hands appeared bent and gnarled, like broken branches off a tree. After closer examination, he looked down and shook his head.

"No, I think that one's yours. I have everything I need."

The smile on the man's face traveled over to Hal's as he lowered the coin to his eye level. A dime! He thought. A whole dime. Then suddenly the dime vanished out of his fingers. Christopher stood over Hal and flipped it in the air.

"Thanks Hal!" he said as he slapped it down on the counter. "We're taking this," Christopher said as he held up a rolled-up copy of *Adventure* magazine. "Don't say we don't pay for nothing," he said as he playfully smacked Hal on the top of the head with the rolled-up magazine. "Come on, little brother. Let's get out of here." The bell already banged the ceiling, signaling his older brother Tim's exit.

Hal shrugged and followed Christopher until he heard Mr. Shiller cry out. "Hey, wait a minute! What do you say to him?" Mr. Shiller asked, pointing to Hal. Hal turned around embarrassed.

"Thank you, sir." Hal said, giving the man with the broken hands a smile. Mr. Shiller appeared confused.

"No, I was talking to your brother," he hollered. "Come back here!"

Christopher turned around, annoyed, as he thumped the magazine on his leg. "What else do you want? I already paid."

Mr. Shiller grabbed a brown paper bag from under the counter and opened it. "Since this is the first time you ever paid for anything in your life, let's make it official and put it in a paper bag."

Christopher strolled over and threw the magazine on the counter. Mr. Shiller stuffed it in the bag and handed it to Christopher. Christopher reached for it but Mr. Shiller would not let it go. His thick grip and face were both swollen with rage. "I don't want to see you or your older brother in this store again. You hear me?" He looked down at Hal. "Your little brother can be in here. But not you two." Christopher yanked the bag out of his hand. "If this is how you treat paying customers, fine. We won't come back and pay for anything again, Fatso."

Christopher turned on his heel and bounced out of the store. As soon as Hal walked through the doorway, Tim reached around and slammed the door behind him, causing a slew of magazines to slide in a wave off the shelves. Tim and Christopher laughed as they walked ahead of Hal down the sidewalk. Christopher took the brown bag off and flung it in the air.

"Eat dirt, you old windbag," he said. Hal watched the bag coast in the air but fall with a distinct thud on the ground. He walked over to the bag and saw something shiny peek out of the top. He reached down and slowly pulled from the bag a candy. But not just any candy. It was a row of his favorite chocolates encased in its cellophane sheathing. He held the candies up to his eyes in shock. Hal's brothers kept on walking as he looked to his left and right for a possible explanation. The only eyes he found were the same little hazel eyes he saw in the candy store. The little girl in the purple coat. Surrounded by her siblings she had stopped and looked at Hal with the same shocked look. She too saw the magic candy appear and acknowledged the miracle with a smile.

Hal put his teeth between two of the chocolates and drew one out of the package and into his mouth. The chocolate eviscerated the taste of smoke. It wasn't a memory. It was real. And it tasted sweeter and more wonderful than he remembered.

CHAPTER 12

Jacob's Lane – Southold, New York, 1944

"Could you please go into the basement and get me the..." Oscar stumbled over his thoughts as he waved his free hand in the air. "The thingamajig."

Ray looked down the workbench at Oscar and scratched his head. "The what?"

"You know? The whoziewhatsit." Oscar tried to illustrate by making a clamping motion with his hand.

Ray shook his head in confusion. He couldn't decipher Oscar's hand movements, the tone of his voice, or anything else he said through a mask. "What's a whoziewhatsit?"

Oscar lifted his welding mask up, slapped his hands on his knees, then began to whip the air around in front of his face as if he could form the word out of thin air. "Come on. It's the whatchamacallit!"

Ray kept looking at Oscar's movements for clues. His words certainly weren't giving him the answers. "Pliers? Clamp? Wrench?"

Olive cried out over her shoulder, "Scissors?"

"No, no, no!" Oscar said, clenching his hands in frustration. "You know, the thing that snips the tin."

"Tin snips?" Ray said with his one eyebrow raised.

Oscar slapped the table. "Did I need to spell it out for you? Yes, the thingamabob. Be a good man, go to the basement and grab me my old pair. They're on the workbench."

Ray nodded, stood up, wiped his hands on his apron and headed toward the back of the room. He stopped suddenly and turned around. "Wait. Where's your basement?"

"Go down the hallway by the kitchen. The door is at end on your left. The light switch at the bottom of the stairs on a...on a," Oscar didn't turn around as he held is arm up and made a fist. He brought it up and down as if he were hammering a nail with his hand. "On a..."

"String?"

"No, Smarty pants. A pull cord."

Ray looked at Olive, who sat hunched over a model zeppelin, meticulously painting a red letter "Z" on its canary yellow side. He crossed his eyes and shrugged. Olive let out a silent giggle before refocusing on the aircraft. They were getting used to Oscar's funny ways and sayings. His tone often sounded harsh and gruff, as if everything he said or that was said to him was a bother. But he never acted mean or angry. He treated Ray and Olive more like adults than kids. He even let them come in the house without knocking. They would just walk in, throw their books on a chair, find their aprons, and get to work. Bottles of root beer were always in the fridge for them and they could drink one any time they wanted. He even let Olive take home an extra bottle for Paley, since he was doing such a swell job protecting the neighborhood from the "Not-so Germans." He said the Germans who came to America before the war and the ones who didn't belong to the Nazi party, like himself and his family, were the good Germans. The "Not-so Germans" were the bad kind. He said any group of people that called themselves a name that sounded so much like the word "nutsy" or "not see" had to be either off their rockers or blind.

Ray headed down the hall until he saw a room lit by only the fading sunlight. He turned around to see if Oscar or Olive could spot him from the living room. When he saw only a wall, he placed his feet gently in the doorway, grabbed the sides of the doorframe and leaned in as far as his balance would take him. Looking around the room, he saw a bed carefully made with a cream-flowered comforter and two pillows neatly tucked into the sheets. Long lace curtains hung from the ceiling and ended in pools on the floor. The vanity held a lace runner with a mirror tray filled with small bottles of women's perfume, a hand mirror, and a long-handled hairbrush. The room, decorated in gold and yellow tones, seemed to be stained by years of sunlight, like an old piece of parchment paper. Dust danced in circles in the air as light filtered in through the lace curtains. The room was just like the other rooms of the house, filled with furniture and lovingly decorated but no longer in use.

Ray looked down and saw a picture of a pretty woman with light hair and large soft curls on the bedside table. She smiled at someone off camera with her head tilted to the side. Her features were soft and round, like her curls. Ray thought she seemed nice and looked like a mom who could make good cookies. Wedged in the frame was a picture of a baby. The photo curled from age and leaned away from the glass. Ray reached over and pushed it gently forward to see the back. Behind it were words written in a female's handwriting which read, "Friedrich Albert Taglieber, eight pounds, four ounces." A strange pull came over Ray. His eyes automatically drifted to the corner of the room. Propped up against the wall sat a folded bassinet. That must have been Friedrich's, he thought. The abandoned rooms no longer served a purpose. Oscar could not fold them up like he could the bassinet so he kept them untouched, hoping that time and sun would bleach them into a memory. Ray pushed himself out of the doorway and checked for fingerprints. He thought it was odd that a room that gold could make him feel so blue.

He continued to the white door at the end of the hallway. The area around the doorknob was stained from constant use. Ray opened it and descended the dark basement stairs until he saw a string hanging from the rafter. He pulled it and a light came on, illuminating the area. Oscar's basement looked no different than the one at his house. A workbench sat in the corner covered in tools, paints, oils, and wood blocks. A stack of logs sat in a large wooden bin ready to be used for his little potbelly stove. Hooks lined one side of the wall holding various ropes, saws, brooms, and even a coat. Ray walked over to the workbench and picked up the old pair of tin snips Oscar requested. Before he turned he noticed that above one of the hooks was writing. Ray recognized the words as soon as he read them.

> *Angel of God, my Guardian Dear,*
> *to whom God's love commits me here.*
> *Ever this night, be at my side,*
> *two light, two guard, two rule, two guide. Amen.*

Ray cocked his head to the side. Why did Oscar have a prayer written above his workbench? And why was it "two light" instead of "to light"? Beneath the words "light," "guard," "rule," and "guide" were four hooks each holding something that look like a harness for a large dog or reins for a tiny horse. Then Ray's question was answered. Each hook held two harnesses. Except for the hook under "light," which only had only one. He looked down on the workbench and saw its mate lying flat on the surface. Upon closer inspection, it appeared to be a small bridle. The straps smelled like earth and animal but were not heavily worn. After Ray inspected the reins he turned and noticed a sheet hanging over a doorway.

Ray walked over to the large cloth and ran his hands over the material. He thought for a second that maybe he shouldn't go inside that room. If Oscar wanted anyone to know what was in there, he certainly wouldn't have put a sheet over the entrance. But then Ray thought he wouldn't ask him to go in the basement if he wanted to hide something. If Oscar thought it was a big deal, he would have gotten the tin snips himself. Ray gently pushed the sheet over to the side and let the light from the bare bulb flood the small room.

The musty smell of rotten wood filled the air. In the center of this small room sat a large wooden frame sitting on long steel rails. It looked like an old carriage or something the guys from Mick's shop would have dragged out of an old potato barn. Whatever it was, it would need years of work for it to turn into anything resembling a car. There were no wheels or even axles. Then a thought came to mind. Maybe this could be something he could work on with Oscar after Christmas. It surprised Ray how appealing the prospect of working with Oscar seemed. Ray loved being around cars and working with tools. It would be worth it to work on this project with Oscar, if only for the free root beer.

Then a voice came into the basement which made Ray jump. It wasn't a voice he heard in the house before. Not Olive or Oscar. He flung the sheet down, yanked the light's cord and ran up the stairs. His feet sounded like a hammer as he banged up the steps. When he reached the top steps he smiled. He did recognize the voice. It was Johnny Mercer.

Olive sang "Ac-Cent-Tchu-Ate the Positive" as she stood in the middle of the room, pointing a paintbrush at Oscar. She moved her arms in the air as if she were conducting an orchestra as she danced in her oversized smock. She found Oscar's old Philco radio and the only station that came in clear. Ray knew Oscar had a radio but didn't think it even worked. He never heard music in the house. By the looks of it, Oscar was not a fan. Oscar stood up in a huff and put his hands on his hips.

"I don't pay you to sing and dance in my living room."

Ray put the tin snips down and began to knock his hips from side to side. "You don't pay us at all!" he said laughing. Olive and Ray sang in tune and clapped in circles around the room. Ray liked the music. It was better than the constant ticking of the second hands that seemed to scream throughout the house. Oscar didn't seem so thrilled.

"Mr. In-between," Oscar pouted. "I AM Mr. In-between."

Then he dropped his hands and started to shuffle back and forth. He leaned from one side to the other with his elbows bouncing gently in the air. Then he began to sing. Ray couldn't figure out how he knew all the words to the song. But it didn't matter. Olive and Ray laughed as much as they sang. They all yelled the lyrics out over the clanging of the bells which rang at four o'clock, letting them know it was quitting time. Olive and Ray headed out, grabbing their root beer and hollering a thank you back to Oscar as they scurried out the door. When they got to the street, Ray looked back through the window and saw Oscar walk over to the radio. Oscar dusted off the top of the wooden Philco and turned a knob. He must have had enough of music for one day, Ray thought. But instead of walking back to his stool, Oscar closed his eyes and smiled. His head bounced to the tempo as his arms floated in the air, cradling an invisible partner. Maybe it was the woman in the frame. Maybe Friedrich. He looked calm and happy as they waltzed around a room that normally held no noise other than the sound of alarms, chimes, and work.

❋ ❋ ❋

It was 10 p.m. and still Ray couldn't sleep. He figured it must have been the two root beers at Oscar's place. He would ask him about what he saw in the basement tomorrow, only he didn't know how he would bring it up. He certainly didn't want it to seem like he had been snooping. If he thought that, he might never trust him to come over again. Worst yet, he might not let him work on that wooden carriage hidden in the backroom of the basement. Ray looked aimlessly and waited for the lights to go out on the lampposts on Ship's Drive. As he stared at the Van Dusen's light, he noticed a light appear between the Goldsmith's house and the Jernick's. Maybe the Goldsmiths were putting their Christmas lights up early, Ray thought. His attention went back to the Van Dusen's light when he noticed the light disappear. Ray shook his head and thought they must be testing the lights for their colossal Christmas yard. He looked back at the Van Dusen's house when the light appeared again. This time it was between the Jernick's house and the Van Dusen's. He rubbed his head. The sequence of the lights going out on that street at night never changed.

Ray looked at the light and watched it go off. Ray tried to focus through the dark until the light appeared again. This time it was in the middle of the woods. It flashed on for only a few seconds and then went out into total darkness. Fear gripped Ray's chest. What if it was them? The Not-so Germans. What if they were the soldiers coming for them? The soldiers Paley asked him to look out for. Ray pulled the curtain down as he flung himself onto the floor. He took several deep breaths into the floorboards. Ray knew he needed to go back and look. He promised Paley he would keep an eye out for the enemy. Paley would not cower on the ground in fear. Ray puffed out his chest and lifted himself up. The curtain rested on top of his head as he slowly raised his eyes over the window sill.

The woods were pitch black. Ray waited only a few moments before the light appeared again. This time, behind the Mott's house. Ray dropped down and moved to the window on the other side of the room. He grabbed his flashlight and held it up in the direction of Olive's window but didn't turn it on. He knew that she was fast asleep. Besides, he didn't want to draw attention to himself. He remembered to breathe as he focused on the glow.

Now the orb was moving. It swooped down and up like an endless string of cursive "Ws." The light illuminated everything in front of it but nothing behind. Anything behind the light remained in total darkness. Ray could not see where the light came from or what it was attached to. It wasn't a fire. It didn't flicker. It was a solid beam and it appeared to be moving towards his backyard. The closest thing that came to mind was a flashlight.

"Mom," Ray whispered. "I should get Mom."

Then came the sound. Twigs breaking, leaves crunching, and thumps hitting the ground. The noise came from a herd of deer as they bounded through the brush. Ray struggled to see through the darkness. They were not just deer. They were bucks. Big bucks. All running through the woods towards the light. The light suddenly moved faster, away from the deer that were charging at it. The bucks, however, were too fast. As soon as the mass of animals reached the light, it disappeared. Ray thought whoever was holding that flashlight must have been run over in the stampede. Ray kept his eyes on the place where the light last shown. Nothing was there. He scoured the backyard. As far as the moonlight would let him see was nothing.

Ray stayed awake until the sky began to turn into the purple of daybreak. He told himself he would look in the morning. In the daylight he would examine the woods and see if there were footprints in the snow. If there was a trampled enemy soldier or a broken flashlight. There had to be something. White lights don't just appear in the woods. And if they do, they are put there by someone. He knew the only someones who should be in that woods. All of them were asleep. Or gone.

The next day, however, only provided more questions than answers. Ray walked into the backyard staring at the ground. The prints the animals made in the snow were beginning to melt into the yard. His mother opened the door and yelled from inside.

"Did you lose something?" she asked. Ray looked around and stuttered.

"Yeah…yes." Ray needed to think faster. He didn't want to tell his mother what happened. He didn't want to scare her. Not until he knew there was something to be scared of. "Thought I dropped a tool Oscar gave me. Some weird metal thing he uses for the clocks."

He saw his mother put on her coat and walk towards him. Ray could feel his face turn hot.

"What was it? Let me help you."

"Nah," Ray said, trying desperately not to seem so concerned. "It was a small whoziwhatsit tool. I thought I took it home and now I can't find it."

"It will go faster if we both look," she offered. She carefully placed her dainty, high-heeled feet over the piles of leaves in the snow. Her concentration focused on finding a small tool that couldn't be found even if Ray did drop it in the leaves.

While his mother was on a wild goose chase, Ray looked around the snow for signs of a person. He tried not to disturb anything in fear of covering up footprints or tracks. But the more he looked, the more he saw only hoofprints the deer made in the snow. No marks on trees, no carvings, no cigarette butts, nothing.

"Found it!" cried his mother. Ray's head shot up to see his mother's cheerful face. She held up a small metal object in the air. Ray ran over to her as she proudly held out the random piece of metal. "At least, I think I found it."

In her hands was a five-inch piece of metal that looked like a drumstick bone made of brass. Ray's gut turned. Something about that light and this object were connected. Only Ray had no idea what this odd object could be used for. But he knew who would.

"Oscar is going to be so happy you found this," Ray said as he took the object from his mother and tucked it safely into his coat pocket. "He wouldn't know what to do without it."

CHAPTER 13

Oscar's House – Southold, New York, 1944

"It's a bit," Oscar said as he examined the piece of metal under the light of an ornate wrought iron-curled standing lamp. Oscar's oily black fingerprints dotted the lace and fringe shade as Olive, Ray, and Oscar huddled under its glow.

"A bit of what?" Ray asked.

"It's a bit of a bit." Oscar ran his thumbs over the bumps in the brass, as if the tough old fingers could smooth out wrinkles in metal. "That's what it looks like. Off a bridle. Or," he paused in thought as he stretched his back to stand up straight. "Or it could be a nogginthumper."

"A noggin whater?" asked Olive, pushing up her glasses.

"A nogginthumper. That's what I call something when I don't know what it is." Oscar illustrated this by crossing his arms and tapping the metal to his forehead. "I thump my noggin until it comes to me. But this here thingy is a bit. It's a small bit. My guess, it belongs to one of Doctor DiNapoli's miniature ponies."

"I love them!" Olive cried. "He sometimes lets Paley and me pet them when he's out on a ride."

Doctor DiNapoli owned two miniature horses, Bev and Early. Almost every night in the summer you could see him being pulled like a Roman general in his red chariot by the two tan, tiny, trotting ponies. Ray's mind didn't go to the doctor's horses but rather to Oscar's basement and those small bridles. Maybe Oscar was working on bridles for Bev and Early. That could be the only explanation for their small size. But why he wasn't claiming it made Ray curious. And nervous. Oscar raised an eyebrow and shoved the piece of metal into the side pocket of his overalls. "I'll see him this week. Got a check-up on Wednesday. I'll ask if this belongs to him."

"Wait," Ray jumped. His arm reached out for a moment but he pulled it back. "Can I keep it?"

Oscar kept his eyebrow high up on his forehead. "What do you need this for?"

Ray shrugged his shoulders. "I don't know. It's neat."

"Neat?"

"Yeah," said Ray timidly.

Oscar pulled the bit out of his pocket and held it up to Ray. "You know, the doctor might really need it. And besides, what are you going to do with it?"

Ray could feel himself begin to stammer. Ray knew what he was going to do with it. He was going to find an excuse to go back in the basement and check it against those tiny bridles hanging over his workbench. Ray could never tell a lie well. His cheeks would redden and words would tumble around his mouth like blocks. He could feel both happening in his head until Olive jumped in to help him.

"If he needed it then it wouldn't be in Ray's backyard," Olive said matter-of-factly. "And anyways, finders keepers."

Oscar raised his other eyebrow at Olive. "Finders keepers?"

"Yes! Losers weepers," Ray said before grabbing the bit away from Oscar. He looked over at Olive and they both nodded in agreement.

The brass bit, still warm from Oscar's grasp, went right into Ray's pocket, where he gave it a slight pat to confirm its rightful place. Oscar crossed his arms and began to open his mouth in rebuttal until he was interrupted by a knock at the door.

"Hello, Oscar! May I come in?" a friendly voice called out.

Oscar stood with his arms crossed and let out a breath of exhaustion. He turned his head and yelled out. "Would it matter much to you if I said no?"

"Of course not!" said the cheery voice as it made its way towards the living room. "I wouldn't come in if I didn't see you all through the window," said the tall and slender man as he strolled into the living room. His tan suit didn't seem thick enough for the frigid weather, which explained why his arms were glued to his side and his hands buried deep into his pockets. The only thing keeping him the slightest bit warm seemed to be the leather satchel tucked under his arm and his thin short beard. "Well, hello there. I see you have company."

Oscar turned and shuffled back to his stool in a mild huff. Ray couldn't tell if the grumpiness that suddenly took over Oscar was due to losing the bit or the smiling man in his living room.

"Meet Olive and Raymond," he said with his back towards the man. He then stopped, turned around and pointed to Olive. "This one's Olive," he barked. Then he pointed to Ray. "And that one's Raymond. They are helping me this year."

Ray and Olive smiled nervously at the man. Oscar's grouchiness, however, seemed to have no effect on his cheerful demeanor. He nodded at the two.

"A sincere pleasure to meet you both. My name is John Charles."

"Do you have two first names or is your last name Charles?" Olive asked with her head cocked to the side.

"Two first names. You can call me John Charles," he answered as he put down his worn briefcase and loosened its straps. "And might I say, it is wonderful to see you both helping out Mr. Taglieber. I'm sure you both…"

Oscar hollered again. "I'm not paying them. They call me Oscar."

"I'm sure you both are a huge help to Oscar," he continued. "Maybe someday you will work for us at INR Industries," he said as he pulled out a stack of papers from his satchel. As soon as Ray saw the lines and block writing he knew what they were. Ray felt himself walking towards the papers, as if they belonged to him.

"What's INR Industries?" asked Olive.

"Well, I'm glad you asked. Ever wonder where all those letters to Santa go?" he said as he proudly held up a stack of papers. "Children write to Santa but they get sent to us. International Network Resourcing Industries," John Charles said as he lifted up the top corner of the stack and let the letters flap down like a fan. Olive's eyes grew wide as she too walked over to see the huge pile. John Charles handed a portion to Ray and a portion to Olive. Each page had the same thick red markings as the letters strung up over Oscar's workbench. Some gifts were circled. Some were crossed out. Some even had notes in the margins.

"Wow," uttered Ray. "Does every letter to Santa go to you?"

"As many letters as possible. We start getting letters in June, if you can believe it."

Olive's jaw dropped. "Wow. It's Christmas even in the summer. You must really love Christmas."

"I do. Especially since Christmas is my birthday."

Ray and Olive looked at each other and made a face.

"What's wrong with being born on Christmas?"

Olive and Ray answered in unison as they thumbed through the letters. "You get stiffed."

Ray looked down at the letter in front of him. It was from a girl named Franny. She wrote that she had been mostly good this past year but found it hard as she spent most of her time chasing around her little sister. She asked for three things: a tea set, a new dress for her doll, and a canteen. The word "canteen" was the only one circled. Ray crinkled his nose. What girl would want a canteen over a tea set? Ray pointed to the letter in confusion.

"How do you pick which present to give?"

John Charles shrugged. "We just know."

"Oh," said Ray, still confused. John Charles did not seem to want to go into any more explanation than that. Ray handed the stack back to John Charles but froze in shock when John Charles reached for them. How could he have not noticed this before? Ray's eyes widened as he stared at John Charles's mangled hands. The ring finger and middle finger on both hands looked like it had been sawed in half. The right hand held no pinkie and the left, only a half a thumb. What was left of the remaining fingers curled inward at such a hard angle that would make buttoning a shirt impossible. Ray took a step back and forced his eyes to look at the ground. He felt embarrassed for staring. He was signaling to Olive in his head, wondering if she noticed the man's hands as well. The telepathic flashlight must have worked because as soon as the man reached for Olive's stack of letters she let out a yelp.

"Your hands! What happened to your hands?" she said behind her own as blue paint from her fingers smeared on her cheeks.

"Happened a long time ago," he said as he walked over to Oscar. "I'm sorry if they frightened you."

Olive dropped her hands away from her mouth as a defiant air came over her, as if she were angry at herself for being scared. "They don't bother me. Do they bother you, Ray?"

It took all of Ray's concentration to shake his head "no" when his mind screamed "yes." It wasn't that the hands were deformed, they just looked so pained. He knew his face gave away his feelings. He looked at John Charles and swallowed hard. He couldn't act tough like Olive

in front of him. Something about the man just wouldn't let him. "It...
it just looks like whatever happened to you hurt a lot."

John Charles handed the stack of papers to Oscar. For the first
time, Oscar looked up at the man with sympathetic eyes. The two
exchanged a look that made Ray feel as if he brought up a painful
memory, only he couldn't tell for which one.

"It did hurt a lot. But they don't hurt anymore," John Charles said
softly as he looked down at the letters. There was no trace of anger
or fear in his voice, as if whatever nightmare that caused his hands
to break apart ended before he could even have a memory of it. John
Charles looked at his hands and then at Ray. "They get cold, though.
Gloves don't really work."

"What about mittens?" asked Olive.

John Charles rubbed his short beard with his wrist in thought. "I
never considered mittens."

Ray let out a laugh. He knew the man was too polite to answer
Olive. "Come on, now," Ray said as he walked over to his stool. "A man
wearing mittens would look silly."

"No he wouldn't. He'd look warm," answered Olive as she returned
to her paints. "And cute. Especially if they had kittens on them."

Ray looked back at Olive in horror. "Kitten mittens? On a
grown-up?"

"With a pink nose and black whiskers."

The thought of it popped into Ray's head. A short laugh burst from
his mouth. Then another. Then another. Then he couldn't stop. The
idea of a man running around town hall wearing mittens with white
fluffy cats on it tickled Ray's funny bone so hard that he doubled over
the workbench. He composed himself for a moment until he noticed
Oscar's body turned away from John Charles. Even though he couldn't
see his face, his shoulders bounced up and down from laughter. John
Charles just nodded at Olive as he tucked his lips, trying not to laugh.

"I can see your point, Olive. Mittens could be a possibility. Maybe without the cats."

Olive did not see the humor. "Ok then. No kittens," she turned around and faced her paints. "Do you like puppies?"

Then Ray and Oscar burst out in unison so loud that Ray thought they'd blow the glass out of the bay window. Ray wiped tears from his eyes as Oscar pressed down on his stomach as if to push the laughter in. John Charles shook his head and smiled.

"Don't you listen to them, Olive. Puppy mittens would be lovely." He then playfully knocked Oscar on the shoulder. "Hear that, Santa? Puppy mittens. Put that on my list."

❄ ❄ ❄

The mitten debate lasted until Olive and Ray saw Paley in the front yard. As they turned up the Mott's driveway, Ray stopped Olive.

"Did you see anything weird in the woods last night?"

"Weird? Like what?"

Ray's voice lowered to a hush. He didn't want to get Paley nervous or upset. He gave a quick glance over to Paley, who stood staring up in the sky and tapping his cereal box. Ray turned his back towards Paley. "Like a light. A bright white light."

"No. I didn't see a light. Are you sure it wasn't a car?"

"I'm sure. Someone was in the woods."

"Did you tell your mom?"

"No, I don't want to scare her," Ray said.

Olive's eyes got even bigger behind her glasses. "Do you think it's..." she cupped her hands and whispered in Ray's ear. "The Nazis?"

Ray shrugged. "I don't know. But be by your window. If you see anything, get the flashlight and beam it my way. I'll do the same."

Olive pursed her lips and nodded hard in agreement. She looked worried as she walked over to Paley. Ray felt bad. He didn't want to worry her but there was too much at stake. They needed to be more like Paley. Like soldiers. They needed to look long and hard at what other people only give a fleeting glance.

❄ ❄ ❄

Ray turned the flashlight on and off, making sure it worked before putting it under his bed. As he lifted the sheets he heard a voice from his doorway.

"Do you want to read a book?" Ray's mother asked, clutching a large red hardcover book to her chest. Her voice sounded light and hopeful. "Thought it might be nice to read a Christmas story."

"I don't need you to read me a book, Mom. I can read fine on my own."

"Well then how about you read it to me. It's your favorite." She held out a copy of the book his dad read to him every Christmas Eve before he fell asleep by the fireplace. *The Night Before Christmas.* The story about a dad who believed in magic after a visit from St. Nicholas.

"But it's not Christmas Eve?"

"I know. I just thought it would be nice."

Ray shook his head before he could even get the words out. "No. We can't. We just have to wait." Some things were sacred. This was one of them.

"Alright. Not until Christmas Eve then," she said softly as she laid the book down the dresser between two of Ray's model cars. Her eyes lingered on over the little racers as her fingers glided over the tiny detailed hoods. Everything he made, everything he touched, everything that came from him was good.

Ray's mother turned and walked slowly towards the door. Sadness seemed to fall like a shadow in her wake. Ray reached over to the stack of books by his bed. He called out before she made it out of the room.

"Mom? How about *Donkey Daniel*?" he said, holding up the book. "We can take turns reading."

She turned and smiled. Whatever sadness clung to her seemed to lift as she headed back towards Ray. She sat next to him on the bed as he laid back and read the story of the donkey that carried Mary to Bethlehem. As Raymond read he could smell his mother's day. The chicken she made for dinner. The starch she used at the shop. The talcum powder she put on her arms to keep her skin dry. It felt safe and strong. Like she carried her family and town everywhere she traveled. She rested her cheek on the top of Ray's head. Ray read to the end of the page and paused for his mother to take her turn. She said nothing. When he felt a drop of water hit his ear he kept reading and didn't stop until the book ended. He figured a mom sometimes needs a bedtime story too.

CHAPTER 14

Ray's Backyard – Southold, New York,
two weeks before Christmas 1944

After he kissed his mother good night and bounced a few beams of light back and forth with Olive to make sure the lines of communication were open, Ray spent the first hours of the night guarding his window with both his hands wrapped around his flashlight. The quick waddle of a raccoon across his backyard was the only thing moving in the dark at this hour. Ray did not check the clock but figured he heard about a million clicks of the second hand as he listened to time chip away the night. Nothing was out there. No animal. No soldier. Not even a breeze. Not even a deer. Ray got to thinking. He was glad it was Olive that he told about the light and not his buddies at school. If the light never showed up again, Olive wouldn't make fun of him or bring it back up years later like Ted. Olive would believe him if he said he saw a dinosaur in the woods. Or at least act like she did so that his feelings wouldn't be hurt. She heard things a hundred times crazier from her brother, so if nothing came of it, she wouldn't look at Ray differently.

More ticks from the clock echoed in the room. Each one persuaded Ray to rest his cheek on the cold glass and draw his eyelids closer together. It wasn't until he heard a loud snap that he jerked his head up and wiped off the fog his breath made on the windowpane. It sounded as if a large branch broke off a tree but there was no sound of it hitting other branches on the way down or the shaking thud when it hit the ground. Ray looked over at the ground for a horizontal shadow over the snow, then up into the branches in hopes of seeing it dangle from above. Nothing.

Then another snap. A snap so loud it produced an echo. Something was out there. Ray ran to the other window and began turning on his flashing repeatedly in the direction of Olive's bedroom. Her window remained dark. She must have fallen asleep. He flicked the switch on the light on and off as fast as he could until he heard another, even louder crack. Ray dropped to the floor and shut his light off. It sounded like treetops were snapping in half. He crawled back to the window and peeked over the sill. Now it was there. The white light. Bright and steady as if someone had planted a headlight on the top of a four-foot fence post in the center of the woods. He couldn't tell where the light came from. Like before, it shone so bright it hid everything behind it in shadow. Everything ten feet in front of the light, however, was awash in its glow. Tree trunks, snow, branches, everything the light touched became outlined and visible in the darkness.

Ray waited for the light to move. He held his breath in this throat so it wouldn't fog up the window again. His heartbeat banged so loudly in his ears that he could no longer hear the clock ticking on the wall. Then movement. Not from the light but an animal. A buck casually walked through the light's beam without a startle or fit. It stopped for a moment and ran its snout along the ground. It proceeded on its way until it left the light's range. Then another buck walked across the light's path in almost an identical fashion. It too poked at the snow, and then kept on its way out of the light's path. Then another, much larger buck walked through the light. The rack on the stag was so large it turned back into darkness over the buck's head. Ray's mouth dropped open as one buck after another walked through the light. He counted seven. Whatever turned the light on did not bother or scare the animals. Rather, it seemed to draw them in, as if it were lighting a path for them through the woods. But it bothered and scared Ray. His teeth clenched together as tightly as his hands gripped the sill. He realized he would be of no use to his mother being as frightened as he was. He needed to tell her. If he couldn't do anything about this, maybe she could. If ever there were a time to warn her, it would be now.

He slowly stood up and backed away from the window. Ray thought if he kept his eyes affixed on the light, it wouldn't move. Slowly and silently, Ray slid his feet backwards on the wood floor until he reached the door. As he carefully reached behind him for the doorknob the light began to shake back and forth like a metronome. Ray quickly abandoned his plan and darted back to the window and crouched low. The light stopped moving for only a moment, as if it were waiting for Ray to get back in his seat. Then, like a shot out of the flare gun, the orb flew up the air in a straight line through the branches and up towards the night sky. No sparks, no flame, just a pure ball of light soared in a straight line north until it cleared past the tops of the trees. Once it reached its maximum height it stopped momentarily. Then the light arced and slowly began to fall back down to earth with a streak trailing behind it like a ribbon. The light's speed picked up pace until it reached the middle branches of the oaks. Without fading or flickering, it suddenly went out. Ray's eyes followed the rate of speed which the light was falling and waited to hear it hit the ground. He stared at the floor of the woods but nothing landed. Maybe it got stuck in the tree, Ray thought. But as the light of the moon illuminated the woods, Ray saw nothing out of the ordinary. No light. No bucks. The trees stood peaceful and silent. The animals hidden. The birds asleep. Everything was just as peaceful as it was before the light turned on. Except for Ray.

❄ ❄ ❄

"Then it went way, way, way up like this," Ray explained as he reached his arm high into the air over his head. He curved his hand and watched it come down slowly. "Then out." He sliced his arms through the air like an umpire over a batter sliding safely into home plate. He plopped down on a wooden cafeteria chair and grabbed his milk. "I looked outside this morning for footprints. Nothing. I found nothing." He took the last glug of his milk, then slammed it back on the cafeteria table in frustration.

Olive stared at Ray as she chewed her peanut butter sandwich. Fear glued her elbows firmly to her side as she clamped down on the sides of bread. "What do you think it is?"

"That's the thing! I don't..." Ray's caught himself shouting and pulled his voice down to a whisper. "I don't know. I just can't figure it out. It looked like a firework when they first shoot it up into the sky. It had like a ribbon behind it."

"Like a tail? Jeez, I'm so sorry I missed it. I stayed awake as long as I could."

Ray shook his hand and dismissed it. "Don't worry. It's going to happen again. I just know it."

"What's going to happen again? A kiss from your girlfriend?" mocked Ted as he walked up to the two. He puckered his lips and shut his eyes as he stood over Olive. Marty jumped next to Ted, waved his hands in the air and began to sing.

"Ray and Ol-live sitting in a tree..."

When Olive told Ray that her mother was picking her up after school to get new glasses from the doctor, Ray racked his brain all through their math lesson on how to tell Olive about what happened in the woods. Writing a note was out of the question as anyone who found it would think Ray was nuts. Recess wouldn't work since Olive would be in the library and it was Ray's turn to throw out the pitches in kickball. Lunch would be the only time. Ray thought if the two hid in the far corner, nobody would get wind of their conversation. Only it seemed the further they sat from everyone, the more they stuck out.

"Quit it, will ya?" Ray said as he rubbed his forehead. "We're just eating." Olive carefully put down her sandwich and began to neatly fold it back into its wax paper.

"So? What say you, four eyes?" Ted said as he straddled the chair next to Olive. He was as big sitting down as Marty was standing up. "Do you have a crush on Ray, here?"

Olive gently put her sandwich back into her paper bag and looked at Raymond. Ray could feel the blood drain from his face. He asked Olive to sit with him and now she was being razzed for it. Ray also knew that Ted found any excuse to tease Olive because he had a crush on her. If Ted thought Olive liked Ray or the other way around, he would never hear the end of it.

"I said, quit it Ted," Ray ordered. "Or I'll…" Ray let his sentence drift off, hoping the thin veil of the threat would work as he had no idea what he would do. He was so tired from not sleeping the night before he couldn't punch a pillow. Besides, Ted was the biggest kid in the fifth grade and at least a foot taller than Ray. Any fight started by Ray would be ended by Ted.

"Or you'll what?" Ted stood up and put his hands on his hips.

"I'll…" Ray could feel himself grasping. "I'll…"

Olive turned and yelled at Ted. "He'll throw you bad pitches at kickball. Now go away!"

Ted dropped his arms in a huff and looked back at Ray. "You wouldn't, would you?"

"If you keep bothering us I'll throw every pitch at your knees."

Ted rubbed his chin in thought, then hit Marty on the arm. "Come on. Let's leave these lovebirds alone."

Ray glared at the two as they slinked away from the table. He grabbed his empty milk carton and squashed it between his hands. "I'm sorry they are such jerks."

Olive shrugged as she took her sandwich back out of the bag and unwrapped it. "It's alright. I just wish Ted didn't like me so much."

CHAPTER 15

The Woods Across the Street – Southold, New York, 1944

Ray still fumed over Ted and Marty as he marched alone to Oscar's place. He wasn't sure why he felt so mad. Was it because they were teasing him, teasing Olive or that it was the second time Olive found the words that eluded him? He couldn't think as fast as Olive or be as tough as Ted. Now he couldn't sleep because he didn't know who was in his backyard. And he was tired. He kicked up snow as he marched over the bridge and looked out over the bay. This thing that scared him at night might make him lose his friends. Or his mind. He couldn't let it happen. He lost too much already.

As he tramped up the hill with his hands shoved deep in his pockets for warmth, the tired feeling that fogged his head suddenly lifted. It took him a second to realize that he stopped walking. His eyes fixed on the truck parked on the edge of the road by the woods. He kept as still as possible. Something felt wrong. Very wrong. The truck was not parked by his home or Oscar's. He'd seen the old pickup before but racked his head on where. His eyes drifted over the empty road and the row of trees. What was wrong? Why did every bone in his body feel like it wanted to leap out of his skin? A crow cawed above him from on top of a telephone pole. He watched the bird look around from the bay to Jacob's Lane. The bird lifted its legs, then took off. It only traveled a short distance to the old tree stand where Olive and Ray hid from Fluffles. The crow cawed again. Then Ray remembered.

Ray took off towards Oscar's. His legs stretched wide to cover as much ground as he could. He knew why the truck looked out of place. They were hunters. They were in the woods. The idea of them putting the dead body of his buck in the back of the truck struck a chord of fear in Ray's heart that he had only known once before. He never told Oscar, so he didn't know if Oscar would even care but something in his head said he would. He had to at least try.

Ray leapt up the front steps in one jump and barged into Oscar's house without any knock or greeting. When he got into the living room he saw Oscar standing by Olive's station holding new pots of paint. Oscar froze at the sight of Ray's fear. Ray could only pant out words.

"Hunters…" Ray heaved. "Hunters." Ray pointed at the wall as he stared at Oscar. "Now. In the woods."

Oscar dropped the paint and ran after Ray, who was already out the door and running down the street. Ray turned to see the old man run into the cold without a coat, his old legs taking him as fast they could. When Ray darted from the road into the woods he heard Oscar call out.

"Let them hear you, Raymond!" Oscar shouted. "They are hunting. Let them hear you!"

Ray ran into the woods across the street from his house. This section of woods wasn't in anyone's backyard and was open to bow hunting. There was no road cutting through it, like Ships Drive. It was a thick section of woods that surrounded an old abandoned horseracing track. There weren't as many paths as there were behind his house but whatever one he took he needed to stay on it. A deep ravine filled with prickers and thorn bushes ran through this section of the woods. His father used to dump grass clippings and yard brush down into this massive pit. Ray stopped running when he reached the edge of the ravine and waited for Oscar. Once he saw him huffing and puffing he pointed to the ravine. Oscar nodded, acknowledging the hole in the earth as he ran past Ray. Ray followed him as Oscar started to yell out.

"Hup!" Oscar cried out in a deep voice. "Hup! Hup!" The words had force and vibrated through the trees.

Ray joined in the cry. He didn't know why this word seemed to work on the deer but now was not the time to question. Ray yelled as he ran. "Hup! Hup!"

As they continued their shouts a wind began to pick up and stir, causing little whirlwinds of leaves to spiral in the air. Ray looked up at the treetops. None of them moved. The breeze seemed to come from the ground rather than the sky. The more Oscar cried out the word, the faster and harder the wind spun.

"Hup!" Ray cried as a strong wind pressed his back and pushed him towards the edge of the woods. Then he heard the crunch of hooves beating on leaves. Ray looked around. Everything in the woods was moving. It was as if the ground woke up and wanted to shake everything off of it. Ray stopped and stared at the hurricane erupting from the earth. He momentarily forgot about the hunters until a massive beast darted past him and almost knocked him over. Ray looked around when he felt another animal fly past him on the other side. They were bucks. Huge ten-point bucks. Ray tried to steady himself when two more grazed him on either side. He turned around and saw four more charging at him. He dropped to his knees and put his hands over his head. He could feel the animals leap over him and land as they bolted towards the old racetrack.

Ray scrambled to his feet and ran after the stags until the woods stopped and the race track began. There, twenty feet away from a hunting, stand stood Oscar, panting, with his hands on his knees. Once the bucks ran into the clearing Ray saw a man stand up on the deer stand, draw his bow and aim the arrow. The bucks were now in a small stretch of open field, in clear view of all the hunters. Ray cried out as loud as he could.

"No! Stop!" The wind that spun around his legs seemed to pick up his voice and carry it in the opposite direction. Oscar, however, didn't seem to have this problem. He squatted down and cried out in a voice that seemed to travel for miles.

"HUZZAH!"

Ray saw the line of deer reach the edge of the woods and jump into the trees. Then whatever whirlwind that spun on the ground seemed to lift into the trees and travel up towards the sky. The hunter released his bow. The wind took his arrow and sent it straight towards the ground. Ray ran into the field and only stopped once he heard one of the hunters begin to curse.

"What do you think you're doing, you old coot?" yelled the hunter in the tree stand at Oscar. Oscar sat on a tree stump, his hands shaking and out of breath. "That was my family's dinner this winter."

"There … were … kids," Oscar panted. "Kids … in the woods. You shouldn't hunt where kids play." Oscar pointed to Ray as he ran towards them, his fingers blue from the cold.

Another hunter with a bow and quiver walked across the field towards Oscar. "What in the hell just happened?" he yelled.

Oscar kept his head down, trying to catch his breath but didn't answer. He didn't say a word as the men barraged him with questions and insults. Ray stood silently next to him and put his hand on Oscar's shoulder, letting him know he was by his side.

CHAPTER 16

Air Raid Drill — Southold, New York, 1944

The sirens always cheered their own arrival. The warning's low growl climbing to a constant high-pitched wail assaulted the ears and inserted fear into a human heart just as much as the sound of any low-flying plane. Ray unhooked the tie-back on the black fabric that his mother bundled on top of the windows and let the instant wall of darkness flap over the living room window. The menacing curtains did their job well, eradicated any light the moon tried to toss into the house. Being the son of an assistant air raid warden, he would be in more danger from his mother than a Japanese bomber if so much as a nightlight was seen during an air raid drill. Ray was left alone these nights. Before, during, and after the wails that screamed over the North Fork occurred, his mother would be hunkered down in the basement of the high school, feverously calling all sorts of people to check their whereabouts. But her first call was always to Raymond, making sure he was home and ordering him to blacken out the windows, triple check that the oven was turned off, and sit in the basement until the sirens stopped or he smelled horseradish. In that case, he was allowed to grab a flashlight and run for the hills.

The siren screamed on as Ray finished covering the windows on the first floor and ran up the stairs to do the second. He remembered halfway upstairs he was doing it wrong. The upstairs should always be done first. Doing it second would insure that Ray would have to navigate a pitch black house or use his flashlight. He shrugged it off, figuring he knew the layout of the house as much as he knew the woods. He could walk through both backwards and blindfolded and still find his way to his dad's workbench. Ray paused in front of his mother's bedroom window and looked out into the woods. Nothing other than the siren's scream was out there. No lights from the Van Dunsen's or Jernick's lampposts. No headlights from the Goldsmith's Pierce Arrow or Christmas lights in their yard. No glow from a lamp hung over a dinner table or a reading chair. Just a wail in the night scaring all the light out of a town.

Ray stepped back from his mother's window when a flash caught the corner of his eye. He looked out the door and down the short hall to his bedroom. Another longer flash was coming through his bedroom window. Ray crouched low and scurried to his room. He looked up and saw the white flash appear again, only this time it came on and off in beats. One long flash, then two short. He ran to the window and looked at the Mott house. There, in the room directly across from his, came another white flash. When the light went out he saw the silhouette of a small girl. Olive was signaling to Ray.

"Is she nuts?" Ray uttered to himself. There's an air raid drill going on. The trouble they could get in from the government, let alone their moms, would be beyond anything they'd seen in the fifth grade. Then Ray thought she might be in trouble. Ray scoured the Mott house for movement. When he looked back into the woods is when he saw what Olive must be signaling about. Excitement gripped his neck. He didn't know if it was from fear or thrill.

There it was. The light. Bright and constant, piercing through maples in Olive's backyard. She had seen it too. Ray grabbed his flashlight from under his bed and flicked the light on and off in her direction. Once he got her attention, he opened the window and stuck his arm out into the cold. He reached below the window so that she could see where he was pointing. He stretched it down as far as he could and pointed toward the ground. Now was the time for courage, he figured. He faced hunters and crazy dogs and survived. Something was out there and whatever it was, wanted him to know it. It was high time he found out what it was.

Olive's light flashed twice signaling her compliance. He pulled his arm in, slammed the window shut and flung the black curtain down. He set his flashlight down where he grabbed his coat. He couldn't take it with him. They couldn't risk being caught by the person holding that light or the police. There were some fast-moving clouds in the sky but the moon shone bright. Besides, Ray knew those woods. He closed the back door gently and kept his body pressed flat against the cedar shakes of the house. The siren's cry sounded even more ominous outside. His eyes darted from the spot where he last saw the light and Olive's back door. He saw no movement until he felt a hand grab his elbow. Then he saw his arms fly in the air from fright.

"I'm sorry. I thought you saw me," Olive said over the siren's cry.

Ray gripped his ears and steadied himself. If Olive were a boy, he'd punch her shoulder for scaring him half to death. But he would never hit a girl, let alone the one who was about to go with him on the biggest adventure yet. He tried to whisper through the siren.

"It's ok," he said as he took another breath. "Just tell me you saw it."

"The light in the woods? Yes. It was right over there." She pointed towards the empty woods that lay behind the tire swing. "But I don't see it anymore."

Ray looked out in the woods and saw nothing. "Get behind me but stay close," Ray whispered. He positioned Olive behind him and started to walk towards the light's last location. They didn't get halfway between the two houses before he felt Olive yank his sleeve.

"It's there!" she said as she pointed to the light glowing in Ray's front yard. The two froze in their boots. The light seemed to float at the bottom of Ray's driveway. It remained there for a few moments before it traveled across Jacob's Lane and into the woods that lay beyond it.

Ray gulped. He hoped the sound of the siren covered it. What they were about to do began to dawn on Ray as the two ran across the paved road. Now he regretted not taking his flashlight. He knew the woods behind his house like he knew his bedroom. The woods in front of the house, however, was a different story. The last time he ran through this brush was hours ago with Oscar. There were hunters, weapons, angry animals, and a ravine in these parts. He remembered how relief flooded over him when he and Oscar reached the road. What happened with the hunters shook Oscar to his core and made Ray nervous. Nothing scared him like seeing a grown-up upset. Ray didn't want to step foot in those parts anytime soon, let alone at night during an air raid drill with no light coming from any houses marking the way home.

"Can you see who it is?" Olive said as she jogged next to Ray. "I can't see who's holding it."

The moonlight reached through the branches but still kept whatever was holding the light in shadow. Ray needed to look periodically down at the path to make sure he didn't fall onto or into anything. The farther they ran, the more Ray began to get his bearings. The woods grew brighter and he knew they were going towards the old racetrack. When they broke through the branches and into the clearing, they stopped. The light was gone.

Ray put his hand out in front of Olive to stop her. Their panting breaths that puffed up to the night sky were the only movement on the field. Ray squinted to see if he could get a better view of the person holding the flashlight. As his eyes began to adjust its aperture to the moonlight, the field grew black as pitch.

"Ray, look," Olive whispered. "In the sky."

Ray looked up. It seemed God untied his blackout curtains and let them fall over the moon. Clouds began to drift over the light of the night sky, leaving them completely in the dark. But there was one thing in the sky. A streak of light. One end started above their heads and led across the field to the other side.

"Is that a shooting star?" Ray asked. "Or a plane?"

"No," said Olive. "It would have disappeared by now if it were either. It looks like … well, it can't be."

"Looks like a what?"

"It looks like a comet."

Ray remembered what his mother said about the Star of Bethlehem. If you're looking for direction and you see a bright light, you follow it. Ray grabbed Olive's hand. "Let's go," Ray urged.

He could feel Olive nod in the dark as they started across the field hand in hand. Don't separate, Ray repeated in his head. If they did, they wouldn't be able to see each other in the woods or hear each other with the sirens going. The more they jogged, the more the nothingness of the field surrounded them. Ray could tell they were somewhere near the center, somewhere around the spot where Ray saw the bucks begin to sprint towards the woods' edge. Somewhere in clear view of the tree stands that held those hunters. The thought of their arrows pointing at him and Olive as they ran sent a sad chill through Ray's heart. That is what war must feel like. His dad must have felt like this. Except hunters over there held weapons far more sinister. They didn't know his dad or Olive or himself but someone on the other end of the world, at the other end of a gun, wanted to see them dead in a field. And for what? For working on cars? For wearing glasses? For playing kickball in school? The thought made him grip Olive's hand harder and his feet move from a jog to a full run.

When they reached the edge of the track Olive yanked Ray's arm to stop. The clouds began to part and moonlight came out again. Ray turned around and noticed Olive staring at something with her mouth open.

"What?" Ray pleaded. "What is it?"

Olive said nothing as she let go of Ray's hand. She slowly walked past him and towards a large branch that lay on the floor of the woods.

"Olive!" Ray cried out. She seemed to not care about the light or even the comet but what lay in front of her, as if something was calling or drawing her towards it. She knelt down on all fours and began to crawl slowly towards the branch. Finally, Ray's feet became unglued as he ran over to her side. Then whatever breath that came out was instantly sucked back in.

"He's hurt," Olive said as she reached her mitten out towards the animal. "We got to help him."

Inches away from the tips of Olive's knitted fingers laid the enormous buck. With the bright moonlight Ray could make out the stick coming from the buck's neck. One of the hunters landed their shot. The buck moved its legs and blinked but the dark stain around the snow meant it wasn't running away soon.

"Watch out," Ray said as he grabbed Olive's hand and pulled it back. "That's a wild animal. He could kill you with those things."

"He's not going to kill anyone," Olive insisted. "We have to help him."

"What are we going to do?" Ray said. "We can't take the arrow out of his neck."

"But we have to!" Olive's face began to contort into the beginnings of a cry. Ray ran his hands over his head to grab his thoughts. He knew what they needed to do. He snapped his fingers and pointed at her.

"We'll tell Oscar. He'll know what to do."

"Will he hurt him?"

Ray shook his head. "Promise he won't. If there's anyone who won't hurt him, it's Oscar," Ray said as he looked up at the comet and spoke to it, more than to Olive. "I promise we'll tell Oscar."

"Let's just take the arrow out first." Olive began to reach for the arrow when the siren's wail drifted down into nothingness, leaving room for the noise that was underneath it to be heard. The two froze in the snow as the low sound of growls surrounded them. Olive let out a gasp and Ray's mouth let out a silent scream as they saw Fluffles and his two other mangy brothers crawl into view, their evil snarls showing off all their drool dripping from their pointy teeth. A hum of fear began to come from Olive as Ray himself wanted to cry. He could feel his lips begin to quiver and said the only words that came to his mind.

"Dad, help…" he begged.

The moonlight grew even brighter, illuminating more of the dogs. One of the hounds turned around suddenly and barked viciously at something behind it. Ray's eyes broke from Fluffles and saw the two enormous bucks behind him. Both stood in a fighting stance, their antlers low and pointed at the dog.

"Christopher Columbus," he heard himself say as he looked around. Two more bucks came into view, one behind each dog. One banged its rack against the tree, causing snow and a few loose branches to fall on one mutt, giving it a start. Then the smell of earth and animal jumped into the air as two more bucks emerged from the woods, one on his left, then another next to Olive on the right, each buck snorting and stomping their hooves on the floor of the woods. Fluffles and his stray brethren lost their minds as they turned their barking and snarling towards the deer. Ray grabbed Olive's shoulders and started to walk backwards. He looked up to see another cloud about to drift in the way of the moonlight. Ray leaned towards Olive.

"Run. Now!"

The two turned and ran back towards the direction of the clearing and away from the horrific sounds of angry, fighting animals. Once in the field, Ray let Olive run in front of him. Even though she ran like lightning, he wanted to make sure he didn't get past her. With no sirens, he heard their panting and their feet stomping over the flattened weeds and rye. Then he heard another sound. More running. Only it wasn't coming from them. It was hooves. Ray didn't need to turn around to see what was behind them. The next sound was him crying out to Olive.

"Faster!"

But as soon as they got to the other end of the field, Ray stopped. He didn't know these woods like the woods behind his house. He had no bearings and could barely see Olive.

"Come on, Ray!" Olive yelled as she faded into the brush. Ray looked up at the comet above them. They just needed to follow that streak in the sky, he thought. That's the way home.

Ray began to run when the clouds drifted back over the moon and encased the woods in darkness. When he turned his head upwards to see if the comet was still there, a log reached up and smacked his feet out from underneath him. Ray's shoulder hit the ground and his body followed. He rolled quickly onto his back and looked up only to see the underbelly of a deer. Ray yelped and tucked himself into a ball.

"Go! Go away!"

Ray opened his eyes. Although he couldn't see much he could smell the animal. It had to be almost on top of him. He scrambled to his feet and saw a faint outline of the buck in front of him. When Ray moved to the left, so did the deer. He quickly tried to dash around him but the deer got in his way. What if they killed those dogs and now were coming after him? Ray tried to stay calm but he could feel the panic rise.

"Move," Ray urged. The deer was not spooked. Each time Ray tried to pass it, the buck would block his path. The sounds of dogs barking grew louder. Fear gripped Ray's chest.

"Please move," Ray begged. "I'm scared."

The deer did not obey but the clouds did. The clouds flew out of the moon's way and light began to make its way to the ground. Ray could see past the buck to the road. A police car sat in the distance. Then the beam of a flashlight cut through the trees. Finally, the deer leapt away from Ray and bounded back into the darkness. The flashlight must have scared him, Ray thought. A wave of relief started to wash over Ray but stopped as he began to walk towards the beam of light.

"Christopher Columbus," he said again as he stared down. A few more steps and he would have landed at the bottom of the ravine, torn to shreds by thorns, briars, and all sorts of horror that lay at its floor. If that buck hadn't been there, Ray thought, I would have been cut to pieces. He turned his head to see if the deer was still there. The light of the moon and the flashlight gave nothing up.

Ray carefully navigated around the ravine's edge, jumped over the logs that stood in his way and ran towards the paved road. As his feet hit the street the light beamed in his face.

"That you, Raymond? What are you doing outside so late?" asked Officer Boland in his thick Irish accent as he stood outside his police car. "I just chased the Mott girl off the road for being out here. Jesus, Mary, and Joseph you should both be home in bed."

That wave of relief finally hit Ray. Olive made it out of the woods safely. He turned one last time to the woods he just exited. Not that far off stood the outline of a buck.

"I'm sorry, Officer," Ray panted. He tried to think of something to tell Officer Boland that wasn't a lie. "Olive and I went to the old track to see the comet."

Officer Boland rubbed his cap with his flashlight. "Comet? What are you talking about, a comet? There was nothing about a comet in the papers."

Ray looked up at the stars. The light in the sky that pointed them home was gone. And so was the buck.

CHAPTER 17

Oscar's House – Southold, New York, 1944

Morning couldn't come soon enough. Ray counted every second that ticked off the wall after his mother kissed him good night and left his room. Officer Boland escorted him home but didn't give him the third degree since Ray's mother worked during the drill. Ray explained in partial truths to Officer Boland why he and Olive were running around in the dark so soon after the air raid drill. They followed something that looked suspicious. That was all true. Upon closer inspection, they believed it was someone walking their dog. That part was not true. Olive and Ray lay in their respective beds staring up at their respective ceilings trying to sift through the details of what they both saw that night. Both worried about a buck: one with an arrow lodged in his neck, one with a white streak on its face. Both were eager to get up with the sun's first rays and tell the same person.

Ray was dressed with his coat half on before his mother even turned on the kettle.

"Where do you think you're going, Mister," she said as she shuffled through the kitchen, fastening the tie on her robe.

"Oscar's," Ray answered as he slid an arm into a coat sleeve while jamming a foot into a boot.

"Oh no, you don't. It's not even seven o'clock in the morning. And it's Saturday. I'm sure Mr. Taglieber would like some extra sleep. Sit down. Let me make you some pancakes."

"But Mom? It's almost Christmas! There's so much to do!" Ray whined. His mother stood in the middle of the kitchen with a frying pan in one hand and her other over her heart.

"I'm happy you like to spend time with him and that you are serious about the work. But Raymond, it's only six…"

Then a light fast rapping broke his mother's train of thought. They walked to the front door and saw Olive standing on the stoop, tired and bundled for the cold. Her glasses sat crooked on her face as she bounced impatiently on her toes.

"See, there's Olive. I have to go."

"But…but what about pancakes?"

Ray ran towards the door as he called out. "I'll just be there for a few minutes. I'll come back for breakfast. Promise."

Ray let the door slam as he rushed to Olive. She didn't even wait for Ray to reach her before she turned and started to run towards Oscar's house. She ran with one hand up to her face. Ray looked over at her puzzled.

"What happened to your glasses?"

"I stepped on them last night when I got home."

"So your mom didn't catch you?"

"Nope. Nobody knew I was gone. But now she's going to kill me."

"Don't worry. Oscar should be able to fix them," Ray said hopefully as they rounded the corner to Oscar's driveway. Olive stopped and grabbed Ray's arm.

"You promised he wasn't going to hurt that deer."

Ray bit his lip. He didn't know if that buck even made it through the night. The arrow looked like it was in the neck pretty deep. But if he had lived, Oscar would not hurt him. His brain knew it. His heart knew it.

"I promise."

Olive tore off to the front door, removed her mitten and knocked feverishly. She didn't stop until a very tired Oscar, still covered with a large blanket, opened the door. Rubbing sleep out of his eye with his palm, he yawned as he spoke.

"What's on fire? Who's on fire?"

Olive looked back at Ray as tears began to pool in her eyes.

"Oscar, they got one," Ray said.

"One what?"

"A deer. One of those bucks. With an arrow."

Oscar's sleepiness evaporated. He shot up straight, his shoulders squared and his eyebrows crumpled into an expression of concern and anger that made Ray nervous.

"Where is he? Is he dead?"

"No. Not yet. He's in the woods across the street. Where the hunters were sitting. Just beyond the racetrack."

Oscar shrugged the blanket off his shoulders as he ran back into the house, leaving Ray and Olive on the front stoop. The two just looked at each other as they wrapped their arms around themselves for warmth in the cold morning air.

"What's he going to do?" Olive said as she blew warmth into her mittens.

"I don't know. But if anyone can help him it's ..." Ray's voice faded as he saw a police car pull up Oscar's front yard and stop. Officer Boland, who stood about six and a half feet tall, slowly unfurled out of the car and walked up to the two.

"Late night. Early morning. When do you kids ever sleep?" he said, chuckling to himself as he sauntered across the yard towards the two. He seemed to stop short once he noticed the looks of concern plastered on the kids' faces. "Hey, what's wrong with you kids?"

"Nothing, Officer. We're just swell," Ray said. He tried to keep his voice from shaking but could not control his knees. "We just needed to tell our neighbor about something we saw last night." As soon as the sentence came out, Ray regretted saying anything about last night.

"While you were out?"

"Yes. I mean no," Ray stammered.

Officer Boland folded his arms across his chest and rocked back on his heels. "Ah, the comet. And what *did* you see out there last night?"

Ray's mouth opened but only vowels and awkward sounds tumbled out. Then Oscar stepped out of the front door dressed in a heavy coat and hat. In one hand he held a metal pail and in the other, a shotgun. Then nothing came out of Ray's mouth.

Olive's tiny cold hands gripped Oscar's sleeve through her mittens. Her eyes pleaded behind her broken glasses. "Please, Oscar. Please don't hurt him. He's ok. I know he is."

Oscar looked over Olive's head at Officer Boland and nodded. "There's a wounded deer out in the woods," he said softly. Officer Boland covered his mouth and nodded, now understanding the concern. Oscar bent over and set the pail down. Ray looked inside to see it was filled with rags and a large knife. Even though he was freezing, a sweat began to form on Ray's neck. How could he have judged Oscar so wrong?

Oscar put his hands on Olive's shoulders and made her face him. His voice was stern but gentle. "Olive, honey, I need you to listen to me. If that deer made it through the night in fine enough shape, I will help him. If he isn't, then, well, I have to put him out of his pain."

"No, Oscar. Please…"

Oscar shook his head but did not change his tone. "It isn't right to let an animal suffer out there like that."

"But he has friends. We saw them. They will help him."

Officer Boland stepped up and put his hand on Oscar's shoulder. For a moment, Ray thought that maybe he could talk some sense into Oscar.

"Oscar, let me take care of it. We can't have a maim deer wandering around here."

"No, no. Thank you, Aiden, but I will handle this," Oscar insisted.

"But my brothers hunt these woods. I could do it and they could…"

"No," Oscar said firmly. "I will take care of it." He bent over to Olive and his reassuring tone came back. "Please, go home and come back with Raymond around lunch time. I'll tell you all about your deer then."

Olive sniffled as she stared at Oscar. "Ray promised you wouldn't hurt him."

Oscar looked over at Ray, let out a sigh and shook his head. Ray couldn't tell if Oscar was mad or just tired. "Whatever suffering that poor animal is in, I will take care of it." And with that he patted her hat sweetly, picked up his pail and gun and waddled off into the woods.

Ray's and Olive's heads hung low as they began to walk home. Officer Boland nervously waved to the kids and called out. "You kids have a good day now!"

After the hum of the police car left the street Ray turned to Olive. "I know he won't hurt that buck. I just know it."

"I believe you," Olive said as she sniffled. "I believe you, Ray."

Ray's mother already had a place set for Olive at the breakfast table when the two plodded into the kitchen, both sad and tired, neither with the enthusiasm and urgency which they left with only minutes earlier.

"Everything alright with you two?" she asked as she scooped the pancakes out of the pan and onto a plate.

Ray and Olive flopped into their seats and stared at their forks. Ray's mother set the plates down in front of them and tried to change the subject.

"Ok then. I'll say grace," Ray's mother said as she sat down and folded her hands. She bowed down but looked back and forth between Olive and Ray as she spoke. "Dear Lord, thank You for the food we are about to eat. Bless this house and all who dwell in it. We ask for your love, protection, and guidance for ourselves and for our country, through Jesus Christ our Lord, Amen."

Ray and Olive muttered an "Amen." They hadn't even unclasped their hands before they heard the shot go off.

❄ ❄ ❄

Oscar's beard was covered in gravy when he answered the door.

"Just in time! I have plenty of stew!"

Olive's eyes, already red from crying all morning, let out another flood of tears. "Why did you do it?"

"Stew? I don't know. It felt like a stew kind of day," Oscar said happily. Music bounced from the old radio around the house as the three made their way towards the kitchen. The warm soft smell of meat and potatoes filled the house. John Charles sat at the kitchen table with a red pen, making circles and notes on a stack of letters. He smiled at the two until he noticed Olive's tears and Ray's frown. Oscar plopped down at his seat, flapped out a napkin and tucked it into his collar.

"I mean kill that deer," Olive said.

"What deer? I didn't kill a deer," Oscar said incredulously as he turned to John Charles and asked, "You kill a deer?" John Charles kept circling but shook his head, no.

"Come on, Oscar," Ray said. Lack of sleep was starting to make him angry. Olive was sad but she didn't need to be fibbed to like a child. "We know you did. You don't have to lie."

"You saying I'm lying?" Oscar huffed as he grabbed the massive spoon and massive fork that sat on either side of a massive bowl. He jabbed at a hunk of meat in the stew and began to chew. He stared at his food as he spoke. "You saying I'm a liar? Olive, get me my gun." Olive's wet eyes grew wide. She looked at Raymond and then at Oscar.

"Excuse me?"

"You heard me. My gun. It's sitting over there in the corner."

"You're not going to shoot Ray, are you?"

"Of course I'm not going to shoot Ray. Now, go over and get that gun," he said as he shoved another hunk of meat into his mouth.

Olive slowly walked over to the shotgun that rested in the corner of the dining room. Ray could see it from the kitchen. The long dark barrel leaned against a china cabinet like a mechanic leaning on a cigarette machine. Ray watched Olive as she stepped slowly around the weapon, trying to find a safe place to touch it. She reached out tentatively and put her hand around the double barrel. Ray reached out as well, as if he were guiding her hands for safety. But then she stopped. She cocked her head to the side as she felt the gun. Her hands felt all around the stock and handle. She pulled the barrel down and lifted her chin to look in it. Ray yelled out.

"Olive! Don't!"

"Let her be," said Oscar as he continued his lunch. He was not fazed by anything. Ray looked at him as if Oscar had three heads before he ran to Olive. Olive smiled wide as she slid her fingers along the tip of the barrel. Ray yanked it away from her.

"It's fine, Ray. Really," she assured.

Ray looked at the gun closely and then ran his fingers over the stock and barrel. Everything looked the same. Other than different shades of paint, the gun seemed to be made entirely out of wood.

Ray ran back into the kitchen. "But we heard it. We heard the boom."

Oscar pointed with his fork at the pail that sat on the other side of the kitchen. Ray ran over to the pail and lifted it up. He held it up to his face. He could see Oscar through a hole blasted through the bottom.

"It's amazing how loud a big firecracker sounds in one of those things."

Olive marched up to Oscar as he ate. "Did you find him? Is he alright?"

Oscar took his napkin and dabbed the stew sauce off his beard. "Olive, I told you I would help him. And he was there, just as Raymond said. But he only had a flesh wound. Nothing more. I took the arrow out, slapped on a bandage and he went on his happy little way. But I couldn't have Officer Boland think that. If he knew there was a wounded buck out there, his brothers would be on the lookout. Can't have that. Not this close before Christmas."

Olive leaned in and gave him a big hug. "I'm sorry, Oscar. I thought you shot him."

"I wouldn't shoot a perfectly good living animal," he said before looking away in thought. "Well, Fluffles maybe."

John Charles looked up from his papers and shot Oscar a disapproving frown. "Oscar…"

"Alright, alright, I wouldn't shoot Fluffles," said Oscar as the grump came back in his voice. "Would like to but I wouldn't." Oscar got up from his seat and pulled the napkin from his chin and slapped it on the table. "Ok now! There is work to be done. Olive, just sit a minute and collect yourself. Tears and paint don't mix. Try some stew if you're hungry. Raymond, let's get going. Stew for you later."

Ray followed Oscar out of the kitchen and to the workbench, where he saw a new set of letters strung up between two lamps, like a line of laundered napkins drying on a clothesline on a summer day. He grabbed his apron and tied it around himself as he read the round red circles on each page. These particular letters came from little boys hailing from Akron, Wilmington, Altoona, and Mason, all of whom wanted racecars. For some, it was the first on their list. Some, last or second to last. But all wanted, and would get, the same thing.

"Thank your lucky stars it isn't trains. I can't stand when they ask for trains," Oscar said as he slid on a pair of elbow-high leather gloves. "They might as well ask for three planes or six boats. Any train worth being under a tree has three cars. Three!" He tried holding up three fingers through the stiff gloves but gave up in a huff. "No one asks for *just* a caboose or *just* a tender. Not a one. They ask for the whole thing. And with a track! Can't forget about that fun little time sucker. I want to say to them, 'Why don't you make it easy on Santa and ask for a pony.' " Oscar flopped onto his seat and wiped his brow. Just the thought made him exhausted.

Ray thought about trains. He remembered the one that carried his father away from him, alive and yelling and waving his cap in the air. He remembered that he used to love the far-off sounds of the whistle and the clanging of bells heralding its arrival. Then he remembered waiting in the car at the station with his mother for the train that carried his dad back in the large box. Trains took people away and brought them back broken. If he were to ever write a letter to Santa, a train wouldn't be on it. And if he had to make tracks for a little boy, they would be in a circle so that the pretend passengers would always get off at the same place and in the same way as when they stepped on board. There would only be one destination. They would leave but always come back home.

"Hey, will you go back to the basement and grab me a tool that looks like this?" Oscar said, snapping Ray's attention back to the workbench. He looked up at the instrument in Oscar's hand. It looked like a standard hammer.

"A hammer?"

"Yes, but one that looks like this. With this thingy," he said pointing to the pointy ends. "And a that."

"Sure thing," Ray said as he made is way down to the basement. Ray reached in his pocket and felt the small brass bit tumble between his fingertips. If ever there was a time to check his theory, he figured, now would be it.

Ray hustled down the dark stairs and reached for the pull string that illuminated the basement. Everything looked exactly as it did the last time he stepped foot down there. First he searched around the workbench for the tool Oscar needed. Three of the exact same hammers in different sizes hung up on the wall next to the other picks, clamps, and wrenches. Ray took a mental note of their location and walked towards the small bridles. He held the bit in his one hand as he examined each harness intently. His eyes darted back and from the piece of metal in his hand to the others that sat attached to the small straps. When he got to the last one, he saw the identical piece of metal hanging loose off the leather strap. Ray pulled the bridle off the hook and looked at the other side. On that leather strap where a hunk of metal should be was only a loose, chewed strap of broken leather. He put the bit up next to the torn edge and held it up to its twin brother. The wearing, the bumps, and the break fit perfectly. It was a match.

He looked past the bridle in thought. But not many thoughts passed through his head. Why would Oscar lie about this? Ray hung the bridle back on the hook under the words "two light" and stared at the sheet that draped over the not-so-secret room. He walked over to it, pushed it aside and let the light flood into the room. A tarp now covered the old car. As he looked towards the ground he noticed a face staring back at him. After a jump of fright, he realized it was his face. Upon closer inspection, the old railings that held the machine were no longer there. Below the tarp something glimmered in the light. Ray gently picked up the corner of the fabric and pulled it back. Where once sat rusted old metal scraps were two wide, long, shiny, silver blades running flat along the ground and curling up towards his chest. They looked like gigantic man-made metal elephant tusks. Between the two impressive blades sat a large old wooden box. Ray took two steps back and tried to take it in. Once his eyes could focus, he felt his hand let go of the tarp. That could not be what it looked like. Southold never got that much snow.

His feet kept moving backwards, past the sheet and under the hanging light. He didn't stop until he felt his back hit a large belly.

Ray jumped about a foot in the air as he spun around. There stood Oscar with one hand on his hip and the other wrapped around a hammer.

"You done looking?"

Ray felt the moisture drain out of his mouth and into his hands. He saw the hammer and then the eyebrow raised on Oscar's face.

"I'm…I'm sorry. I wasn't snooping. I mean…I guess I was…"

"Oh please, that's not snooping," he said as he dropped his hands and walked over to the sheet. He grabbed the sheet and wrapped it around a hook. "I keep the sheet up because I'm sanding it. Don't want my tools getting filled with sawdust," Oscar said as he flung the tarp completely off the massive sleigh. He stood proudly next to the beast, padding one of its large blades. "What do you think?"

Ray's mouth remained opened. He couldn't figure out what was more amazing: not being in trouble for snooping or this huge storybook sleigh sitting in the middle of an old dirt fruit cellar.

"What's it for?" Ray uttered.

"Baking cookies," Oscar said seriously. "Shushing through the snow in the North Pole! Or Jacob's Lane on a snowy day. Take your pick."

Ray shook his head. Still nothing seemed to make sense. "Is it… yours?"

"No. It's Santa's," Oscar said matter-of-factly. "Made for one little boy who stopped believing in Santa." Oscar looked over the carriage with pride. Ray couldn't even look at the sleigh. Words escaped him as he felt himself tap his chest. Was this for him? Then Oscar continued. "For little Thomas."

Ray's fog lifted. "What? Tommy Goldsmith?"

"Yes, Tommy Goldsmith. Don't say anything to him. His mother wants to keep it a surprise."

"Wait, you're giving him your sleigh?"

Oscar finally stopped looking at the sleigh and looked up at Ray. "Did you use a noggin thumper too hard? Like I said, it's Santa's. Well, that's what the note will say. His mother asked me to make it for him since a certain someone…" he paused for a moment and pointed at Ray. "Someone seemed to convince him that Santa wasn't real. Figured if he saw this on his lawn on Christmas morning it might change his mind."

Air finally escaped Ray's lungs. The sleigh was a commissioned piece for the Goldsmiths. He shook his head as if he were trying to shake off a bad memory or sleep.

"You alright there, Raymond?" Oscar asked. "You look funny."

Ray rubbed his eyes. "Tired, I guess."

"Nothing a fizzy drink won't fix. How about going upstairs and grabbing a root beer? That'll set you right."

Bewildered, Ray kept rubbing his eyes as he headed upstairs towards the kitchen. Nothing seemed to make sense. Was it the lack of sleep? Ray counted the things he knew. He knew what he saw with the light in the woods. He knew Olive saw it too. He knew there was a deer in the woods with a star on its forehead. He knew that a buck saved him from Fluffles and from winding up at the bottom of a ravine. He knew the other bucks saved him and Olive from those dogs. He knew that only a short time ago, that sleigh looked like the remnants of a rusty beaten-up potato combine yanked out of an old barn. Now it looked like something that slid off a snow-capped mountain of a child's storybook. He knew that bit belonged to that bridle. Now wasn't the time to question Oscar. He would save it for later. Oscar was nice enough to not yell at him for looking around the basement. The last thing he wanted to do was get on his bad side and call him out on a fib. If it were even a fib at all.

Ray's thoughts swam in his tired, confused head as he rested against the wall and took a glug of root beer. Olive didn't acknowledge him as she wiped her eyes with the end of her sleeve. John Charles was no longer sifting through the pages. His twisted fingers laid on top of the stack as he listened to Olive.

"And I think that's when I stepped on them," she said, fumbling with her glasses. The side piece, now bent and snapped, completely broke free from the rest of the glasses. "They were brand new. You think maybe Oscar can fix them?"

John Charles smiled and took the two pieces from Olive. His fingers looked more broken than the frames. He could only grasp the pieces with what was left of his index fingers and thumbs. He looked at both parts with his head cocked to the side.

"I know it may not look like it, but believe it or not, I've been known to fix a pair or two of glasses in my time."

"Really?" said Olive. Her eyes swollen and red looked even bigger and greener without the spectacles on. "Did you ever wear glasses?"

"Oh no, but I knew lots of people who did. For some reason, I could always help them see better." John Charles reached in his pocket and pulled out a linen handkerchief. He blew into the cloth and gave it to Olive. "Here. Dry your eyes and let me see if I can't fix these."

Olive took the handkerchief, tucked her chin down and put it to her face. "If you say you can fix them then I believe you."

Then John Charles directed another smile to Olive which she couldn't see. He took the pads of his fingers and ran them around the broken section of frame. Then he folded the ends back and forth inside. Ray pushed his head closer. They weren't just fixed. The glasses looked like they had never been broken in the first place.

"There you go," he said as he held them up to Olive. She reached out for them and rubbed the lenses with the handkerchief. After clicking the sides back and forth she put them gingerly around her ears. She began to blink slowly. With every blink, her smile grew wider.

"Wow! You really did fix these!"

"I told you I could. And you believed in me and that helped."

Olive stood up from the table, walked over to John Charles and gave him a hug like the one she gave Oscar.

"Thank you so much. You saved my hide."

"And you saved mine by painting all those planes. If it weren't for you, we would only be able to give them to boys and girls whose names begin with the letter "G.""

Then Oscar's voice barreled into the kitchen from the living room. "I got ears, you know. I heard that."

Olive and John Charles both put their hands over their mouths and chuckled. Then all the clocks began to ring out, letting them know it was two o'clock and that it was safe, at least for the next ten seconds, to laugh out loud.

CHAPTER 18

The Backyards of Jacob's Lane – Southold, New York, 1944

Ray, Olive, Oscar, and John Charles worked through the blustery afternoon and into the early evening. With Christmas less than two weeks away, the letters began to pour in. INR Industries did not give cutoff times for the letters and collected them all the way up until Christmas Eve. Oscar insisted on making extras in all the toys as to accommodate the last-minute minions. He said kids who believed in Santa had their lists done by Thanksgiving. The ones who pulled one out in the ninth inning were usually older and hedging their bets.

"Amazing," Ray's mother said as she scrubbed a cast iron pot. Ray stood next to her and looked out the window into the darkness of the backyard as he dried the rest of the freshly rinsed dinner dishes. "How do you think he'll get it out of the cellar?"

"I'll help him. It'll be impossible for him to do it alone."

"I'd like to watch that when you do. It'll certainly be something to see," she said as she dunked the pot into a bucket of water. "But be careful. I don't want you to get hurt moving Santa's sleigh. Maybe you should get some reindeer to help you."

Ray rolled his eyes as his mother laughed at her little joke. "There," she said as she pointed with her chin to the pile of vegetable scraps in a bowl on the counter. "Take those out into the woods. I can't make broth out of them. Maybe an animal would like them instead."

Ray complied. He put down the dish, grabbed his coat and headed out into the backyard. He threw the scraps as high and as far as he could into the woods. After they left his hand he heard nothing until the scraps landed with a slight crunch on the leaves. He couldn't see them in the dark but knew that the longer the pause, the farther they went. Ray stood at the edge of the woods and looked into the shadows, hoping to see a light peek its way past a tree. He narrowed and strained his eyes in all directions but all he saw were the lights on the Christmas trees flickering through the windows on Ships Drive.

As Ray turned back towards his house, he noticed a bright white light shine in the backyard of a house a few doors down. It was Oscar's floodlights. Ray walked through the neighbors' backyards towards Oscar's, thinking he might just be pulling the sleigh up out of the cellar and could possibly use a hand. As Ray walked around the side of the house, he felt his feet slow to a stop.

In Oscar's backyard stood the bucks. All of them.

Ray ran to the side of house and peered around its edge. His eyes scoured the yard, counting every buck and every antler tip. Three were far larger than the rest and stood still and solid in place. Each seemed as large as a horse with eight to ten points on their racks. Four shorter bucks milled about, eating what they could find and shaking their antlers and ears periodically, like a batter tapping the mud off his shoes with the tip of his bat before he sets up to swing. Ray kept searching. As quiet as he tried to be, he felt his lips move.

"Where are you, buddy? Come on. Come out," he whispered to himself as he searched. Then, as if on command, one of the large bucks broke from their position and walked forward, allowing the buck with the white markings to come into view. Ray smiled, hoping the buck could see him and maybe come to him. But instead the deer twitched his ear and followed the larger buck. Then the sound of a storm door slamming rang out. Ray flattened his back against the house until he heard Oscar's voice.

"There you go. There you go," said Oscar in a kind tone. "You deserve another helping. You had a rough day."

Ray's eyebrows drew together as he turned back to look at Oscar's backyard. There Oscar stood, a cluster of carrots in his one hand, with his other gently rubbing the bandage on the large buck's neck. None of the other bucks changed their behavior. None moved. None jumped. None were startled or tried to dart away. It was as if one of their own sidled up to them. The rest happily let the large buck munch down on the carrots, content with their lot in the yard. The sight, so unreal, made Ray gasp aloud.

All the deer jerked their heads up in unison, as if they were just a collection of marionettes being pulled by the same string. He slapped his hand over his mouth and his back towards the house. The tone of Oscar's voice changed.

"Hup, hup," Ray heard Oscar say firmly and quickly. The sound of hooves and limbs taking off and hitting the floor of the woods rang out. Ray knew if he turned around to look they would be all gone.

"Hello?" Oscar called out. "Anyone there?"

Ray squeezed his back into to the clapboard siding. Nothing came out of his mouth. Not a word, not a breath. His whole body blended into a shadow on the side of the house. The storm door slammed shut and the light went out, darkening the backyard and giving Ray the opening to exhale. Everything, he thought, is nuts.

Ray inched towards the front of the house. The light that came out of Oscar's bay window faded to a soft glow. Curiosity got the best of Ray as he peeked over the edge of the window. There, in the middle of the room, stood Oscar in baggy pants and a long john shirt. He picked up the small pillow embroidered with the word "love" off the green velvet scrolling armed lounge chair and sat down. The small lamp on the side table provided just enough light to give the room a warm, firelight glow. Oscar put the pillow on his lap and placed his glasses on the side table on top of a book and next to a steaming mug. He let out a long breath and rested his head on the side against the chair. With eyes closed he gave the pillow a hug and said a few words Ray could not make out.

Now Ray knew why the bed in the back room was never used. This living room was his bedroom. His world. Oscar's face looked content as his stomach steadily rose and fell with each breath. Ray didn't worry about getting caught as he turned and headed for his house. Oscar seemed so peaceful sitting with his pillow. So very peaceful. And so very sad.

CHAPTER 19

Southold Elementary School – Southold, New York, 1944

The light tap of a horn from the Mott's beat-up old Ford Tudor cut into the morning quiet as Ray raced around the downstairs gathering his books for school. As he struggled with the buckle that cinched his science and history textbooks together, his mother stuck a lunch bag and a small stack of letters under his nose.

"I'm looking after Paley today for Marcia. Will you drop these off at the post office on your way home from school?" she asked.

Ray grabbed his lunch and letters and grunted a quick, "Yes, Mom," as he bolted for the door. As he reached for the handle he looked down at the top letter and saw the address. This envelope was going to Arkansas. The Kozaks had no family in Arkansas. Ray stopped and looked up at his mother. She stood in the middle of the room, still in her flannel nightgown in front of the unlit Christmas tree. He knew who lived in Arkansas.

"Just wanted them to know they were in our prayers this Christmas. We weren't the only ones who lost someone that day," she said matter-of-factly.

Ray looked back down at the address. Mrs. Samuel Pickett. Searcy, Arkansas. He knew who she was, although he never met her. Samuel Pickett fought in the 9th infantry division and died on September 22 in a building in Saarlautern, Germany, with his father. He knew all the names of the men who were in that building. Now his mother knew all the wives or mothers. Ray didn't realize that he hadn't moved as the horn honked again. Then he felt his mother's hand run along the top of his head, followed by a kiss.

"You have a good day, son," she said. The scent of her cold cream surrounded him and felt even more soothing than the scent of the Douglas fir.

Ray grunted another, "Yes, Mom," as he tucked the letters under his arm and headed out the door. Olive scooted over as he squeezed himself into the backseat. Two of Olive's sisters sat side by side examining themselves in their open compacts as they painted in their eyebrows and lips. Mrs. Mott drove with the window open, letting some of Olive's grandmother's Lucky Strike smoke filter out of the car, only to have a blustering cold wind pull it back into the backseat. After a few seconds of the sisters' complaining Mrs. Mott agreed to roll up the window. While the car swirled in the sounds of the women's lighthearted chatter and smoke, Ray sat with his books and lunch on his lap and thumbed through each letter. He looked at their names. Pickett, Asher, Lonergan, Carrig. He looked at the states: Rhode Island, Pennsylvania, Connecticut, Virgina, Arkansas. He knew his mother waited until all the other Christmas cards were sent before she started this batch. He knew his mother took more time and care with these cards than any cards written to their cousins or aunts. To his mother, these women meant something. Something delicate and important. To Ray, they were all just unlucky.

"What are those?" Olive said softly as she looked down at the letters. Her little frame pressed so tightly between her sister and Ray that she could not move or look away.

"I've got to mail these for my mom. They're Christmas cards," Ray spat as he tucked them into the small opening of his buckle and his history textbook. "I hope I don't forget."

But he knew he wouldn't forget. All day long, the letters pulsed with life wherever he placed them, making him feel as if he were trying to hide a kitten in his desk rather than a small stack of mail. If he had a free moment after rushing through a test or the two minutes before the recess bell rang, Ray would gently pull out the pile and sift through the cards. It wasn't until lunchtime when he had a chance to escape into an empty stairwell and examine the letters more closely. He held each card up to the light at various angles to see if he could look through the envelope and read the words his mother tucked between the folds of a manger scene.

"Are you going to read one?" he heard a small voice echo on the top of the stairwell. Ray looked up and watched Olive walk down with a half-eaten apple. She sat next to him and took another bite.

"No," Ray said angrily. "They're just stupid Christmas cards."

"Then why are you looking at them like that?"

"No reason."

"Who are they to?"

Ray swallowed the air that sat in his mouth. "Mom wrote them. They are to the families of the men who died with Dad."

Olive's eyes widened behind her glasses. "Can I see them?"

Ray gave the stack to Olive. He peered over her shoulder and commented on every name as she gently picked up each card.

"That's to Stephen Carrig's mom. And that family is Allen Lonergan's. I hear he knew how to stitch up holes in shirts as well as people. And that's one's going to Samuel Pickett's family. The army told us that everyone called him Captain Lightening but Mom probably figured it wouldn't get there if she addressed it to Mrs. Captain Lightening."

Olive stopped suddenly at one letter. She studied the name and then put it to the side.

"That's Jack Donner's mom," Ray said. "Dad mentioned him in a letter once. I think they were pals."

The next letter caused her face to scrunch up. She turned to Ray puzzled. "Who is this one?"

Ray looked at the address. Mrs. Paul Rancer. Falls Church, Virginia. "She's the wife of another man in Dad's squad."

Olive looked at Ray, her eyebrows curled down in thought. She took the letters and placed them on the stairs.

"Hey? What are you doing?"

Olive ignored Ray as she laid out the seven letters side by side on one of the steps. She knelt on stairs with her hands on her knees and studied the addresses as if it were a treasure map.

"Seriously, Olive. Stop it," Ray said as he reached to pick up a card. She pulled his hand away and pointed.

"Look. Isn't that neat?"

Ray looked down at the letters but saw only the names and addresses. Whatever she saw appeared only to Olive. Olive pointed to the first card. "Look at the last name."

Ray picked up the card and read. "To Mrs. Kathy Donner."

"Ok," she said. "Now look." Olive took three fingers and covered the middle letters of the next name. "What does that say?"

"It should say Quentin Terence Pudd if you're hand wasn't there."

"No. Read it fast."

"Q. Pudd."

Olive now was smiling at Ray. Noticing that he still hadn't caught on, she did the same with the next letter. She covered over the letters and asked Ray again.

"Donald Asher. Well, D. Asher."

"Now do you get it?"

Ray felt his head cock to the side. A laugh shot out of his mouth. "Olive, be serious."

"I am. Donner. Cupid. Dasher. Paul Rancer," she picked up the letter and covered the letters of the first name. "Look! Prancer!"

The smile left from Ray's face. "That's crazy. Come on, Olive."

"It's right there. You don't think that's neat?"

"Well…well what about the other names?" Ray said, aggravated. "There's an Allen Lonergan. A Stephen Carrig. And Samuel Pickett. There's no reindeer named Carrig or Pickett."

Olive looked down at the letters with her chin in her hand. "I bet we'd find it. Maybe if we knew something about them."

"That's crazy!" Ray shouted, his voice echoed and bounced up the stairwell. "You're crazy."

"It's not that crazy." Olive said as she flipped over the letter in her hand. She put her index finger under Mrs. Henry Lee Kozak's name on the return address then displayed it to Ray. "Your dad's name is Hal. Hal Lee. He's Comet."

Ray stared at Olive, angry and wanting to cry. He scooped the letters off the stairs like a scattered deck of cards. "Don't go to Oscar's today. I'll paint the planes if I have to. I want to be alone."

Ray fought the choke coming up his throat as he ran up the stairs, away from Olive. The cry that he held back seemed to have traveled down the stairs and into Olive's throat. He could hear her voice shake as she called out to him. "Please! I'm sorry, Ray. Really, I am."

Ray said nothing as he bolted through the doors and down the hall back to the safety of the fifth grade classroom. He ran with the cards clutched against his chest, as if he pushed them in hard enough they would absorb into his heart.

❄ ❄ ❄

No music played at Oscar's that afternoon. The only sound heard between Oscar and Ray on the workbench was the whomping of metal sheets and the second hands ticking away from the clocks on the wall. Ray did as he was told. He let the letters slip from his hands down the chute of the mailbox in front of the post office. He was angry at Olive, but did not know why. His father's death wasn't a joke. He knew Olive didn't see it as that. But something about the reindeer names made it seem silly. Nothing about his dad's death was neat.

"You two have a fight," Oscar said as he continued cutting a sheet of tin.

"No. She said something stupid."

"Did she say your breath smells like a dirty diaper?"

"No," Ray pouted.

"That you have the laugh of a wounded billy goat?"

"No."

"That your belly is as big as a tub full of jelly?" Oscar looked up. "That's never a nice thing to hear."

"No," Ray uttered.

"Then whatever it was couldn't have been so bad."

Ray couldn't explain it to Oscar. The idea of the soldiers sounded crazy but it was just one more thing that Ray couldn't explain. Ray knew that now would be the time to start finding out. He was too sad to be afraid anymore. He let out a breath, reached in his pocket and grabbed the brass bit. He put it on the bench next to a can of nails that sat between him and Oscar.

"Here, it's yours. Take it."

Oscar looked over at the bit and stopped working. He slowly reached for the bit, picked it up and put it in his pocket.

"Why didn't you say it belonged to you?" asked Ray. "I must have forgotten," Oscar said quietly. He picked up a pair of snips and continued to cut the metal.

Ray pulled down his goggles and looked at Oscar. He put his hands in his pockets so neither of them would see them shake.

"Oscar," Ray said, his voice scared and soft. "Oscar, are you Santa Claus?"

Oscar let out a hard laugh and turned to Ray. "You don't believe in Santa, remember?"

"I'm not kidding. Are you the real Santa Claus?"

Oscar stopped working again and faced Ray. He pushed the goggles down off his face and removed his gloves. "Is this about the sleigh downstairs?"

"No, it's about the bucks in your backyard."

Oscar just stared at Ray, running his tongue over his teeth in an attempt to buy some time. He blinked a few times, then finally spoke. "What bucks?"

"The bucks you saved in the woods. I saw you with them. They know who you are. They listen to you. Except for one," Ray said as he stood up. "He listens to me."

Noises and breaths in objection came out of Oscar, but no words. Ray continued.

"There's one with a white star on its face. That deer saved us from getting eaten by Fluffles. And … and I also think …" Ray paused as his courage dipped. Oscar lowered his chin and looked at Ray, waiting to hear the next allegation come from his ten-year-old mouth. "And I think those bridles downstairs are for those bucks and not Dr. DiNapoli's horses. I think you made them to pull that sleigh."

Oscar's chin remained low as he looked at Ray. Ray waited for a response. Oscar just looked at him, sucking his teeth in thought. Finally, he spoke.

"Those bridles were from Dr. DiNapoli's ponies. The sleigh is for the Goldsmiths. I know I appear like Santa because I make toys at Christmas, have a white beard and although I'm not jolly, I'm certainly…" he slapped his stomach with both hands. It rippled like a pebble hitting a pond. "Fat."

"What about the bucks?" Ray asked.

"Well, what about the bucks?"

"Why do they follow you?"

"Maybe they think I'm a big head of cauliflower. I don't know," said Oscar as he got up from his seat and headed towards Olive's workstation. "I think you should keep on not believing in Santa. It's easier that way."

"Really," demanded Ray as he got up to follow him. "Why? You said Santa is real. Remember when I yelled at Tommy? You said Santa is very real to some kids."

"Well, yes. Santa is real. Santa is very real. I'm just saying…" Oscar grabbed his hair in frustration. "You shouldn't stop believing in Santa. You should stop believing in me."

The two looked at each other sadly in the middle of the room. The clocks rang out three o'clock, saving them both the time and space to say anything. They stood quietly as they let the bells and chimes ring out. After the echo of the alarms faded they remained quiet. Oscar hobbled in defeat back to the workbench and put on his goggles.

"Come on. We got work to do."

Ray walked slowly back and sat down at his station. He put on his goggles and quietly asked, "Oscar, when did you stop believing in Santa Claus?"

Oscar said softly, talking more to himself than to Ray. "About fifteen seconds ago."

CHAPTER 20

Kozak's Front Steps—Southold, New York, 1944

Neither Ray nor Oscar said much for the rest of the afternoon. Both worked in relative silence until it was time for Ray to leave. After the clocks rang out four o'clock Ray walked home, dragging his feet in thought. Most of what Oscar said he didn't believe. Too much of what Ray saw pointed to his theory that Oscar was, in fact, the one and only Santa Claus. Maybe the storybooks had it wrong. A simple miscalculation in words. Instead of North Pole, it was the North Fork. No one would think to look for him on Jacob's Lane. But if Oscar insisted, however badly, that he was not who Ray thought he was then there was no need to ask anyone else. The only one would believe him would be Olive. Despite being mad, Ray missed her at Oscar's. She lightened the air at the workshop. Whether by humming along to the radio, stumping Oscar with the riddle from *Terry and the Pirates* or talking about the funny things she and Paley would search for with a telescope, Olive knew how to make time fly in the workshop and Oscar not swear when he hit his hand with a hammer.

Ray trudged along until he saw Paley rocking in place in the Mott's front yard, staring up above the treetops. The cereal box clenched in his hands looked worn and soft from the elements and time.

"Hey ya, Paley," Ray said. "See anything today?"

Paley, eyes still in the sky, shook his head. "No planes today. No soldiers today."

"That's good," Ray said with his voice raising. "Bet you're scaring them off."

"No," Paley said. "No. They're not scared of me. I'm not scared of them." Ray patted Paley on the shoulder. Paley would have made an excellent soldier. Fearless, loyal, tireless, keen, and fascinated by planes. Ray believed that he would be dropping bombs over France if he didn't come out on this earth slower than his peers. Some people felt sorry for the Motts and for Paley with his different brain. Not Ray. To Ray, Paley's different brain kept him alive and out of a war.

"I feel safer knowing you're here," Ray said. Paley just smiled shyly with pride and patted Ray's hand, never looking away from what might be coming in the sky.

Ray continued to his home but stopped when he saw Olive sitting on his front steps. Her knees bounced up and down rapidly in hopes of keeping her stocking-covered legs warm. She looked up at Ray with red eyes and waved at him timidly. Ray's feet moved himself towards her as he took a seat on the front steps.

"I'm sorry for what I said today, Ray. I didn't mean to make you angry."

"It's fine," Ray said as he picked blindly at a piece of frayed leather coming off the tongue of his shoe.

"I don't ever want to make you feel sad about your dad. I miss him so much."

Ray looked at Olive in surprise. It never occurred to him that she might miss him too. The only hurt he could see was his own. He really never saw his mother's. He just knew it came out in quiet bits and pieces behind his back or a closed door.

Olive stared ahead over the patches of snow that still clung to the grass. Her voice quieted to a whisper, as if she spoke too loudly someone would come along and take her memories away.

"He called me Sweetheart. Nobody calls me that. I liked that." She looked over at Paley and nodded. "And he called Paley, Son. I liked that too. Father never called us those things."

Olive's father, from the little Ray remembered of him, was a loud man. Ray's dad could get loud, but only when they were running through the woods or playing games. Mr. Mott was loud when adults were usually quiet, like after bedtime or during dinner. Mr. Mott spent all his free time at the taverns and bars. After a while, all of his time became free. Ray heard that he lived around town but he never saw him anywhere. Never at church or at the grocer or post office or even at the barber. Ray asked his mother once why they called him Paley if his name was really Frank Jr. She said Mr. Mott wanted to make sure that no one confused the two. And then, for some reason, she spit.

Olive wiped her nose with her mitten and smiled. "I also missed the way he pitched to Tommy."

Ray let out a laugh. He could picture his dad looking like a human pinwheel as he wound up to throw a baseball to Tommy Goldsmith. Tommy would look so serious at bat. His oversized cap wobbled around on his head and his chubby arms struggled to hold up a bat too big for his frame. Ray's dad would tug on the brim of his cap, lift his leg way up in the air, wind up like a windmill, hop five times to get closer to the batter, then release the ball. Everyone other than Tommy would be in stitches. But Tommy could always hit them. His dad called Tommy the best hitter in Southold for being about to hit a pitch that silly. Since Tommy's cap covered his eyes most of the time, Ray thought his dad might just be the best pitcher.

"And the way he clapped. Like this." Olive put her hands together as if she were packing a snowball.

It felt good to hear someone talk about his dad. Someone who knew him and missed him in the small ways. The way he clapped his hands. The way he threw a pitch. Olive and Paley weren't Ray's brother and sister. His father wasn't their father. But by the way Olive spoke about him in the everyday details, it became clear to Ray that his father might just be their dad.

"Yeah, me too," said Ray. "I miss…" Ray looked back down at his shoe, which he began to pick apart. "Everything."

Olive stood up and smoothed down her coat. "Is it alright with you if I go to Oscar's tomorrow?"

"Sure. That's swell. Olive?" Ray paused and looked up at her. "Olive, do you believe in Santa?"

Olive looked at the ground and shrugged. "I wanted to but my sisters told I me was too old to believe. Why?"

"It's just. I didn't but now… I'm… not sure. I mean, I saw things around Oscar's place…"

"You think Oscar might be Santa Claus?" Olive jumped in.

"I don't know. I asked him."

"What did he say?" Olive said as she stared at Ray. By the tone of her voice, Ray got the feeling that she harbored the same suspicion.

"No. Said he wasn't him."

"You don't believe him. Do you?"

"I don't know," Ray said, confused. "Oscar… or Santa wouldn't… lie. Would they?"

Olive narrowed her eyes in thought. "There's a way to find out." She turned around and marched towards her house. The sun dimmed in the horizon as it turned quickly from dusk to night. Paley had already gone inside as the lights from the Mott's parlor shown through the front window.

"How?" Ray called out. "He said he wasn't!"

"A letter!" Olive hollered back. "I'll write him a letter."

CHAPTER 21

Kindergarten and the Railroad Tracks –
Southold, New York, 1944

A nd she did just that. The next day in school Ray followed Olive as she walked a red envelope to the oversize mailbox that sat in the hallway between first grade and kindergarten. The makeshift mailbox was an old milk crate from Sunrise Dairy painted red, with the words "Letters to Santa" pasted in cotton balls on the side.

"Wouldn't you rather put it in a real mailbox?" Ray asked.

"John Charles said they take letters from schools. They have to take these."

"Did you ask for just one thing, like we talked about?"

"Of course."

Ray leaned in and whispered. "One thing Oscar can't make."

"Yep. Just one pirate telescope for me and Paley."

Ray thought about what Olive said. If Santa could bring him anything then maybe he should write him a letter. The thought stewed in Ray's head all through the rest of their classes and after the last bell rang. Ray sat at his desk and stared at a blank sheet of lined paper and scribbled a note beginning, "Dear Santa." He didn't know what to write. There was nothing he wanted. No toy, no mitt, no game. Nothing under the tree would make it a better Christmas. Olive left Ray with his thoughts as she headed out to find Tommy Goldsmith while his teacher, thinking he was working on his long division, let Ray sit at his desk until she finished cleaning the blackboards. Once she wiped the words off from the day, Ray jotted down the only thing that made sense, stuffed it in an envelope and shoved it in his coat pocket. He made his way through the halls of the school but stopped once he turned the corner to the kindergarten.

The Santa mailbox sat on the floor, overturned by the janitor, who was shoving fistfuls of letters into a large sack. The man was already dressed for the cold as he smashed the letters down into the bag to make them all fit. Ray lingered at the end of the hall, silently watching the man's movements. Once the man finished cramming the last clump of letters in, he slung the sack over his shoulder and headed down the hall towards the doors that led outside. Ray watched as the man opened the doors and walk out as a frigid blast of wind rushed inside.

Ray thought for a moment, ran down the hall and followed the man's path outside. He trailed him across the parking lot of the school and towards the intersection that led towards town. Ray figured the man might be on his way to the post office but as the janitor came to the crossroads, he turned left onto Horton's Lane, the street that leads away from town and towards the railroad tracks.

"Maybe he's taking the letters home?" Ray uttered to himself as he followed the man. But that area held almost no homes. The only homes by the tracks were rundown and filled with people with dogs that didn't stop barking.

The man walked the tracks until he reached two men standing next to a smoking metal barrel. The men stood with their hands out, warming themselves by the smoke. They stepped back once the janitor walked up to it. Ray watched in shock as the man pulled the sack off his shoulder, yank the cord and dump every one of the letters into the fire. The new addition to the barrel caused the flame to burn high. He slung the empty sack back over his shoulder and began to rub his hands next to the now roaring fire. Ray stood motionless until he heard one of the men cry out to him.

"Hey kid? Need to warm up? Fire's going now."

Ray walked stunned over to the barrel and took his place in the circle next to the janitor.

"I never remember it being this cold in December," the custodian said. "They reckon it's going to storm on Christmas Eve. Shame."

Ray didn't listen to the man as he peered into the fire's contents. Curling and crisping in the flames were the letters addressed to Santa. Each carrying a hope, wish, or desire from a kid in his school. And somewhere in there was Olive's. Ray felt the crunch of paper inside his jacket and took out his letter. He looked at it for a moment before tossing it into the fire.

"I hope that wasn't your homework?"

Ray recognized the voice. He broke his gaze from the fire to see John Charles standing on the other side of the barrel. His eyes and smile seem to cut through the billows of gray smoke and yellow licking flames.

"Just one more to add," Ray said as he watched flames dissolve his letter into ash.

"Are you on your way to Oscar's?" John Charles asked as he held his mangled hands out to the fire for warmth. "I'll give you a ride. It's too cold to walk today. Give me a moment and I'll meet you by my car."

Ray nodded in agreement and walked to John Charles's old Packard. As Ray waited for John Charles to finish saying goodbye to the men around the fire, he saw him shake one of the men's hands and give him a note or bill. Then the man thanked him and put it in his pocket. John Charles walked over to the old Packard carrying his worn leather briefcase. He tossed the bag in the backseat as the two rode off in the direction of Jacob's Lane.

"You know that fire was full of letters," Ray said, looking out at the trees whipping past the window. "Letters to Santa Claus. From kids at my school."

"I know," John Charles said with a hint of a smile on his face.

"Why didn't you say something? You should have stopped him."

"I can't stop a man from doing his job."

"His job was to throw those letters into the fire?"

"Yes, Raymond. It was," he said as they drove over the Goose Creek Bridge. Ray looked out over the fading sun's icy reflection on the water.

"Don't worry about those letters, Raymond. Those kids will get what they asked for."

"How do you know, huh? How do you know they will get what they want?" Ray's thoughts went to Olive's letter. It would be a miracle if that appeared under her tree.

"Ray, you need to trust me. I know."

"Olive's letter was in there. So was mine."

"Well, why don't you tell me what Olive wants?"

"Olive wants a telescope. For her to share with Paley. He likes looking for planes and she likes the stars. It's not something Oscar can make."

John Charles nodded in thought. "Ok, that makes sense. Now what about you? What do you want for Christmas?"

Ray didn't say anything. He wouldn't tell John Charles what he wanted. He didn't write what he really wanted on that letter anyway. He wrote what he should ask for, what would make him smile if he saw it under the tree, but it wasn't what he really desired. Ray hesitated before the lie squeaked out of his mouth.

"A new… a new bat."

John Charles said nothing as they pulled into Oscar's driveway. He shut the engine off but did not make a motion to get out of the car.

"Raymond, what is it that you really want for Christmas?"

Ray couldn't hold it in. His face crumpled up like those letters burning in the fire. Hot tears burned his cold cheeks as he felt them melt a crease down his face. What he wanted he would never get.

After giving Ray a few moments, John Charles kept his eyes out over the steering wheel. His voice grew serious, as if he were giving him directions to a place that he'd already visited.

"Raymond, I want you to listen to me very carefully. I promise you there is a heaven. It's where everything you lost, you get back. Every baseball game, every Christmas morning, every Wednesday, everything. I promise you. You will get it all back." John Charles then turned and looked at Ray. "Do you believe me?"

Raymond looked up at him. Through his tears he could see both seriousness and sympathy come from John Charles's eyes. Ray nodded his head. He did believe him. Not because he wanted to but rather something in his heart knew. As sure as snow was cold, John Charles was telling him the truth.

"Yes, sir. I believe you."

Then John Charles gave him one of his broken hands and they shook on it.

CHAPTER 22

Oscar's House – Southold, New York, 1944

Ray walked into Oscar's living room to the two working in full swing. Ray grabbed an apron as he watched Olive carefully line up the racecars she had painted on the mantel above Oscar's fireplace. Oscar sat at his usual stool. His glasses dangled from a chain around his neck as he struggled to read a letter he held up at arm's length.

"Says here Tony wants a red car with his favorite number 139 on the side," Oscar said as he dropped his hand to knee in disgust. "What kid's favorite number is 139? A strange kid, I'd say."

"Maybe that's his weight?" answered Olive.

"He's six," said Oscar as he swiveled back to the bench. "So he's a very large, strange kid."

Olive looked up at the ceiling in thought as she wrote in the air with her fingers. "One. Thirty-nine. Maybe that's his birthday? January, 1939."

Oscar let out a huff. "That's not a favorite number. That's a radio station."

Olive smiled. "Don't worry, Oscar. I'll be happy to paint 139 on the side of a car."

"It'll look silly." He put back on his glasses and grabbed a set of tin snips. "Oh my guts, what do I care. You can paint my telephone exchange on it if you'd like."

John Charles walked over to Oscar, dropped off the new stack of letters in front of him and patted his shoulder.

"Come on now! Where's your Christmas spirit?"

Oscar turned to him and showed him his hands covered in small cuts. "I snipped it off eighty zeppelins ago."

John Charles just chuckled and gave Oscar another pat. He then looked over Oscar's head and gave Ray a smile as he put one of his mangled fingers to the side of his nose and gave it a slight tap. Ray knew their conversation would not leave him so he pursed his lips together and nodded his thanks before John Charles quietly left the room.

"My cousin from Detroit weighed 108 pounds when he was eight," Olive said, as her voice floated through the air. "Lots of things are heavier than they seem." Olive walked over to Oscar's bench, took one of his mallets and made her way to a hanging scale Oscar attached to the side of a curio cabinet. "See, this weighs a hair more than four pounds. Doesn't look like it, does it?"

"No, I guess it doesn't," answered Oscar. "Feels like it weighs 80 pounds after an hour."

"And this," Olive said as she grabbed a small block of nails. "It's only a few inches but it weighs…" she paused as she dropped the block on the scale. "Well, guess, Ray?"

Ray's stomach still hurt after his talk with John Charles. He didn't feel up to it but tried to join in the happy mood. "Three pounds?"

"No!" she cried. "It's seven pounds. Isn't that crazy?"

"Certifiably," answered Oscar.

Olive then walked over to a chair and picked up the pillow with the word "love" embroidered on it. She struggled with its weight as she plopped it on the scale. After the needle stopped moving she called out, "And this! Oscar, guess how much this pillow weighs?"

Oscar didn't answer. His silence caused Ray to look down the bench at him, wondering if he heard Olive. Oscar had stopped working. His head hung low. His hammer and snips were still in his hands but he held them on the bench, the same way he would hold a knife and fork at a dinner table before devouring a steak.

"Come on! Take a guess?"

Oscar closed his eyes and let out a sigh. Slowly he answered. "Eight pounds. Four ounces."

Olive looked at the scale closely and yelled. "Hey! That's right!"

Ray kept his eyes on Oscar, who had yet to open his. Ray quietly asked from the end of the bench. "Are you alright?"

Oscar still didn't move or answer. He sat there in silence with his eyes closed as Ray got up, took off his apron and whispered to Olive that it was time for them to leave.

CHAPTER 23

Estelle Kozak's Bedroom – Southold, New York, 1944

A soft light shone from under the door of his mother's bedroom. He knocked quietly as he was supposed to be in bed over an hour ago.

"Come in," she answered as she ran a comb through her hair. Ray's mother turned around from the vanity as she continued her nightly ritual of combing out the lint that kicked up from the sewing machines. "You should be asleep, Mister."

"I was wondering about something," asked Ray as he sat on the edge of his parents' bed. "Do you know much about the other men from Dad's squad? You know, the ones who died?"

His mother looked around in thought. "Well, I know a little bit. I've heard from a few of their wives." She put her hairbrush down. "What would you like to know?"

Ray picked at a hangnail on his finger. "I don't know. Just things. Like, you know, where they lived. What they did before they were in the army."

His mother looked at him and narrowed her eyes in thought. "I think I might have something. One woman, Kathy Donner, sent me an article from her local paper," she said as she got up and made her way to a bookshelf. She took down a shoebox, which held a stack of letters. "I think I put it in this box," she said as she thumbed through the cluster of opened envelopes.

Ray walked over to his mother and looked over her shoulder as she searched. All addressed to her. All written in different handwriting. She picked up several only to file them back until she reached the one from a Kathy Donner. Sandwiched between the pages popped out a clipping from a newspaper. She handed it to Ray, who became immediately rapt.

"Something like this?" she asked. "I think all of the men are mentioned in there."

Ray held up the delicate cutout like Olive would a paper doll. The title of the article was "Hometown Son Dies a Hero." Ray's eyes skimmed the piece and immediately noticed his father's name jump out. "Henry Lee Kozak, 32. Southold, New York. Mechanic. Beloved husband to Estelle Agnes Kozak and father to Raymond James Kozak." Pickett, Lonergan, Rancer, Asher were all mentioned. Ray looked up at his mother.

"Can I bring this to school to show Olive?"

"Sure. I don't see why not."

"Thanks," Ray said as his attention focused on the paper.

"Good night and God bless you," his mother said as he walked out of the room, fixated and fascinated by the paper in his hand. "And right to bed."

But he couldn't sleep. Ray pulled the blankets over his head and turned on the flashlight to read the article. His fingers traced the words as he read.

"...*Donner quick with his fellow officers ran to the aid of children trapped in a building weakened from sustained aerial bombardments...*" Ray read quickly through the tale of bravery but skipped Jack Donner's family facts until he reached the list of the other soldiers. When he got to Stephen Carrig and read his description, his head shot up so high it knocked the blanket off.

The clipping read: *"Sergeant Stephen Carrig, 25. Providence, Rhode Island. Dance instructor for Cipri's Swing and Ballroom Studio. Beloved son to Audrey and Geoffrey Carrig."*

"Dancer," Ray said dumbstruck to the thin air. Christopher Columbus, he thought. Olive was right.

CHAPTER 24

Grigonis House – Pittstown, New Jersey, Last year

Ava laid the yellow newspaper clipping carefully on top a small stack of letters next to the old shoebox. The clipping, held together at the crease with a clear piece of tape, had grown stained and faded by constant handling and time. Pop-pop often rummaged through the old odds and ends that rattled below the paper at the bottom of an old Florsheim box in hopes of finding a missing part for a racecar or an old memento from his days as a boy. Sometimes, one of the papers would catch his eye and he would take out it out for a moment, smile, then put it back. Other times he would take the page, let out a long sad breath and shake off a frown. Ava noticed the older and darker the pages looked, the sadder his expression.

"Is this it, Mister?" asked Ava as she held up a small brass fitting she plucked from the box.

"Nope, that's close but not it," said the man, scrapping the rust off the corroded axle of the racer. He looked back down to his work when he noticed the clipping. "Excuse me, may I see that?"

Ava called out to her mother for permission as her mother sat with John Charles at the kitchen table, looking through an old photo album. She broke her concentration with the photograph she was explaining to John Charles and Berta to answer her.

"Why, yes. Just be careful, Ava. That is very old."

Ava treated the clipping as if she were handling the wing of an injured bird, passing it gently to the man on the tops of both her palms. He examined the clipping with the same intense interest as Ava had seen doctors examine her grandfather's medical charts. Like those doctors, he also shook his head in the same sad way.

"Wow," he uttered. His eyes dug into the words as his fingers gently grazed the old newsprint.

"Those were the men who died in the war with Grandpa Kozak," Ava's mother said with her chin hung over her shoulder and her glasses halfway down the bridge of her nose.

"Yes," the man said again. He did not look up from the paper. "I never realized how young they all were."

"They were just boys, really. Except for Grandpa Kozak. He was really the old man of the bunch at 32."

The corner of the man's mouth shot up in a silent chuckle. "Yes, Ma'am, I imagine he was."

Ava studied his face as he read. He mouthed some of the sentences as he went through. Some of the words would even cause him to show a hint of a smile. Once he finished, he turned the page clockwise and noticed the child's handwriting in the empty margin. He held the clipping closer to his eyes and saw the word written over Allen Lonergan's name. Ava leaned closer to the man to look at the paper.

"What does that say?" Ava asked as she put her tiny finger on the word written in pencil.

"That says 'Vixen,'" he answered.

"Why?"

"Well, let's see…" The man held the paper closer to Ava for her to examine as he read aloud. "*Allen Lonergan, 19. Medic. Wilton,*

163

Connecticut. Beloved husband to Louise Lonergan and son to Victor and Marianne Lonergan." He pointed to the word "Victor" and then at the word "son."

"I guess that makes him Vic's son."

Ava took the paper and nodded in agreement as that seemed like a reasonable answer. Ava's mother let out a laugh.

"I like that one," she said as she returned to thumbing through old pages of the album. "I just figured that was a nickname."

"I like that. Vic's. Son. Like the reindeer," Ava said as she began to place the paper down on the stack. Suddenly, the man's hand reached out to stop her. Ava looked at him to see his eyes fixed on the small sheet of mustard-colored paper that she was about to cover. Without asking, he carefully pulled the paper off the stack and drew it towards him. Ava got up and sat by his side as he looked at the old note.

"Now that's a piece of history right there. A very sad piece," Ava's mother said as she took the glasses off her nose. "We have to make sure that gets into a scrapbook."

The man tucked his lips under his teeth as his eyes grew large. He then put his hand up to his mouth as if he were trying to rub the frown into his face. The small square, marked with crooked type, was filled with lines and bumps from being crumpled and smoothed. Two words sat large on the top of the page like a marquee. After a moment, he handed the paper back to Ava.

"What is it?" Ava asked the man. This time he would not look at her.

"It's called a telegram," he uttered as he picked up the racecar. He wiped his temple with his wrist before continuing to scrape the rust off the toy. "The worst kind."

CHAPTER 25

The Worst Day – Southold, New York, 1944

By the end of September, the summer had already passed its fading torch over to autumn. The low clouds stamped and scattered the sky while the air, which once smelled like freshly mowed lawns, now smelled like a hint of firewood that the cool air carried over from the chimney tops. The men at Mick's garage yelled at each other over the noises in the shop. A song from Bing Crosby tried in vain to compete with the banging that came from thrown tools and revving of engines. The men whirled and whizzed around the hive like every other Wednesday afternoon, thinking of nothing other than whitewall tires, oil filters, baseball games, and swinging on a star.

Except one. Mick stood as motionless as the unlit cigarette stapled to his lips in the center of the commotion. His eyes fixed on the teenage boy pushing his bike in the front of the garage while staring down at a letter. The official hard cap on his head tilted to the side as he looked up at the street sign and scratched in his head in confusion.

"Keep…moving…" Mick uttered over the cigarette as he stared at the lad, as if his words would keep the young man from turning down Youngs Avenue. The mere sight of the Western Union messenger turned Mick's blood cold. He knew what direction he did not want the boy riding in. Turning down Youngs Avenue put him in the direction of Jacobs Lane and the Kozak's house. Mick abandoned Christian prayer as he began to sell pieces of his soul to any voodoo god that would make the boy pick up his bicycle and ride back down Main Street.

It would not work. The boy looked up at the street sign on the corner, then back at his letter. He then leaned his bike up against the pole and walked into the shop. Mick could not get his feet to move as he watched the boy open the door. He did not hear the bell over the shop's door clang or the men gab or the metal banging. He only saw Betty filing her nails at the front desk. Her file methodically and quickly hummed back and forth as it coasted over her fingertips. The boy leaned over the desk to Betty, who quickly looked down at what the boy pointed to. Her file began to slow. The rhythm stopped. She put down her file and her eyes, as large as headlamps, found Mick's.

Mick did not know how he got to the desk. He looked down at the letter and at the address of the house where he and his wife played marathon games of pinochle.

"I don't know where this road is," the boy said as he pointed to the words "North Bayview," a name of an old dirt road the town renamed to Jacob's Lane years before.

Mick looked at the clock on the far side of the wall, then at Betty. Her red-lipped wry smile turned downward and began to quiver.

"Get Raymond," Mick said. "Bring him home to his mother." His voice seemed to come from the back of his throat. "I'll take you there, son," Mick said as he walked aimlessly to his nearby truck. He almost ran over the boy's bike as he headed out of the parking garage and down Youngs Avenue, towards the direction of Jacob's Lane.

❄ ❄ ❄

The last bell rang and the kids scurried down the hall in a race to leave the building. Raymond began to run too until he noticed a young woman silhouetted by the sunlight coming in through the front doors of the school. As he got closer, he noticed the blond curls and red fingernails of Betty. She was talking to his principal. Ray was curious and happy to see her at school. She had no children but she always had gum for Ray when he came into the garage. As he approached he saw her face. She smiled a nervous smile as she reached out to give a Ray a hug.

"Betty here is going to take you home," said Ray's principal. "Is that ok by you?"

"That's swell," said Ray as he looked up at Betty's face. Her lips smiled but her eyes did not. They looked terrified. As soon as the words came out, he wished he could take them back.

The interior of the Lincoln Zephyr filled with Chesterfield smoke before they even left the parking lot. As she drove, Betty tapped the steering wheel nervously with the two red talons that held the cigarette.

"You have a good day at school, Big Ray?" she said. Her voice shook as much as her fingers.

"Yes," Ray said as he stared at her.

"Mr. Polywoda still teach art? You know, he can't smell nothing," she said, her happy voice trembled when she spoke and smoked, making Raymond more and more uneasy. She took a long drag of her Chesterfield and kept on rambling. "We used to smoke cigarettes in the dark room. Guy never noticed. We think he stopped smoking and liked the smell. I mean, how can you not notice something like that?" Ray looked out the window at the bay. He'd never been in a car with Betty before. He wondered if this is what she was normally like or if something had happened to her. It had been a year since he spent any length of time with her. Maybe something had changed. It wasn't until they reached the Mott house that he realized the reason for her concern.

Cars. Everywhere. Packards, Fords, Lincolns, every car he'd seen at Mick's shop seemed to be parked on the side of the road. It looked like Christmas day at his Aunt Carol's house as the cars lined the street and took up every available patch of grass on their front lawn. For a moment, he wondered if the Motts were having a party. When he saw his driveway filled with cars and the Mott's empty, his chest began to hurt. He didn't wait for Betty to stop the car before he jumped out.

Ray zigzagged through the cars until he heard a far-off cry. He knew that cry. He heard it many times before over skinned knees and hurt feelings. He looked over at the Mott house and through the parlor window and saw Paley. Paley rocked back and forth fiercely, crying and smacking his ear. Mrs. Mott struggled to hold him close to her but his force was too much. He kept beating his head and wailing, not wanting his mother's comfort as he tried to rock and beat the pain out of his body.

Ray ran up to the front steps to his house. The stairs were lined with filthy men, covered in oil stains and overalls fresh from the garage. All were smoking and looking down. Bobby looked at Ray, then turned away. Some said nothing as Ray walked past them. Some said his name softly into their chests as he walked by. It wasn't until he saw Mick when he heard anyone speak above a whisper.

"Raymond," Mick said in a low, steady voice. He placed a firm grip on Ray's shoulder. Mick's arm seemed to stretch for a mile from down his shoulder to Ray's. "Your mother is upstairs. She needs to speak to you."

Ray did not like Mick's tone. Mick never called him Raymond before. He always called him Big Ray. Raymond sounded grown-up, as if he was now the man of the house. Ray nodded as he looked at Mick's face. He wanted his expression to give something up. To tell him something before he saw his mother. But Mick's large face looked more like a vault. Whatever was inside stood behind a foot of steel.

Ray ran up the steps to see his mother's sisters, his Aunt Carol and Aunt Annette, at the top of the stairwell. They clutched handkerchiefs in front of their mouths. He could not tell if they were coughing or crying as their eyes were squeezed shut. He had never seen his aunts cry before. His heart began to hurt more.

"Mom?" Ray called out as he turned the corner to his parents' bedroom. Once he got in her doorway, he stopped. His eyes found his mother sitting on the bed with her back to the door. Her purple coat was still on as her arms stretched outwards like tent ropes on the bed. In her one hand was a fistful of sheet. In the other was a crumpled piece of paper. His Aunt Beth and grandfather stood next to Father Freeman, who all looked up at Raymond in unison. Ray's mother whirled around.

"Raymond," she said. Her face looked as if she dunked it in a baptismal font. Everything, except for her ears and hair, was soaking wet. Her expression was a cross between anger and confusion, as if she were suddenly being dragged off a beach and thrown into the cold waters of the bay.

"Raymond," she said again. This time her voice choked. She didn't need to say whatever it was she needed to tell him. He knew. His heart knew. His head knew. More than anything, his feet knew. He felt himself walk backwards out of the doorway and into his room at the other end of the hall. He did not turn around. He wanted to make sure no one followed him inside. As soon as he got past the safety of his threshold he closed the door and locked it. His Buster Browns continued their march backward until the bed stepped in and stopped his stride. He sat down on his patchwork quilt as a force drew his eyes up towards the yellow number eight racecar idling on his bureau. He asked God if he could make him small. As small as a racer that would fit in that tiny toy car so he could drive away from this house.

A soft knock came from the door's edge.

"Raymond," his mother's voice said firmly. "Raymond, I need to come in there."

Ray said nothing but shook his head "no." He wished and willed for her to go away. Not forever but just for now. He could live on his own until his dad came back. All he needed was for God to make him into a miniature man so he could drive away in his racecar. Away from his scary house with all the sad people in it. Once they left, maybe he would think about coming back for his mother.

She continued to call for Ray but he did not get up. After a minute, he felt her presence leave the other side of the door. For a moment he thought God would answer his prayers. That he would shrink or even disappear. But then the sound of a large man creaking up the stairs filled the air. After the creaking stopped, more mumbling came from the hall. First from a man and then from his Aunt Annette, who he had seen in the hallway. He did not hear everything she said. The only word that seemed to get through the hum of her lips, through his door and into his ears was the word "killed."

Ray opened his mouth. Nothing came out. His scream seemed to make no sound. He placed his hands over his ears like Paley as the tears exploded out of his eyes. Ray's prayer would not be answered. He did not disappear.

But his father did.

CHAPTER 26

The Last Day of School Before Christmas –
Southold, New York, 1944

Kids scattered and weaved around Ray as he plodded out of the classroom. The excitement and buzz for Christmas hummed through the halls as the kids ran towards the exits, eager to get their Christmas vacation started. The halls grew more colorful and Ray grew taller as he walked out of the middle school and towards the hallways of the elementary school. Ray hoped the Christmas mailbox would still be there, along with some stray letters added by last-minute doubting Thomases. The kids, Oscar said, were "hedging their bets." Ray thought if he got to the mailbox after the final bell, he could take those letters before the janitor got them. Even if Oscar couldn't make those toys, they were better off in Oscar's and John Charles's hands than in the fire of a burn barrel.

But he was too late. Ray turned the corner and saw the big red mailbox still propped up in the center of the hallway. When he reached it, he saw a piece of paper covering the slot. It read, *"Sent to the North Pole."* Ray's hands held the edges of the box as he eyes reread the note.

Right, he thought. Sent to the North Pole. By smoke signals. The air left his lungs as he dropped his arms. Another lie.

Ray turned to leave when he saw Tommy Goldsmith standing obediently in front of his teacher. Tommy looked up at her as if in pain as she methodically weaved a scarf around his head and neck.

"Make sure you cover up. It's getting colder by the minute out there," she instructed as she flopped and folded the scarf around his face. "But remember, even if it storms, Santa can get through it. He always does."

"Yes, Ma'am," Tommy answered in a sad, sing-song tone. She turned him around and patted him on the back in the direction of the exit and into the tide of rushing children.

"Hey, Tommy," Ray said as he walked up to him. "Excited for Christmas? Just a few days away!"

"Hey ya, Ray," Tommy said, dejected. "Yeah, I guess I feel excited. But now I just feel hot," he said as he pulled on the scarf choking his neck. "Are you coming home with me? Is that why you're here?"

"Nope, I'm here to see if there are any letters for Santa."

Tommy stopped and turned to Ray. He lifted the scarf wrapped around his eyes to get a better look at Ray. Then he looked both ways, leaned in and whispered, "You don't believe in him."

Ray too looked around for stray kids and leaned in towards Tommy.

"Actually, I do."

Tommy's eyes got bigger. Then his eyebrows curled. "Since when?"

"Since…well since…" Ray didn't know how to answer. Since he started to believe he was working for him? Since he saw the sled in Oscar's basement? Since he saw the bucks hanging around Oscar's backyard like sophomores at a soda fountain? Since he saw the light in the woods? Ray looked down at Tommy and his chubby cheeks spilling out beneath the edges of his red woolen wrap. He wouldn't lie. Not like every adult seemed to do this time of year. "Since I saw him."

Tommy shrugged off Ray's declaration and began to walk away. "Me, too. But it's Mr. Terry with a fake beard. Dad told me it was Santa but I know it's Mr. Terry. His eyes are red like Mr. Terry's and he smells like ham."

Ray followed Tommy and put his hand on his insulated shoulder to stop him. "Wait, no. That's the butcher your dad hired for the store. That's just for show. There is a real one."

Tommy stopped and turned. "Where?"

"Here! In Southold!"

"Can we go see him?"

Ray thought about it. Tommy knew Oscar Taglieber. If he took Tommy to Oscar's and told him that he was Santa Claus then both Tommy and Oscar would think Ray lost his marbles. And Oscar would just say he wasn't Santa anyway, even to Tommy. Ray's eyes dropped to the floor.

"No, we can't," he said, looking at the scuff marks on the floor. "He's busy."

Tommy patted Ray on the elbow. Their gloomy expressions seemed out of place amongst all the Christmas tree cutouts and paper snowflakes lining the hallway.

"It's okay, Ray. You were right. Babies believe in Santa. I'm a big boy now."

The two walked out of the school and towards the Goldsmith's gleaming Pierce Arrow parked in the lot. Ray still could not get in the car with Tommy so he stood back and watched Mrs. Goldsmith fawn over Tommy as soon as the door opened. She tried in vain to keep up the Christmas excitement, telling him that they shoveled part of the roof to make sure Santa's sleigh would land safely and that she would make pinwheel cookies because the mothers around the store said that's what Santa liked. But Tommy's flat expression didn't budge. Tommy did not believe in Santa anymore. Not because he grew out of it, or an older sibling squawked, but because of him. Ray knew it and the glares that Mrs. Goldsmith shot at Ray through the window told Ray that she knew it too. She was trying her hardest to keep up the game. But the magic was all but gone out of Tommy's eyes. Mrs. Goldsmith didn't have to make Ray feel bad about it. Ray felt horrible enough as it was.

By the time he got to Oscar's door, Ray was fighting back tears. He felt rotten. Like a bad kid. He never pictured himself as a bad kid but he couldn't shake Tommy's expression. He did that. Ray finally knew why his mother got so smoked when he told Tommy there was no Santa. She knew that this is what happened when the jig was up. She knew that only adults should undo the lies they tell. Even if they were pretty and covered in tinsel.

"What's with the sour puss?" Oscar yelled as he walked through the workshop. "You can't make toys looking like that."

"Sorry," Ray uttered as he took off his coat. He walked over to the closet and reached for a hanger. "Hard test at school."

"The last day before Christmas vacation? Don't they let you just eat cookies and run around like hooligans on the last day?"

Ray put his coat on a hanger and hung it up. As he lowered his arm he noticed a garment bag puffed up and hanging in the back of the closet. He hadn't seen it there before. He pulled it closer on the rod and pulled the zipper down slowly. After just a couple of inches a big tuft of white fur popped out of the top. Ray's eyes widened as he turned back in Oscar's direction. Oscar sat on the bench with his back to Ray, his voice still calling out.

"I can't even get my doctor on the phone the Friday before Christmas. How could a teacher expect a kid to sit in their seat! Tests, my guts," Oscar called out.

Ray turned back to the closet. He continued to lower the zipper until he reached halfway down the bag. After another look in Oscar's direction he gently pulled the bag open and noticed that inside was a thick, red coat. The fabric felt like his grandmother's velvet winter curtains and its white collar like a bunny's tail. He didn't need to go any further. He knew it was a suit. And exactly what kind of suit it was. Ray quickly zipped up the bag, pushed it back into the closet and shut the door. No need to ask Oscar, he thought. He would just lie about this, too.

"Well, I know what will make you happy, Raymond," Oscar said as Ray took his seat. "Last batch of letters, my good man," he said as he patted a stack of paper on the workbench. "I can see the light at the end of the tunnel!"

Ray reached over and took the small stack. As soon as he looked down at the first letter he could tell these were different. They did not read any differently than the letters he had seen before. The toys they were to make were the same. Racers, zeppelins, cars, planes were still circled in red or written in John Charles's handwriting across the center. They felt different. Something with the paper. The color wasn't stark white as he had seen in others. These were all written from the same stock, like they were cut from the same piece of parchment. Ray ran a page between his fingers and felt a slight grit. He put the page down and looked at the ash-like residue cling to his fingertips.

"Yeah, something happened to that stack," Oscar said flatly.

Ray picked up the same page and drew it to his face. As soon as the page came closer to his nose he knew what happened to this batch. It smelled like smoke.

"John Charles must have stashed those away by a woodstove," Oscar continued but Ray wasn't listening. He looked at the top of the page. He knew the handwriting. It was from Thomas Goldsmith. Age 6. Grade 1.

"This is from the elementary school," Ray said in a fog of thought.

Oscar leaned over and took the letter from Ray. He grabbed a set of reading glasses from the bench and held it in front of his goggles. "Hey, it's Tommy's letter! Wonderful news. Look, the kid wants another train. A train. My guts."

Ray stood up in a haze. His eyes glazed over as he looked at Oscar. "I saw them burn."

"Burn? What burn?"

"The letters. These letters. I saw them in the fire."

Oscar flipped Tommy's letter over and examined the back. "Well, they look a bit dingy but I don't think they burned…"

"They did!" shouted Ray. "They did burn! I saw them!"

"Raymond," Oscar's voice lowered. "If they were on fire they wouldn't be sitting right in front of us."

"They did burn! They did!" cried Ray. "I watched them. The janitor took them from the box and put them in a burn barrel. I saw it. So did John Charles."

"Calm down, Raymond," Oscar said softly. "Maybe those were other letters you saw in a fire."

Ray grabbed the stack and feverishly thumbed through the pages.

"Where is it? Where is it?" he uttered to himself and his fingers flew through the cream-colored pages. His fingertips grew darker and darker with ash as he searched.

"Raymond, what on earth has gotten into you?"

Then he stopped. He found what he was looking for. It was a simple letter buried in the stack. He knew the handwriting and he knew it only had one item on it. He knew because it was his own.

"Here! I threw this in the fire," Ray said, nearly in tears.

Oscar stood up and took the letter from him. As he read it, his weight plopped him back on the seat. The item Ray wrote was crossed out in red and the word "clock" written over it. He then rubbed his forehead in exhaustion.

"This is what you asked for? I never thought of you as a budding astronomer," Oscar said quietly.

"This was burned up," Ray said pointing to the letter. "I saw it."

Oscar shook his head. "You…you must have thought you saw it…"

"You think I'm making this up?"

"No. I just think there is a logical explanation for this."

"Is it the same explanation for the suit in your closet? For the sled in the basement?" Ray shouted, his face turning redder with anger by the moment.

"Yes, Raymond. I thought I explained all that."

Ray stomped around the room, unfazed by Oscar's calm tone. "There's an explanation for the deer who listen to you? For the one who listens to me? For that light in the woods?"

"I…I…I'm sure there is a reason for all of it."

"Alright then, Oscar. Explain this?" Ray walked towards Oscar's easy chair and grabbed the pillow embroidered with the word "love" and held it out to him, like a steak in front of a hungry dog. Oscar's face melted into that of a timid boy.

"Please, Raymond. Put that down."

Ray struggled to hold his arm up as the pillow was heavier than it appeared. It felt more like a bag of sand than something you would use to rest under your head.

"Santa isn't real, but this? This is?"

"It is special to me," Oscar begged. "Please just put it down."

"It's not real, Oscar. I know what you want this to be but it's not him. It's just a pillow."

"Please, Raymond. Put it down," Oscar's tone turned firm, as if giving an order.

And for a brief moment, Ray's anger flashed. He wanted Oscar to know how it felt to be told that what he saw, what was in front of his eyes was not real. He didn't see or care that he dropped the pillow or that his foot flew up to kick it. He wasn't kicking anyone. His angry feet didn't mean to kick Oscar or his dreams, but rather every lie told to him. As soon as his foot connected with the pillow he wished he had held onto it tighter. He wished the white knit embroidered sack did not leave his hands. He wished he lovingly gave it back to the kind man who let him and Olive in his house every day after school and gave them jobs and root beer. But those wishes faded once he saw his foot rip through the pillow, scattering the stuffing and beads across the room.

Ray just stared at the destruction in horror as little beige nubs rolled and bounced on every surface. Oscar dropped to his knees, reached his arms out like a fishing net and tried to pull the million rolling pearls towards him. He didn't yell or cry. Instead he made pained noises that sounded like he was battling an aching back. But Ray knew it was not his back that was hurting. Ray didn't want to be near that much pain. Pain that he caused. Again. He just walked backwards, stunned.

"I'm…I didn't mean to…" Ray mumbled before running down the hall and out of Oscar's front door.

The cold only burned his cheeks. Tears stung once they dropped out of his eyes and hit the frosty air. The rest of his body radiated heat from sadness and shame. He figured he couldn't go inside. His mother might skin him alive for being mean to Oscar. He wanted to go back and help Oscar but he was afraid. But there was a place he could hide. A place where he could cry without anyone to comfort him or ask questions. The woods.

Ray crunched over the snowy ground on the path behind his house. Buried under a small coating of frost was a fort made of two fallen trees and a dozen large broken oak branches. As Ray began to walk towards the wooden mound he heard another crunch in the snow. His sad red face turned around and saw the only sight that could bring a smile to it.

There, six feet behind him in the center of the path, was his buck.

CHAPTER 27

The Fort – Southold, New York, 1944

The buck twitched his ears as he faced Ray on the path. His glassy eyes examined Ray, wondering why water poured from this little boy's face. Ray held his breath as he studied the buck as well. He had not been this close to the animal before, except for when he was leaping over him in the dark. The buck turned its head to the side, displaying its antlers, but then gracefully turned back to face Ray. The buck made no sudden movement. Nothing jerked or flinched. The animal did not seem afraid or timid or agitated. So Ray took a step closer.

No movement. Its snout gently puffed out white streams of steam into the iced air. Ray took another step forward with his eyes fixed on the buck's antlers. If the buck felt threatened, he could stab him with the rack on his head. But each small step Ray took towards the animal did not change its temperament. The buck seemed to be waiting.

"Hey, buddy," Ray said quietly as he held up his hand. "Can I touch you?"

The deer answered by taking a few steps forward. Its long legs gently picked up and settled its posture in the snow. With only an arms-length separating the two, Ray reached out and touched the side of the deer's snout. He stroked the short-haired hide, following the grain of the brown and ash-colored coat. The buck just kept looking at Ray. It blinked slowly as it lowered its head, making it easier for Ray to touch him.

"That's a good boy," Ray said, his eyes fixed on the white markings on its face. Ray didn't want to touch it in case it was an injury.

"What happened to you? Did someone hurt you?" Ray said as he gently petted the area around its nose. The buck remained calm as Ray ran his hands up to the bridge of its snout to the soft wide space between its eyes. His hands traveled over the brilliant white star scratched in the deer's face and up along the faded white streak that traveled from the star to a space behind its ears. "Don't worry. I won't hurt you."

Everything about the buck became seared into Ray's memory. Its antlers, its eyes, the color changes in its hair, and especially its markings seemed to push every awful memory, recent and past, out of Ray's mind for the briefest of moments. The quiet and cold framed the two in their own world. The wild animal in front of him and the wild animal in his chest. Nothing seemed wrong, for the moment. Somehow this deer made it all better. Ray smiled as he let the air out of his lungs.

"My dad had a white patch of hair, just like you," Ray said as he placed his other hand on the deer's cheek. "Yes, sir. Just like you." The deer playfully rocked its rack from side to side as Ray laughed. Ray felt himself smile as he pulled his hands off the buck's face. "Easy, boy. I'm not gonna hurt you."

Ray reached towards the deer again until a gunshot sliced through the air, causing the buck to jump up and away from Ray's hands. Ray fell to the ground in fear as he watched his deer tear off through the woods. Ray cried out for the invisible hunter to stop until he saw where the bullet had come from.

"What are you doing?" Ray screamed as he ran towards his backyard. His mother looked confused as she ran towards him, coatless, holding his father's rifle.

"Are you alright, Raymond? Are you hurt?" she cried as she ran her hands over his face.

"Are you nuts?" Ray's anger boiled back up again. He could see a hunter shooting at him, but his own mother? "Why are you shooting at me?"

"Did it hurt you?" she asked again, her voice shaking as she struggled to keep hold of the rifle while examining Ray for cuts and bruises. "I fired in the air. I wanted to scare him off."

"You did! He ran away. Are you happy?"

But she wasn't listening to Ray. She kept searching him for marks. "Raymond, did it hurt you?"

"No! I'm fine! Except you scared my friend away."

His mother turned around in a daze and walked into the house. Ray had never seen her shaken. He followed her inside, wishing that the gun was made of wood, like Oscar's. He didn't even know where his father kept the rifle or that his mother even knew how to shoot it. Once she reached the center of the living room she stopped. Her knees buckled as her hand covered her face. The gun held her up until Ray took it away from her. He placed it safely in a corner then put his arm around her shoulders.

"It's fine, Mom. I'm fine," Ray said, his voice now soft with concern.

Then his mother flung her arms around him and sobbed. She gripped the back of Ray's head and held him so tight he could feel the breaths heaving out of her chest.

"I was so scared," she cried.

Ray held her tight and patted her back. "Not as scared as I was," Ray said.

She pulled away and held Ray's face in her hands. She did not look sad. She looked terrified. After blinking away frightened tears she smiled. They both let out a chuckle.

"I thought that animal was going to hurt you," she said through a sniffle. "I saw those antlers from the window and your legs and I thought… I thought that wild thing…"

Ray's mother pulled him back to her and said nothing, as if the mere outcome of her assumption was too painful to say out loud. Neither would let go. Even when Mrs. Mott knocked feverishly at the door.

"Everything alright in there?" she yelled.

But his mother didn't budge. She just kept Ray close in her arms and he let her. All the anger he felt stopped as he let another feeling take its place. He didn't know what it was but it seemed like pride. His mother thought he was in danger and came charging in like an army. She knew how to be a dad.

Ray's mother could not see his smile as she cried the remaining fear out of her small frame. Ray smiled because he felt safe. There were two soldiers in the family.

CHAPTER 28

Oscar Taglieber's Basement – Southold, New York, 1944

The walk to Oscar's house seemed painfully short. Ray dragged his legs as he made his way to Oscar's front door, much the same way he did when his mother trucked him there the first time. Ray liked it better when he would run into the house with Olive, grab an apron and a root beer and get to work. How John Charles made Oscar's grumpy funny. How the smell of machines and stew filled the air. How hammers rested on doilies, couches were workbenches, and kids built racecars. How the chaos of all these people lived in one room yet somehow it all moved perfectly, like one of the many clocks that watched them from the walls. He didn't realize how much he'd grown to like it. How much he looked forward to seeing Oscar and listening to him teach and grumble. He didn't want to be kicked out of that world but figured his kick might have done just that.

Ray did what he normally did. Knocked twice and walked in. He slowly crept his way past the untouched parlor into the lights of the living room. As he leaned in the doorway, he looked around and found that world already gone. Oscar's workbench once littered with scrap metal and tools was wiped cleaned. All the tools, nails, nuts, and screws had been put away. Olive's paint station returned to its original state as a dining room chair. The clothesline that the letters hung from was no longer strung up between the lamp and the curtain rod. All the airplanes, racers, and zeppelins evacuated the fireplace mantel, making it look like an abandoned runway. Ray's eyes searched in vain for the love pillow. It too was gone. The happy Christmas chaos of Oscar's house seemed to vanish overnight. It no looker looked like Santa's workshop, but a widower's living room.

Oscar stood in the corner of the room with his back to Ray. He held a piece of paper in his hand and appeared to be counting items in a large cardboard box. Ray cleared his throat to let Oscar know he was in the room but that did not cause him to turn around. Instead, Oscar stuck his arm out to silence Ray as he continued to count. Ray watched him finish, write down something on the paper, then fold the corners of the box shut. He put his hands on his hips and stared down at the box in thought. Ray could hardly breathe as he waited for Oscar's well-deserved wrath.

But it did not come. Oscar looked out the bay window at something Ray could not see. After what seemed like an hour, he spoke.

"When I was a boy, a long time ago, I walked into my neighbor's shed after he had just killed a buck. I can still see him hanging from the rafter. What a beautiful creature. He seemed as big as an elephant to me at the time. And he had the most majestic set of antlers," Oscar said as he stretched his fingers out over his head. "Well, as a boy, I was upset. I had never seen anything that large dead so I ran home, sat on my bunk and cried." Oscar turned and looked at Ray. "I was a pretty wimpy kid in those days."

Ray let out a little smile as Oscar continued. "My father came in and told me a story. He said that when every living creature is born, no matter if it's a person, a porcupine, a bug, or a bird, Jesus sits down with them and tells them the greatest struggles they will ever face in their life. Lays it all out there for them. The thing is, they must agree to it before they can be born. If they think it's too hard or too painful, well then they can say 'no thanks,' hang around in heaven and fly around from cloud to cloud playing their little harp thingy," Oscar said as he plucked the air. "My father said that before every deer agrees to be born Jesus tells them the same thing. That out of all the animals around, they are destined to be the greatest gift to his people. He will tell the stag or doe that their body will be used for meat. Their skin for warmth. Their head for sport. That their voice will never be loud enough to cry out. Their antlers were not made to defend themselves against their greatest hunters. No expression on their face will warrant sympathy. And none of their deaths will be mourned."

"Sounds like a raw deal to me," Ray interjected.

"Yeap. Sure does." Oscar turned around and faced Ray. His eyes looked tired. "But, because they were so good to his beloved humans, they would go to a separate heaven. The heaven for those who gave their lives for another. Whether it's animal or human. They would not have to wait by the pearly gates. They would not have to answer St. Peter's questions. They would just…show up. And he'd be there to greet them when they did."

"Did that make you feel any better?" Ray asked. "You know, when you were a kid?"

"Of course not! I still cried like a ninny. It's a horrible thing to tell a child after they see a dead animal. But you know something, Raymond, I believe it. Crazy enough, the older I get, the more I think that's true. That we know the path of our lives before we let out our first wail. We know every pain and heartache before it ever happens. And we agreed to it."

"Why?" asked Ray.

"Because we know the love we get in return will be worth it. It will be worth it to be a mechanic in a tiny town. Or a clockmaker. Or a mother. Or a girl who wears thick glasses."

"Or a dad," Ray said, looking down at his hands. "Or a kid whose dad dies."

Oscar smiled a tired smile. "Or Santa Claus."

Ray looked back up at Oscar. What he said made sense. It sounded right. Even though his dad was gone, he wouldn't trade him for any dad living. Not Mr. Goldsmith or Mick or even Oscar. If Jesus told him to pick a dad, he'd pick Henry Lee Kozak every time, hands down. Ten years with him would be better than a hundred without. Oscar was right. Santa was right.

"Oscar, are we done?" Ray asked quietly. Oscar looked around the room filled with clean surfaces and boxed up toys. His gaze settled back on Ray as he let out a breath.

"Well, that depends on you," he said. "I told you I would need some help with the sled. You feel up to helping me paint?"

A smile stretched across Ray's face as he stood up straight. "Yes, sir!"

"Ugh, don't call me that," Oscar growled as he hobbled past Ray towards the cellar door. He patted his shoulder as he walked past. "Grab a smock and let's get to it."

Ray followed Oscar down into the cellar stairs. The sled was now pulled out of the small room and sat in the center of the cellar. Its blades pointed towards the wood slabs that rested on the stairs leading up and out of the exterior cellar doors. Ray stood beside the sled and admired it from end to end. The sled looked nothing like the gnarled mass of a few weeks ago. The shiny silver runners looked sleek against the freshly sanded wooden frame. Ray ran his hand over the curve of the carriage. The wood curled and arched like a wave frozen before it broke on a shore. The black leather tufted seat inside looked just as nice as any interior Ray had ever seen in a Cadillac. Oscar opened a can of fire engine red paint and handed Ray a paintbrush.

"I do what I can reach. You can do underneath. I'm not that small…or thin," he said as he placed the can on the floor. "Don't let paint get on anything that isn't wood, a drop cloth, or you," he said as he laced up his smock. Ray grabbed the brush and hustled underneath the carriage. He dipped the brush in the paint, wiped the end and stopped. He could only see Oscar's wide legs from under the belly of the carriage.

"Hey, Oscar," he called out.

"Don't tell me you got paint on the runner already?"

"No," he said as he sucked in a breath. Ray wanted to say that he didn't mean to yell at him or kick a hole in his pillow. He didn't mean to accuse Oscar of lying to him or make him feel bad. Or make him admit he was Santa when he wasn't ready. He wanted to say that he was sorry. As sorry as he was for yelling at Tommy Goldsmith. As sorry he was for making Olive sad. Maybe even more so. But all Ray could squeak out were three simple, quiet words.

"I'll miss this."

He heard the shush of strokes from Oscar's paintbrush stop. Ray waited to hear if he would say anything. Finally, his old voice spoke three words in return.

"Me too, son."

❄ ❄ ❄

After an hour of painting, Ray left Oscar's floating on air. He didn't know if the feeling came from the fumes of the paint from his basement or being forgiven for the worst thing he'd ever done. Or maybe it was because Christmas was only two days away. There would be nothing under the tree he would care about but his heart still seemed hopeful. Hopeful that something good would come. He walked into the door and saw his mother and Olive at the kitchen table. His mother wore her hair like she did at the shop, piled on top of her head in a tight knot. Thimbles topped on her fingertips as she pulled a needle and thread through a black glove. Olive sat next to her, her elbows on the table and her chin resting on her knuckles.

"What are you doing?" Ray asked as he hovered over his mother.

"Making a birthday gift for John Charles," said Olive proudly. "Those were my dad's."

"What? But he can't wear gloves."

"He'll wear these," Olive said as his mother cut off one of the fingers. "And we won't add the kittens."

Ray held up one of the finished gloves. Half of the fingers were sewn together while one finger looked drastically shorter than the other four. It looked crazy. As crazy as John Charles's hands.

"It will be his most favorite birthday gift ever," Olive said.

Ray's mother looked up at Ray with her eyebrow raised. Ray's face lit up. She was right. It would be his most favorite gift ever. Then a thought popped into Ray's head.

"Hey, Mom, when you're done, could you help me with something?"

CHAPTER 29

Christmas Eve – Southold, New York, 1944

Downtown Southold was abuzz from more than just Christmas spirit. After every greeting and well wishes for a Merry Christmas came talk of the storm expected to hit during the night on Christmas Eve. People's fears of midnight mass being canceled due to the storm caused a small panic in town. There was a rush on scallops and turkeys as people found themselves doubling up on their groceries in case they couldn't make it to their relative's home Christmas Eve night or Christmas morning.

Ray accompanied his mother as they rushed around Main Street, dropping off peanut brittle to the women who worked at the dress shop and a large tin of cookies at Mick's garage. After they got through the hour-long line for bread at Bohack's Grocery they finally ventured to Oscar's house to drop off his Christmas present.

Ray helped his mother take the gift from the backseat as they both carried it to his front door. For the first time, the lights were off and the curtains in the bay window were drawn. No one was home at Oscar's.

"He didn't say he was going anywhere for Christmas," Ray said as he held his face up to the glass door. He tried to search through a small window but only saw the dark, lonely parlor.

"He's probably on line at Bohack's," she said as they gently placed the red and silver wrapped package under the small awning. "You think we should leave it here with the storm coming?"

"Nope, he'll be back. He's got things to do tonight," Ray said. "I'm sure of it."

That evening, Ray and his mother went to church, then across town to their Aunt Carol's and Uncle Bill's farm on Young's Avenue. Their Polish Christmas Eve dinner of twelve different types of fish, breaking the opłatek, the blessed Christmas wafer, and exchanging gifts was cut short by the howl coming through the cracks of the doors. The snow and stray leaves that didn't have a chance to hit the ground cluttered the air as the wind whipped anything up that it could carry. Before the weather got bad, his mother and Ray jumped into their Ford and made it safely home.

Ray listened to the wind whirl around the house as he looked at the Christmas tree light up the dark family room. His mother walked into the room and looked at the glow from all the colored lights that sparkled off the tinsel. In her hand was the book, *The Night Before Christmas*.

"You promised me we would read this," she said as she held up the large pop-up book. "I know I won't read it as good as your father, but I'd love to give it a try."

Ray sat and looked at his mother. "Mom? Could you tell me another story?"

"Sure," she said as she hugged the book. "Which one?"

"Dad's Most Magical Day," he said as his eyes popped around the tree.

"You mean the day your father got a piece of candy from Mr. Shiller?"

Ray's sat up on the couch, his expression screwed up to horror. "What? No. He said candy magically appeared from the bag."

"Oh, no. Mr. Shiller put it there. He used to have a set of bags by the register that had an extra piece of candy in them. For kids that he liked, he would grab a bag from the left. For older folks, he'd grab a bag from the right. He didn't want anyone to think he was a softy." His mother tapped the book on her chin in thought. "I haven't thought about him in years. My stars he was mean."

"But I thought..." Ray's face melted. "But if he put it there, it wasn't magical."

Ray's mother smiled as she sat next to him on the couch. "It was still a magical day."

"But how? How can it be magical if someone put it there?"

"Well, for starters, it was the day I fell in love with your father."

"What?" Ray said. His nose swished up as he rested back on the couch.

"Yes, well, I wouldn't say I loved him the way I loved him later. But I sure did like him," she said as her gaze went up to the star on top of the tree. "He was so poor. And his brothers were so...loud. Your father looked and smelled like a kid who was being cared for by two rowdy teenagers. But when I saw him give that dime back to that man I thought, that boy has character. Even Mr. Shiller thought so."

"But you said Mr. Shiller was mean?"

"Mean as they get. You know, your father wound up working for him. Since he told your father that he could come by, he would go there and hang around the front of the store. I think it was the only store a Kozak boy was welcome in back in those days. Anyways, Mr. Shiller got tired of looking at him so he would ask him to clean the gutters or fill the candy jars. Whatever odd chores he needed to be done. I think he'd pay him in licorice. He even used to give him the old comics for his brothers but I think that was more to keep them out of the store."

"But Mom, how is that magic?"

"Because the only person he trusted to work for him was a Kozak and he hated the Kozaks with every fiber in his big old body. Mr. Shiller and your father were good friends to the day Mr. Shiller passed. Mr. Shiller even came to like your Uncle Tim and Uncle Christopher, once they were old enough to stop being hooligans. But by working there, your dad was safe. He wasn't spending hours in dirty pool halls with his brothers or at home with his mean father. He was busy eating candy and getting my sisters and brothers gumdrops with his extra pennies. That's how he won my heart. And if that's not magic. I don't know what is."

Ray gave it some thought as he looked up at the tree. Maybe it was magical. Maybe a candy store was a good way to spend the afternoons. Mr. Shiller was like his Oscar. And Oscar was magical. As magical as could be to Ray. Ray kept staring at the tree until his mother poked his shoulder.

"Hey, there. I still would love to read this book," she said. "Although with this storm, I think every creature will be stirring. Even a mouse."

CHAPTER 30

Ships Drive – Southold, New York, 1944

I think every creature will be stirring.

His mother's words looped in his head. Ray stared out of his dark room into the storm outside and waited to see if the light would appear in the woods. His mother was right. This storm would have all the animals running for cover. The Christmas lights on the trees outside from the houses flashed and disappeared as their branches bent and twisted in the howling winds. Through the woods, he could still make out the lights from the lampposts from the houses on Ships Drive. All the houses were dark except for the Goldsmith's, as they were deep in the throes of their Christmas Eve party. Mrs. Goldsmith started preparing for the party after Labor Day. Nothing short of a direct hit from a tornado would stop Mrs. Goldsmith from throwing a party and unleashing a tidal wave of her spiced eggnog on friends and family.

Ray's eyes combed the dark as he waited for something to appear. A light, a silhouette of an antler, the shadow of a deer on his lawn. He stared so hard into the woods he thought his eyes were making things up for him to look at. People walking, men shooting pool, kids playing jump rope. His eyelids began to sink into sleep until something did show up. A figure of a man in the Mott's backyard. The person kept looking at the house, then back into the woods. The light from the upstairs bedroom window did not cast enough light to give his identity. Once the figure began to rock slightly back and forth, Ray knew it had to be Paley.

Ray grabbed his coat and snow boots and tiptoed downstairs. The grandfather clock chimed the half hour bell as Ray dashed through the kitchen and into the breezeway. Ray put on his coat and boots while looking out at Paley, whispering a prayer to himself that Paley wouldn't move or go wandering off into the dark. After readying himself for the storm, Ray gently turned the handle. He tried desperately not to make a sound but the wind yanked the door open like an angry parent, causing it to swing with such force that it threw Ray outside. The air burned as he felt the snow burrow into the corners of his eyes and under his collar, as if it too were trying to hide from the storm. After a tug of war with Mother Nature to close the door, Ray turned back and noticed the square patch of light from the Mott's second floor was out. Paley's silhouette, thankfully, remained.

Ray ran over to Paley in the dark and placed his hand on his arm. Ray could barely make out his expression but his chin faced the woods.

"What are doing out here?" Ray asked, trying not the shout.

Paley remained silent and focused, like a cat spying a field mouse through the crack of a wall. Ray looked at Paley as he stared off into the woods. The wind swirled around them but not between. Even the storm couldn't seem to shake Paley's resolve. Finally, Paley spoke.

"They are in the woods."

"Who?"

Paley nodded to the trees. "The soldiers."

Ray looked into the woods but saw nothing but the dark outlines of branches and trunks. He craned his neck from side to side but all he got was pelted by snow.

"There's no one out there, Paley," Ray said. "You better go inside."

The sound of the Mott's backdoor slamming shut made Ray whip his head around. From the distance, he saw the small silhouette topped with a pompom run towards them. Paley still would not move.

"What are you guys doing?" Olive said, her teeth chattering through the cold. Ray looked down and noticed the hem of a nightgown peeking below her coat and over the tops of her rubber snow boots. "Paley, Mommy is going to be upset that you're outside."

"He says he saw soldiers," Ray said, throwing his hands up in the air. "I didn't see anything but..."

But Olive did. She thrust her arm out past the two boys and yelled, "Ray! Over there!"

It caught Ray's eyes before he even had a chance to turn around. The light. Shining bright and clear from Ships Drive through the center of the woods. This time, though, the light had facets, as if it were twinkling like a diamond. The three stood motionless and fascinated by the glow filtering through the trees and illuminating the storm. Ray felt himself drift from Paley's side toward the edge of the Mott's backyard, as if the light was egging him closer. Then he saw it. A buck stepped into the beam and began to walk towards the three, its body turned towards the road but its face pointing back towards the direction of the three. Ray walked closer to the animal and could barely make out the white mark on its face. This was his buck. And he wanted Ray to follow.

Ray lifted his feet higher with each step. As soon as his foot hit the leaves under the white powder he caught himself. Ray turned around and called out to the two.

"I'm going," he said to them.

Olive stood glued to Paley's side, clutching his arm. The two looked at each other and without saying a word, grabbed each other's hand.

"Us too," she said as they walked over to Ray. Paley's eyes never left the animal as it started to head deeper into the trees.

Ray was happy that the wind hid the sound of his chattering teeth. Where his buck would take them, he did not know. But no great voyager knew what they would discover before they left the safety of their home. He looked at the moving light and then back at his fellow explorers.

"Adventure awaits," Ray said as the three stepped hand in hand into the storm.

❄ ❄ ❄

The three brave friends said nothing as they followed the deer. The trees buffered the snow from hitting their faces but still none of the three could see far in front of them. With no moon and blinding snow, the light was the only way to navigate the paths. Everything in front to the light looked like ribbons tied to a fan. It was as if they were all in a scene in a massive shaken snow globe.

The deer did not hesitate as it made its way out off the dirt path and onto the pavement of Ships Drive. The three stood at the end of the path and watched the buck head down the center of the street away from them and towards the Van Dusen's house. The white light of their lamppost seemed to be shining ten times brighter than normal as the group stepped onto the road.

"What do we do now?" asked Olive over the wind.

Ray looked at the buck for clues. Suddenly it stopped, turned around and looked back at Ray. It seemed to be waiting. For what, they did not know. Ray wanted to call out to the deer and ask what he would like them to do. As his mind began to form questions the answer came riding in on the wind in the form of Christmas carols sung off-key. The buck was waiting for one more person to show up. Ray knew who. He leaned towards Olive.

"Stay with Paley," Ray said as he took off running down Ships Drive away from Olive and Paley and towards the bright lights and bad singing of the Goldsmith's house. Once he reached their yard he pulled some snow off the ground, packed it into a ball and threw it at the end window of the second floor. After the third hit he heard the slide of the window and Tommy's voice.

"You're not Santa," Tommy said as he chewed on the end of an enormous candy cane.

"Would you like to see him?" Ray called out as he hid behind a tree. "I can take to you him if you'd like. Olive and Paley are with me. Want to go?"

"You said you couldn't show me Santa," Tommy said. "Remember?"

"I can and I will show him to you," Ray answered. "Grab your coat and boots and meet me by the backdoor."

"What about his reindeer? Will I see them too?"

"Yes. Promise."

"Cross your heart?"

Ray made an "x" on his chest and kissed his two gloved fingers. Tommy answered by shutting the window and turning on his light. Ray watched Tommy's tiny shadow walk across the room before the light went out again. After a minute the backdoor opened and Tommy emerged, followed by a blast of drunken "Angels We Have Heard On High." The party was so loud in the front of the house Tommy could yell out he was leaving and taking the Pierce Arrow and no one would be the wiser.

"Are you sure it's Santa and not Mr. Terry?" Tommy yelled as Ray took his hand and dragged him as fast as his little six-year-old legs could take him.

"I'm positive," Ray called back. "But first you'll see his reindeer."

"Really? All of them?"

"First you'll see just one," Ray said as he stopped in the middle of the street and pointed to the lamppost light at the end of the road. Ray couldn't see Tommy's expression but his voice raised about two octaves.

"God...bless...America," Tommy said dumbstruck. Ray grabbed Tommy's tiny mittened hand and led him over to Olive and Paley, who remained huddled together in the cold. "Which one is that?"

"That's Comet," Ray answered. "He has a star on his face."

"Really? Can I see? Can we pet him?" Tommy asked as he started to walk closer to the deer. "I want to pet him."

"Nope," said Ray over the wind. "We don't want to scare him off."

"Well, where are the others? Where's Donner and Prancer and Blitzen? And Santa? Where's Santa?"

That was a good question. Ray looked up the street but didn't see any of the other bucks, a sleigh, or Oscar. With the snow falling heavier and faster, even if they were around, Ray figured they might not see them. Ray tore his eyes away from the buck and crouched towards Tommy.

"Look, you might not see Santa but you'll definitely hear him. When he wants the reindeer to run he'll say, 'Hup Hup.' And when he wants them to fly he yells, 'Huzzah!' "

"Really?" asked Olive.

"Positive. I've seen him do it." Ray could feel Olive look at him through the blowing snow. Then Tommy let go of Ray's hand, took a step forward and yelled as loud as he could.

"Hup! Hup!"

Immediately the three felt the road rumble beneath their feet. Each grabbed each other's arm as they turned around, ready to yank each other out of the way of an oncoming car. The light suddenly grew brighter, casting a wider net. As they tried to focus through the snow he heard Tommy cry out.

"It's them! There they are!"

Like a stampede, seven enormous bucks came barreling down the road. Their antlers perched solid, fierce and regal on their heads as they leapt and raced towards the four. The kids pulled into each other as the deer ran around them like the tide pulling a wave around rocks. Ray held his breath and Olive covered her glasses as they anticipated getting trampled. Only Tommy and Paley did not appear to be afraid for their lives.

"One, two, five, eight," Tommy yelled. "Look, Ray, that's all of them!"

Ray lifted his face that he had buried in the top of Tommy's cap. He was right. They were all there, prancing proudly in front of the lamppost light and shaking their racks from side to side. Ray knew these were the same as the ones that were in Oscar's backyard. They had to be. Ray noticed one with a square patch on the side of its neck. He tapped Olive on the shoulder.

"Look, Olive, there's your deer. That's the one Oscar saved," Ray said as he pointed to the large buck standing next to the light. Olive wiped the snow off her glasses with her scarf and leaned forward.

"Wow," Olive said, in a voice almost in a squeal. "That's the one."

Then Tommy broke from the pack and began yelling again. "Hup! Hup! Hup! Hup-hup-huppity-hup!" The sound of his voice made the bucks rear up on their hind legs and pace frantically around each other.

Ray pulled Tommy back. "Stop it, Tommy. You'll spook them."

"No, I won't. Look!"

Tommy was right. They weren't spooked. They appeared to be forming a line. Two lines actually. Each buck walked to its own place in the queue, like thoroughbreds taking their respective gate before a race. After they all found their place, the lamppost light grew brighter as if it were turning up the volume on a radio, causing the bucks to fall into the darkness behind it. The only ones lit on the street now were four terrified and thrilled children.

Then a familiar voice in the distance called out deep and loud.

"Huuuup!" the voice bellowed. The bold command cut through all the sounds the world could make in a storm. "Huuuup!"

"Oscar?" Ray yelled as he stepped away from the group and towards the voice. His own could not compete with the wind. "Oscar, is that you?"

The voice did not reply to Ray but kept its marching orders like a drill sergeant. "Huuuup!"

"Is that you, Oscar?" Ray repeated as he kept walking. The only voice Ray could hear reply was Tommy's.

"That's not Mr. Taglieber, Ray. It's Santa!"

The voice in the distance kept its instructions. The silhouettes of the bucks got larger and the voice, louder. Ray stopped. His eyes widened as he realized he wasn't moving closer to them but they were coming closer to him.

"Huuuup!" The command was getting louder, too.

Fear hit Ray's chest as the black shadows grew taller. The wind whipped around his legs, pulling them down and cementing them into the snowy street. The only thing Ray's body could do was turn away from the locomotive speeding in his direction. He could hear hooves smack the pavement like applause in the movie theater as he hunched towards the ground. Then another voice cried out loud and clear. Ray looked up and saw Paley standing with his hands high in the air as a twister swirled around him. His voice was so clear that nothing could miss him or ignore his command.

"Huzzah!" Paley cried.

Ray saw the faces of the three turn sharply upward. Then a loud pop and burst of light. The Van Dusen's lamppost exploded. But instead of burning out, it shot up like a flare, leaving a white trail in its wake. All their mouths dropped open in shock. Ray began to stand up straight until something hit him on his back, knocking him into the ground. His mouth that only a moment ago was filled with awe was now filled with snow. He rolled over and saw the white ball of light slingshot across the sky. No storm could stop it. Against the backdrop of the clouds a long streak remained, just like the night over the field, an arrow of light pointing in the direction they needed to go. It was their Comet. Their North Star. Their Star of Bethlehem. He crawled up to his feet and ran over to the three who were cheering with joy.

"Santa! It was Santa!" cried Tommy as he grabbed Ray's elbows. "Did you see him?"

"Told you, Tommy. I told you he was real," Ray said as Tommy's face became illuminated in the cold. He could see all three of them clearly now, their faces a mix of thrill and joy. Faces he'd only seen on summer afternoons on that very street after they hit one of his dad's home run pitches.

"Look! He came back!" Tommy yelled as he pointed behind Ray.

Ray turned around and saw another light, only it was accompanied by the two white headlights of a police car. Ray winced as soon as he heard the thick Irish brogue.

"Have you kids lost your minds?" he cried out before the door even slammed shut. Officer Boland was so fit to be tied he was asking and answering his own questions. "Jesus, Mary, and Joseph, what are you doing out in this storm? Looking to get all your gifts taken back before Christmas, I reckon. Tommy Goldsmith, do you know how mad your mother is going to be? I'll tell you. She's going to be madder than two dogs with one turkey leg…"

"We saw Santa!" Tommy cried out.

"You'll be seeing your mother in about two minutes. I'll be seeing your mother in two minutes. Oh Jesus, Mary, and Joseph," Officer Boland said as he ushered the excited kids into the shelter of the police car's backseat.

The only person who shared Officer Boland's concern for Mrs. Goldsmith's impending fit of rage was Ray. Ray thought he would be able to get Tommy back without her noticing. Now they were going to be escorted into her house by a police officer during her Christmas party. She would certainly notice now. If Mrs. Goldsmith didn't pluck and baste him in boiling butter like a Christmas goose, his mother certainly would.

Officer Boland pulled into the Goldsmith's driveway still muttering to Jesus, Mary, and Joseph and any available saint to save the kids' hide from a nightmarish Christmas death at the hands of Mrs. Goldsmith. As soon as the car stopped he took a deep breath and turned around.

"All you kids, out of the car and into the house to warm up."

"I'd like to stay in the car," Ray said with his chin tucked into his chest.

"Would you now? Me, too. Get out," he ordered as he opened the door.

Tommy was already jumping up the front steps by the time Ray stepped out of the car. Tommy flung the door open, excited and unafraid about the trouble they were all in. The rest of the gang cautiously stepped into the grand foyer as the crowd of guests turned their heads and lowered their punch glasses. Their "Go Tell it on the Mountain" faded into a whisper that wouldn't have even made it over an anthill. Officer Boland took off his hat and began to wring it in his hands.

By the time Ray stepped into the room, Mrs. Goldsmith's arms had enveloped Tommy in its folds, smothering his excited cries of Santa. She stared down at Ray with utter distain. She took a deep breath between every word that came out so she would not faint before finishing her sentence.

"Why. Was. My child. Outside. In. A storm?" she said through clenched teeth as she struggled to hold Tommy close.

"Anta! Anta!" Tommy yelled into Mrs. Goldsmith's bosom. She released him but kept him at arm's length. "Santa!" Tommy cried. "Ray said he'd show me Santa Claus and he did! We saw Santa!"

The guests clutched their drinks to their chests and laughed nervously. Mr. Goldsmith walked over to Officer Boland and handed him a glass of punch.

"I'll call their parents," Mr. Goldsmith said softly before ducking out of the room. Officer Boland sniffed his drink then discreetly poured it into the tree stand. Tommy, however, wouldn't let Ray answer the question. He broke free from his mother's grip.

"Mom! Didn't you hear me? We saw Santa!" he yelled. "Didn't we guys?"

"We sure did," Olive said boldly, tugging at Paley's sleeve. "Right, Paley? Didn't we see Santa and his reindeer?" Paley, who couldn't stop rocking and smiling, just clapped his hands joyfully. He didn't need to answer Mrs. Goldsmith. His excitement was affirmation enough.

Mrs. Goldsmith's attention, however, did not veer from Ray. Her seething stare, flared nostrils, and heavy breathing seemed to bring the storm that raged outside, in. Tommy remained oblivious to his mother's anger. He ripped off his hat as he slapped his head with both hands.

"My gosh, I gotta get to bed! He won't stop here if I'm awake. Everyone go home! He won't come if you're here!"

The crowd erupted in laughter as Tommy threw his coat on the floor and ran towards the stairs. Before heading up, he ran back to Ray and flung his arms around him, pinning Ray's arms to his sides. Tommy closed his eyes as he gave Ray the biggest bear hug.

"This is the best Christmas ever, Ray. I'll never forget it. Even when I'm a hundred years old, I won't ever, never forget it."

Ray smiled as Tommy released him and dashed towards the stairs. His feet and hands slapped the steps as he took them two by two up the winding staircase.

Ray turned his head slowly towards the crowd. Mrs. Goldsmith stood in the center as someone handed her a cup of punch. She put her hand up and wouldn't take it.

"Wait here one minute," she ordered as she turned on her heel and disappeared into the kitchen. Ray was happy Officer Boland was standing there. He didn't know what weapon Mrs. Goldsmith would emerge with.

The kitchen door swung open as she appeared with a silver square. She walked over to Ray and thrust it out with both hands.

"For your mother. It's my fruitcake," she said as she handed it to Ray.

Ray took it from her but almost dropped it from its weight. Like Oscar's pillow, the loaf looked far heavier than it appeared. "And tell her I will drive you home from school after the break. They said it will be a stormy winter. You shouldn't be out in this cold."

Ray could not seem to make his face relax as he looked up at her in mid-wince. "Thank…you. Merry Christmas?"

"Merry Christmas, Raymond," Mrs. Goldsmith said cautiously. The music started back up and swelled around her as Officer Boland ushered the kids outside and into the police car. As soon as the driver side door closed Ray heard Officer Boland let out a sigh of relief. The sound of the engine starting up pushed the noises of the storm away and made the crowd fade as they began to belt it out again, over the hills and everywhere.

❄ ❄ ❄

"Did she fill it with coal?" Olive asked, lifting the fruitcake above her knees.

"Not sure," Ray answered as they pulled into the Mott's driveway. He could see his mother and Mrs. Mott standing on the front porch, arms tightly crossed in front of their chests. Ray didn't know what to expect. If his mother would be angry, relieved or both. This time, Officer Boland stood back from the three as they stomped up the Mott's porch. Ray's mother pulled him close but did not hug him. Mrs. Mott grabbed Paley by the shoulders and examined his face for clues. Still in her nightgown, she spoke to him in measured tones, the way Ray only heard people speak when they were gearing up to cry.

"Paley? What were you doing outside? Tell me."

"I saw them. In the woods," he said, staring up in the air as the smile still clung to his face.

"Who? Who did you see in the woods?"

Paley laughed and put his hands over his mouth. "Santa. It was Santa." Joy radiated from every corner of his face.

"Tommy Goldsmith was spouting the same nonsen...thing too," Officer Boland chimed in before taking another step back. Ray looked at Olive, who stood with her mitten to her mouth in thought.

Mrs. Mott shook her head in confusion as she looked at Olive for a better explanation. Only Ray seemed to notice Olive switching gears.

"Mom, something was out there. Honest. Ray tried to get Paley back inside but Paley wouldn't go. He really saw something. We all saw something," Olive pleaded. She straightened up her little frame and nodded the facts. "I think it might have been Santa Claus."

Mrs. Mott put her hands on her hips and cocked her head to the side. "Olive Marie Mott, you know better."

"Santa!" It was Santa!" Paley cried as he bolted past her into the house. Mrs. Mott ran after him, leaving Olive on the porch. Olive looked at Ray and shrugged her shoulders. Although she was speaking to Ray, her words were not for him.

"Thanks for trying to help me bring Paley back in, Ray," she said smiling.

Ray tried to hide his thankful grin as he pulled his coat collar up above his mouth. He wasn't sure it would work but he wanted to hug her for the effort. Olive ran into the house and slammed the door behind her, leaving Ray out in the cold and in hot water with his mother. Ray did not move but his eyes drifted up to his mother. Her arms were still crossed, either for warmth or in an attempt to hold in her rage.

"Fruitcake?" Ray said, handing the loaf out like an olive branch to his mother. She studied him with her eyebrow raised and her mouth jilted to the side as she took the silver brick. Ray knew his mother always believed Olive but this time she didn't appear to be too sure. Her gaze broke from Ray as she turned to thank Officer Boland for her son's safe return and to wish him a Merry Christmas. She then put her arm around Ray's shoulders as she led him back to the lights of their home.

"If Mrs. Goldsmith let you live, I guess I can too. It is Christmas, after all."

CHAPTER 31

The Most Magical Day – Saarlautern, Germany, 1944

Hal Kozak pulled out the dog tags tucked underneath his field jacket and ran his thumb over the raised letters of his last name. Kozak. Seeing the word made him feel all the memories that came with it. His brothers, his wife, and his son. For some reason, he missed them intensely that morning, more than any other day, although he wasn't sure why. It was no one's birthday or anniversary. School had already started and baseball was ending. Hal searched his brain as he walked in lock step with the others. They had formed two large lines as they marched through woods and past small villages to the next bombed out town. His squad had grown quiet in the walk, lost in their respective thoughts and various states of alertness. When he would see a town sitting peaceful in the distance or a tree untouched by bullets or blood, he let his mind fall back to the woods behind his house where he would see Ray and the neighborhood kids building forts. This day, the town of Saarlautern loomed in the distance. He knew it would not be peaceful when they arrived but from their view along the path, it looked like it could be another Tuesday in a town where people busied themselves with going to work, fixing cars, building clocks, making pies, learning their math lessons. A busy town on a sunny day. He wondered if it were sunny in Southold. He couldn't take out a picture of his Estelle and Raymond that he had tucked up inside the straps of his helmet. Taking off your helmet was suicide. He just pulled the shiny silver nubbed cord of his dog tags and looked down at the name. For now, just looking at the name they all shared would have to do.

"Can you fix this, old man?" asked Private Donner as he turned and passed him an old rusted headlamp. "I can't get it to work. Sometimes it turns on. Sometimes not."

Hal looked down at the miner's headgear. He pulled the switch that turned on the lamp. The white light did not come on. He heard a laugh from two soldiers up in line.

"It's the switch that reads 'on,' Donner. If you turn the arrow to that, it usually works," chimed Sergeant Carrig. Hal could hear the smile through his teasing.

"Thanks for the tip, Fancy Feet. I know how a headlamp works."

"That's Sergeant Fancy Feet to you," Sergeant Carrig said as he turned and flashed a gleaming white smile. No one knew how his teeth looked so white despite weeks of spotty hygiene. A dance instructor before he enlisted, Sergeant Carrig looked as if he just floated off a USO dance floor with a swooning woman instead of trudging through a German forest with a bunch of tough guys from the 9th Infantry.

Private Lonergan, a wiry blond fellow from Connecticut, tapped Hal on his shoulder.

"Actually, I think it's one of those models where you need to give it a good idea. That's when the light comes on," he joked. Another laugh erupted from the men around him.

"It's Donner's so it probably stopped working years ago," added Asher, shouting from the back of the line.

"Hey now, it's my dad's," Donner said, ignoring the jokes falling in around him. "It's perfect. Just tired of shining, is all," he said, kicking up a cloud of dirt from the path.

Donner was a coal miner's son from Chambersburg, Pennsylvania. No one knew how he snuck the light past the higher-ups as Donner wasn't the brightest bulb in the bunch but if anyone had a problem with Donner carrying his dad's old headlamp, they never said. Donner held on to it like a pacifier. He was far younger than the age of enlistment. The family bible had him at seventeen though most of the men swore he was not a day older than fifteen. Donner was by far the most picked on member of their squad. The rest of the men figured that for the amount grief they gave him about his Pennsylvanian accent, how he pronounced "iron" like "urn," he deserved a small comfort from home.

"You know what I'm tired of?" a voice boomed out. "C-rations and listening to you all yap," Captain Pickett yelled as he marched back to the group. He stood two hands taller than everyone except Carrig. "More walking. Less talking. Except for you, Puddy. If he ever speaks a word other than 'Yes, sir' in English, someone come get me."

Hal smiled. He liked Pickett, or Captain Lightning, as he liked to be called. A chain-smoking, three hundred and seventy-pound giant, he earned his nickname beating the youngest and most athletic men in the company at random foot races. Pickett said if anyone could beat him he would give them his cigarette rations for a month. Hal saw many foot races but never saw Pickett without an Old Gold sticking out of his mouth. Loud, large, and loyal to death to the men who worked for him, Pickett reminded Hal of Mick from the shop. And like Mick, Pickett kept Hal close and his opinions in high regard.

After Pickett left the group for his rightful place at the head of the line, Donner turned back around and whispered to Hal.

"Please tell me it ain't broke."

"I'm sure it's fine," soothed Hal. "Just needs a little cleaning. I'll get it working again. Don't you worry."

After spending much of the day marching through the tall dark woods, the group headed toward the outskirts of the small German town. Most secretly hoped they could steal food as Pickett wasn't the only one tired of the C-rations. But as they came up to the village they soon realized there would be plenty more meat unit cans in their future.

The smell was the first thing that grabbed Hal. It was as if a something unholy came from deep underground to herald death's approach or departure. It was war's smell. The smell of gunpowder and buildings turned inside out. On this street, frames of houses and stores were the only things left standing. An open door banged against a house where the owner once planted lilies. A shell that was once a Sonderklasse automobile rested half on the street and half on the empty sidewalk. The people had vanished. Roads were carved up like a rudder through water with debris in its wake from the aftermath of an air strike. Hal shuddered and thought the same thing he did upon every village they passed. What if this had this been Southold? How would it look deserted? With grocers and garages flattened by bombs? Hal shook his head. Regardless of the outcome, the people of this town lost this war.

Hal saw the explosion before he even heard it. Something shot ash and rock high in the air only two blocks up from the men. They all scattered to the side of the road, their backs plastered to the outside of a brick wall. Pickett barked orders as the men pulled their M1s from behind their backs and held them close to their chest. It could have been a leftover bomb or a fresh attack. Pickett waved Rancer and Puddy from the squad to head up the road with him to investigate as the rest remained with their backs to the wall.

Hal faced Donner on the wall. Donner's eyes were not fixed on Hal but rather on something in the distance over Hal's head. His expression twisted in confusion.

"He shouldn't be there?" Donner uttered before standing up.

"Donner get down," Hal urged. Donner crouched down but kept popping his head up over Hal.

"It's…just…" Donner said standing up. "He shouldn't be standing there."

Hal turned around and followed Donner's eye line. From the fourth floor of a bombed out building he saw what puzzled Donner. It was a boy. A small boy standing up in what was left of a window. He didn't notice the soldiers looking up at him. Instead, he stared at the same black cloud of ash that caused them to take cover. Hal crawled from behind the wall to get a better view. His stomach dropped open once he saw between the buildings. Standing in the windows one floor below the boy were children. All were staring out through the paneless windows at the smoke billowing down the street.

"How many you reckon?" asked Donner from behind Hal.

Hal counted quietly. "That's about twenty kids."

Carrig and Lonergan ran up to the other two. Carrig took out a set of binoculars and counted. "Twenty-three to be exact."

"Don't they know to hide? Or at least get away from the window?" Lonergan asked.

"There must be no adults. If there were then…" Carrig began to say before another explosion rang out. This time on the floor underneath the children.

A collective high-pitched wail came from the building that sounded like kids on a roller coaster. And same as that switch on a headlamp, something clicked on in Hal and in the other men. Something similar to when he would see Ray in the path of Fluffles. Something instinctual. Not from a soldier but as a father. He pushed the gun around towards his back as the adrenaline grabbed his legs. He was off towards the building, his squad at his heels.

The opening of the door was now just a pile of rubble. The men reached for every angle to get some sort of foothold into the building. Looking up he noticed the top of a window not completely caved in. Hal climbed up the rocks and knocked out the remaining glass. He shimmied the top half of his body inside. He winced as he popped his head in. He didn't know if there was anything or anyone in the room waiting to greet him other than a gray cloud of soot. After squirreling into the building, he rolled over the rocks and stones from the fallen walls towards the floor and began to pull debris away from the door, giving the others an opening to get inside. When he finally made an opening, he was shocked to see that that the first face to run through was none other than Pickett's.

"They don't call me Captain Lightning for nothin'," he barked as the other men filed in behind him. Puddy ran to an opening in the wall and yelled out in German.

"*Seid ihr da*?" Puddy called out, asking if anyone was there. "*Wir holen euch raus*!" saying the soldiers would get them out. Everyone stood silently as a small female voice crawled out from between the cracks in the ceiling.

"*Wir sind hier*!" she called out, announcing they were there. "*Tun sie uns nichts*." Don't do us harm.

"*Wirt tun euch nicht*!" he called out, saying they would not. Puddy turned to Pickett but Pickett didn't need to know what the girl said.

"Keep her talking. We'll follow her voice," Pickett shouted as he pointed to the half blown-out staircase. He then turned and pointed at Hal. "I lift. You climb," he ordered as he grabbed Hal. His thick paws grabbed Hal's uniform and with one quick heave, Pickett hoisted him up the second section of the staircase. Hal ran up the other two sections and stopped at a bookshelf that had collapsed across the door. Once he pushed past it the large oak door swung open with ease. He pulled his gun from around his back and carefully peeked into the room. After seeing what was there, he dropped his gun to his side in shock.

Hal was the tallest one in the room. Between and under every blown-out opening in the room was a child, their eyes wide in fear as they clung to each other. None appeared older than Ray. They looked like typical kids. Some dressed like they were going to church. Some were in rags. Some wore birds on their shirts and some wore stars on their sleeves. Hal spun around the room and found the only adult sitting on the floor, clutching her blood-covered legs. She cried out in German.

"*Er ist oben*," she cried. "*Ich muß zu ihm.*" He is upstairs. I have to go to him.

Hal looked at her and shook his head in confusion. Tears cut a path through the ash that covered her face. "I'm sorry. I do not understand you," he said. Hal didn't take his eyes off of her as he yelled out. "Captain! I found them."

The children let out a pained cry. They did not understand that he would not be shooting them. He pulled the strap of his gun so it rested on his back, got to his knees and held his hands out.

"We will get you out," he said patting the air. "It will be alright."

A hundred hopeful eyes did not understand. They looked too young to know any language other than German. His body language tried to soothe them but the orders being screamed from two floors below were anything but calming.

"Get them on the ground, Kozak! Now!"

Hal got on the floor and patted the ground. He looked back at the older woman in the corner of the room. Her head lobbed from side to side in pain as she repeated.

"*Ich muß zu ihm.*"

"Ma'am," Hal yelled. He put his head on the ground, hoping she would be able to understand him. "Tell them they need to get down."

She looked at him in defeat. The tired worn face of a mother nodded. She strained to turn her head towards the children as she mustered the energy to speak louder than a whimper. *"Kinder,"* she ordered, *"zu boden."*

One by one, the children lowered themselves to the floor, looking to each other for permission that it was safe to do so. Hal demonstrated by putting his body close to the floor. He looked up to see if the woman was following suit. A screaming whistle from the air began to drown out her voice. Then he felt a hand grab his helmet and press his head to the floor.

"Runter!" Puddy screamed before the explosion blew the sunlight out of the room. This time the bomb landed in the street somewhere near the front of the building. A black cloud barreled through the window openings, throwing any standing kids to the ground. Hal opened his eyes and through the dust saw leather boots and olive drab pant legs fly over his head and scatter around the room. He was yanked to his knees to see Puddy, Carrig, and Lonergan scooping up as many up as kids as they could carry. Donner's smiling face popped in front of his, blocking his view.

"Sorry to be so rough on ya, old man," he said as he slapped his helmet before running to pick up a child. Hal shook his head in an attempt to stop the ringing in his ears. Each soldier had at least one child in each arm with one holding onto their back.

"Get'em out! Get'em out! Get'em out!" yelled Carrig as he struggled to hold a feisty red-headed five-year-old. "This place won't be standing for long."

Hal ran over to the woman. Her flowered dress ripped to shreds from the waist down. The blood from her knees cast a red dye into the yellow of the dirty roses of her skirt.

"We're going to get you out," Hal said in a reassuring tone but nothing in her face appeared calm. She grabbed Hal's uniform with one hand and pointed up in the air with the other. Her eyes became crazed and she struggled against him.

"*Mein sohn*," she cried. "*Mein sohn ist oben.*" My son is upstairs.

Hal pulled the woman to her feet but she kept crying. She repeated the words over and over. Hal tried to block her out. "Mine zoon," is what the words sounded like. By the time Hal got her to the opening most of the children were gone. The men had passed them down a hole by the stairway to Pickett, Asher, and Rancer.

"Take them to the back. To the back," Pickett bellowed. "Run like me, you young bucks," he hollered as he grabbed the kids, picking them out of the air with one hand as if he were plucking apples off a tree. Captain Pickett looked up past a set of twin boys and caught Hal's eye.

"Separate heaven for you, Private," he yelled. Before any battle, Pickett would say there was a separate heaven for the men in infantry. That anyone sitting in a foxhole and not in the safety of headquarters or a plane or a tank got to cut the line at heaven's gates. Hal nodded to Pickett nervously. He knew where his heaven was. It was a million miles west from this place.

Hal tried to hand the woman over to Donner but she would not let go of his jacket, her panicked expression an inch away from Hal's eyes. Every space of her face creased with desperation.

"*Mein sohn!*" she cried as she pointed up. "*Mein sohn!*"

Suddenly, Hal knew what she meant. The boy. The first one he saw. That must be who she was talking about. Hal nodded and pulled her away from him.

"I'm going upstairs," he said to Donner while looking at the woman. "That boy is still up there."

Donner nodded but his eyes pleaded with Hal not to go. His voice cracked in an attempt to hide his concern. "Go get him," he said as he slapped Hal on the shoulder. Hal nodded in agreement, turned on his heel and disappeared into the dust.

Hal took the stairs by two. The stairwells were surprisingly clear. The higher he went, the more the stone walls hid the barking and crying of children and soldiers. It almost seemed peaceful if not for the terrifying sounds of rock crumbling and the small volcanoes of dust that shot down from the ceilings. Hal reached the next floor and entered every room the same way. Back to the wall by the side of the door, a quick head turn into the room, then enter the room with his gun drawn. But each room he entered held no life. No enemy soldier. No boy. Not anyone. Hal wished he had thought to ask the woman for the boy's name. All she repeated was something that sounded like "mine zoon." Maybe that was his name or nickname. He figured he might as well give it a try.

"Mine zoon!" Hal called out. "Mine zoon, are you there?" Suddenly, another high-pitched whistle pierced the air. Hal crouched down inside the doorway and braced himself. Black ash blew inside from the openings in the wall as the blast shook the building. More crumbles, more cracks, and more dust. The mortars were acting like timers, signaling everyone that the clock was running down.

Hal got to his feet and ran into each room, yelling the same thing. "Mine zoon! Mine zoon!" hoping to get some sort of return call or cry. As he barreled into what once looked like a bedroom he began to yell until he heard a whimper. Hal dropped to his knees and looked under the furniture. Tucked deep under a desk was the little boy he saw in the window. He couldn't have been much older than seven but like Hal, his frame was small for his age. He curled up like a cat behind the foot bar of the desk, his big blue eyes looking at Hal in utter terror.

"Mine zoon?" Hal asked calmly. The boy cocked his head to the side in confusion. Hal reached in to grab him but the boy recoiled tighter behind the slab of wood separating the two. Hal looked at himself. He realized he must look terrifying to the kid. He pushed his gun to his back and took off his helmet. He handed it to the boy and pointed it to his head.

"Here, mine zoon," he said gently. "For your head."

The little boy looked at Hal, then at his helmet. After assessing the situation, he began to crawl out from under the desk and stood in front of Hal. The boy standing was as tall as Hal kneeling. Gaunt and sickly, Hal fastened the large helmet on the boy's tiny head. Hal looked at him and smiled.

"Hold onto me tight," Hal said. He demonstrated by grabbing fistfuls of his uniform. The little boy nodded in agreement as Hal scooped him up and began to dart out of the room. Before leaving the bedroom, Hal grabbed a knitted piece of lace from under a fallen lamp on the top of a dresser. He flung it over the helmet. From a distance the boy might look like an American soldier and an instant target. He tried to cover the helmet as he ran down the hallway and down the stairs. After safely making it to the floor below, Hal ran to the opening he last saw Donner. No one was there. Hal looked around and then down at the hole. He and the boy were both small enough to go through the opening together.

"Hold tight, mine zoon," Hal said as he wiggled his way through the gap. He could feel the boy's grip firmly on the straps on his collar as they dropped through the ceiling. Hal landed square on his feet on a flat surface. Looking down, he realized that the men put a table there for the other kids to get down. Hal scrambled off the table and looked around. There was no opening, anywhere. The little boy lifted his head from Hal's chest and pointed to a doorway on the other side of the room.

"Da," he said loudly. Hal took his word for it and ran through it, entering deeper into the building. Even as the halls turned black as pitch, the boy knew how to navigate them. He would tug at Hal's collar, grab his hand and point the direction for Hal to run. They made their way like this until Hal saw the light at the end of the building. As he ran closer to it, he heard the sweet familiar yelling of the Old Reliables. Hal ran out of the building and into the daylight when he heard another familiar voice yelling.

"*Mein sohn!*" Hal heard her cry. He followed the voice into an abandoned butcher's shop. Once inside he saw all the children on the floor with their backs to the wall. Hal swung his head around to see the woman in the doorway, her useless legs spread out on the floor as she held her shaking arms out to him. Hal ran to her and got on his knees to deposit the boy on her side. She wedged her arms between Hal's chest and the boy. She tried to pull him to her but the boy would not let go.

"*Nein!*" the boy screamed as he struggled against his mother. "*Gehen sie nicht!*" Do not go.

Hal tried to pry the boy off of him but he would not loosen his grip. For such a small twig of a kid, he was strong. Then he heard Carrig's voice outside in the road.

"Captain's got it in the neck! We need to move him!"

Panic ripped through Hal. The boy kept yelling as the woman tried with all her strength to force him away. As she tried to wrench the boy off, Hal's neck jutted forward and began to burn. Then Hal saw why. The boy's hands were wrapped around his dog tags.

"*Gehen sie nicht!*" he screamed but Hal ducked and ripped the chain over his head, releasing him from the child's clutches. Hal rolled onto his side, scrambled to his feet and dashed out of the door towards the voices of his squad. Even as he listened for the various accents of home he could still hear the boy screaming from inside the building.

"*Papa! Papa Geh nicht!*" Dad, do not go.

By the time Hal made it out into the street the others had gone back into the building. Hal ran in behind Carrig to the men crowded around the far corner of the room. Lonergan knelt over Pickett, his hand covered in blood as he held it over Pickett's neck. Pickett looked like a Greek god who fell from the sky. His eyes were alert but his mouth hung open as if he were asleep.

"We're going to lift you in three, Captain," Lonergan yelled into Pickett's face. The other men filled in around him to help lift Pickett's massive frame. Pickett's eyes grew stern.

"Leave," Pickett gurgled but no one could hear him. Another loud shrill sliced through the air. The bomb hit so close the walls moved like a tree in a storm. It took Hal a moment to get the ringing out of his ears. He looked around and saw all the men still huddled around Pickett. All except for one.

"Where's Donner?" he yelled as Asher got to his feet. "Where is he?"

"He's not with you?" he answered, focusing on the Captain. "He said he was going to find you."

"Oh, God," Hal uttered to himself as he jumped to his feet. Hal's legs wanted to sprint through the halls but the darkness would not allow it. He tried to remember the way the boy instructed him to go but when he reached the hallway he could not see. If only he could flick on a light. He suddenly stopped and tapped his pocket. Yes, he thought. Maybe, I can.

Hal grabbed Donner's headlamp and turned the switch. The white light flickered on, then shone as bright as any headlight on a car. He pulled the straps tight around his head and began to run. With a light to guide him he could finally see the dangers that lay ahead. He leapt over every piece of fallen furniture and crumbled wall that crossed his path. He made his way back through the opening and lifted himself up through the hole in the ceiling to the floor above.

"Donner!" Hal cried. "Donner, where are you?"

Hal's mouth dropped when he turned around. It wasn't dark anymore on that floor. Light illuminated every corner of all the rooms.

The façade of the building was gone. The front wall of the entire structure was reduced to a pile of rubble and ash in the street. Hal walked to the edge and looked down into the mountain of debris.

"Donner?" Hal said, this time only in a whisper. He did not expect an answer. He heard one nonetheless.

"Here!" Hal heard Donner's cry from inside the building. Hal took off again into the rooms. Ash and dust seemed to be spewing from every crack as the walls fought to keep themselves together.

"Donner! Talk to me!" Hal yelled as he ran into the stairwell. His light targeted every room in search of his brother. After racing up to the third floor he heard what sounded like someone shuffling through rocks. Hal ran towards the sound and into a large room. There was no light other than what came from his lamp. He stopped in the door and slowly scanned the room for signs of life. In the corner of the room is where he saw Donner. His head and arms were the only parts of him not buried by a pile of fieldstone. From Hal's view, it looked as if he were taking a swim in a sea of bricks. His hand tried to limply push a small boulder off his chest.

"Daddy..." Donner cried. His voice as weak as a kitten. "Daddy, I'm over here."

Hal scrambled over the stones as the sound of thunder began to grow. He knew Donner could not see him. All Donner could see was the light of his father's headlamp.

"I'm coming!" Hal yelled over the rumble. The roar overhead sounded like a racing locomotive baring down on them. "Hold on! I'm coming!"

"Daddy..." Donner cried. This time his voice turned over into tears. "Daddy, I knew you would come to get me."

"I'm here!" Hal yelled as he reached out for his friend's hand. "I'm here!"

Then he wasn't.

Grass. Everything that was in front of Hal vanished and was replaced by vibrant green grass. Jack Donner, dust, rock, ash, the sound of thunder. All gone in a blink and replaced with another scene as quickly and seamlessly as a switch of a movie reel during a matinee. On the grass in front of him was a hand. All five fingers were splayed out on the warm soft fescue. The hand was smaller, smoother, and a bit pudgier than his own. He turned it over to look at the palm. The lines were the same as his. Hal studied the inside of this hand, his hand, until a clanging jingle of a store bell and a quick burst of the smell of sweets rolled into the air.

He stood up and looked around. There were people far taller than him walking around the street. They were running out of Bohack's with full bags of groceries and into the Kramer's Soda Shoppe, chatty and happy. The oak leaves of Main Street shifted in the wind as if waving hello. Hal put his nose up in the air to follow the smell. He turned and saw Mr. Shiller and the man who gave him the dime wave from the white wooden porch of the Penny Candy store. Hal returned the wave with a smile. Mr. Shiller pointed in front of Hal to show him that something was going on that needed his attention. As soon as Hal heard the laughing, he knew.

It was his brothers. Christopher and Tim sat on a bench in front of the barbershop, both reading from the same comic and cackling in unison with delight. Christopher noticed him first and stood to greet him. He looked as tall as a flag post and his smile sparkled as brightly as any firework Hal had ever seen.

"Of course you're here, Hal," he heard a familiar voice say over his head. "Where else would you be?"

Hal looked up. There by his side stood his father. He was dressed neatly in clean dungarees and a white-collared shirt. Hal thought it was odd to see his father so put together but then couldn't remember why he thought it was odd in the first place. This is how his dad always looked. Clean-shaven with bright eyes and a warm smile that greeted him every time he walked into a room. The man who made him feel nothing other than loved and safe. His father's expression, this place, filled every pore of Hal's soul with absolute and complete joy.

Then he heard the sound of a paper crumpling. He looked down and noticed that in his other tiny hand was a paper bag. He reached in and pulled out a piece of chocolate candy. It was his favorite.

The last thought of his adult life came in and out of his head as if it traveled on a dragonfly's wing. Pickett was right. There was a separate heaven for the men in infantry. And then that was it. There wasn't one thought that hurt. Not one memory of any pain. Everything was perfect. Everything was normal, mundane, and magical on this little stretch of Route 25. Hal popped the candy of out its cellophane wrapper and dropped it on his tongue. He let the rich, wonderful taste fill his mouth. He looked up at his father, took his hand in his and smiled. This life, his life, was sweet.

CHAPTER 32

Christmas Morning – Southold, New York, 1944

R ay sat up in his still warm bed and rubbed the sleep out of his eyes as the smell of a turkey roasting in the oven filled his bedroom. Ray could already hear his mother in the kitchen slapping lids on pots, sliding pans, and closing cabinet doors. The clock on the wall read 7:15 but it smelled like he had slept through dinner. This only happened one day a year. Christmas morning.

He crawled over to the window and looked out at the woods. The early morning sun tried to push its way through the high cloud haze. The trees stood motionless, tired and spent from the thrashing they took from the storm. As far as Ray could see, the wind and the snow conspired to conceal Ray's, Olive's, Paley's, and Tommy's adventure by blowing snow into all the tracks they made during the night. The storm wiped all the evidence of Santa Claus away. The only proof now would be four memories.

"Merry Christmas, son," his mother said as he entered the kitchen. She smelled like cold cream and cooked onions as she hugged him in oven mitts. "And don't eat the bananas. They are for the fruit cup."

"Sure thing. Merry Christmas, Mom," Ray answered as he shuffled over to the tree. If his mother was upset from the scare he gave her the night before, she didn't show it. Between all the cutting, slicing, peeling, stuffing, and setting of tables, she didn't appear to have any time to be angry.

"Raymond," she called out as she leaned over a hot pot and blew on a wooden spoon. "Is Mr. Taglieber spending Christmas with anyone?"

"I don't think so," Ray answered. He spied a large box from under the tree. He tried to pick it up but it weighed too much to lift. He pushed it past the others and towards the center of the rug. The paper didn't match any of the other paper from the other presents and the tag only read, "To Raymond."

"Mom, who is this gift from?"

"Let me see," she said, walking over to Ray, wiping her hands on her red polka dotted apron. "I don't remember seeing it before. Must be from Santa."

"Can I open it?"

"Sure."

Ray ripped the paper off in one pull and opened the box. Inside was a cuckoo clock. Ray lifted it out of the box and examined the dark wood carvings around the face. It did not have birds or men holding beer steins like Ray had seen on Oscar's wall. Instead, this one was covered top to bottom in bucks. Antlers reached high over the top like a crown. Ray's finger traced over all the deer as he counted. All eight were present. A smile stretched across his face.

"It is from Santa," Ray smiled.

Ray felt his mother kiss the top of his head. "Why don't you run over to Mr. Taglieber's and ask him to come for dinner. We have plenty of food. And you can thank him for the lovely gift."

Ray gently put the clock down, ran to the closet and threw on his snow pants and boots. He grabbed his coat on the way out the door. As he threaded his arm through the sleeve his mother stopped him.

"Oh, Raymond," she said, grabbing his shoulders as she examined the back of his coat. "You got paint on this."

Ray tried to look over his shoulder at what his mother was talking about but then just took off his coat. On the back of the winter coat was a large cherry red paint smudge. Ray recognized the paint. It was what he used on Oscar's sled. He didn't remember wearing his coat when he painted the sled. He did remember wearing it when he was knocked to the ground and ate a face full of snow.

"I'm sorry, Mom," Ray said as he rushed to put on his coat. "That was from Santa's sleigh."

"From what?" his mother asked as he ran out of the door and into the yard. Ray couldn't answer. He was too busy laughing.

Ray made it only as far as the Mott's front lawn. Once outside, Ray saw Olive standing in her driveway talking to John Charles. Olive tapped her fingertips together in excitement as John Charles held his gloved hands out in front of him.

"Do you like 'em?" Olive asked, her voice high and full of joy as she lifted herself up on her tiptoes. "Ray's mother sewed them but I told her where to put the stitches."

"This might be the best birthday gift I ever received," John Charles said, still looking down at his hands and admiring the fit. "I can't thank you enough."

Olive rolled her shoulders side to side with pride. She looked over at Ray. Her eyes became big again. "Oh, Ray! Stay right there. Don't move a muscle. I want to show you my telescope! It's the best present in the whole wide world. Even better than gloves!"

"Not these gloves," John Charles said as wiggled what was left of his fingers. Olive turned on her heel and ran into her house, kicking a path in the new snow towards the door. Ray had never seen Olive this giddy with joy before. The door opened before she even reached it. A man stood inside, held it open for her and let her run past. He looked out and nodded a greeting to John Charles. Ray looked at John Charles, confused.

"Wait, did Oscar get her letter after all?"

"Nope," answered John Charles as he smiled and nodded to the man in the house.

Ray looked back at the man. He had seen him before. As John Charles rubbed his gloved hands together it hit him where he had seen this man. He was one of the men at the railroad tracks. One of the men by the flaming barrel trying to keep warm. The one John Charles shook hands with before leaving. That was him. That was Olive's father.

"Sometimes a letter to Santa is better in someone else's hands," John Charles said. Ray looked at him in amazement. He was right. No gift from Santa could match that.

The man still had the door open as Olive tore past him on the way outside. In her hands was the small box. She ran to the two, opened the box and produced a small telescope which grew in length when she pulled the eyepiece.

"We can see anything from our rooms now. Planes, deer, comets, anything."

Ray looked through the telescope at Olive's house. He saw her mother step outside with a camera and take a picture of the three. He passed it back to Olive, who took her turn at looking at the tops of the trees. She hooted in delight as she fiddled with the piece. John Charles turned to Ray.

"Merry Christmas, Raymond," he said as he gave Ray a pat on the back. "And thank you for all you've done this season. We at INR Industries will not forget your kindness."

"Happy birthday," Ray answered, as he lifted his feet and headed towards the road. Ray was already at the end of the Mott's driveway when he turned to yell back to Olive. He wanted to say that he would be by later to search for planes with her and Paley with their present and to wish her a Merry Christmas. As he looked at her showing her gift off to John Charles like a prize-winning heifer at a 4H fair, he knew he didn't need to wish her anything. Hers, for that day, had come true.

The shades were still drawn when Ray reached Oscar's front door. He gently knocked before letting himself inside. Other than the ticking and clicking of the clocks on the wall, the house was as still as church on a Tuesday.

"Oscar?" Ray called out quietly as he slowly walked up the hall. He dipped his head into every room he passed. The rooms were clean and quiet. When Ray reached the living room, he stopped and stood in the center. He spun in a circle but Oscar was not in any chair. Ray looked up at the hundred clock faces on the walls for an answer. The pendulums rocked back and forth as if shaking their heads, telling him they would not give up Oscar's whereabouts.

"Oscar?" Ray continued as he turned towards the hallway leading to the cellar. As he headed down the hall a smell reached up and grabbed him. Something smelled burned, like a faded campfire or a wood stove. Ray followed his nose towards the open bathroom door. When he walked in he saw the source of the smell.

Inside the bathtub was a pile of clothes covered in ash and soot. Ray knelt down and picked up a piece of the cloth. It was a sleeve, charred like it had been sitting on a grill. Upon closer inspection, Ray saw that the sleeve was not fried to a crisp. The sleeve was dirty but not damaged. Ray lifted the whole jacket and saw the once white fur collar stained black.

"Blitzen!" Oscar voice cried from another room. Ray dropped the jacket and jumped up. He ran to the unused back bedroom and saw

Oscar lying under the covers. His head tossing back and forth. He kept mumbling until he startled himself awake. "Blitzen!"

Ray stood in the doorway like before, holding onto the frame. "Oscar? Are you alright?" Ray said gently.

Oscar sat up in bed, panting from the nightmare. He wiped his brow and took a few deep breaths. "I'm fine. Storm didn't let me get much sleep last night."

Ray waited a moment for Oscar to catch his breath. "Mom wants to know if you'd like to come over for Christmas dinner. She's making a turkey and extra stuffing. And we're having fruit cup."

"Fruit cup? You don't say," he said with his back still to Ray. "What time?"

"Two o'clock."

"Sounds about the time I could go for some fruit cup. Tell her thank you. I'll be over."

"Alright," Ray said, leaning in the doorway. He looked over at the bed and saw that his gift to Oscar had already been put to good use. Oscar turned and saw Ray looking at the pillow.

"Thank you for my gift," he said as he ran his hand over the word "love" embroidered in red stitching. The pillow had a dent in the center and creased from holding a fretting head. Oscar then patted the pillow firmly. "It's a bit heavier than the last one."

"I know," Ray said shyly. "He'd be bigger now."

Oscar kept his hand on the word "love" as his lips pushed together in a sad, thankful smile. He sucked in a deep breath and nodded. He opened his mouth to say something but he quickly closed it and nodded his thanks. He coughed nervously and shook his head.

"Two o'clock? Is that what you said?" he said, shifting his tone.

"Yes," Ray answered. "And thank you for my clock. It's really great."

"You are most welcome," he said as he turned back around and fluffed his comforter. "If you ever feel like you're going nuts, just look at that clock and say to yourself that the only thing cuckoo in this room is this clock."

"Sure thing."

As Oscar prepared himself for another round of shut-eye, Ray began to leave until curiosity got the best of him. "Oscar, why were you yelling for Blitzen?"

"When?" Oscar said looking around the room confused. "When was I yelling that?"

"When you woke up. You were calling out for Blitzen."

Oscar ran his hands over his beard in thought. After a moment he answered. "Must have been from the storm last night. I still dream in German."

"I don't get it. What does that mean?" Ray asked. "Dream in German."

"It means that when I talk in my dreams, I speak German." Ray shook his head in confusion so Oscar continued. "Blitzen is German. It means lightning."

"Oh," Ray said as he turned and walked down the hall. "Oh."

"See you later! See you at two!" he heard Oscar call out.

Then a fog covered Ray's head.

"Lightning…" he uttered to himself as he shuffled down the hall. Then he heard himself utter another word. "Blitzen." The words repeated in a loop in his mind as if someone was saying one in the left ear and the other in the right. "Lightning…blitzen. Lightning… blitzen," Ray repeated as he marched out into the snow. With each step his mouth spilled out a word. "Lightning, blitzen, lightning, blitzen."

"Blitzen." Ray stopped and looked up. "Captain Lightning."

His feet began to lift and take off into a run. Something grabbed Ray's chest as he raced down the street. They were soldiers. And Paley knew. Paley knew all along.

"I'm not cuckoo," Ray heard himself say. "I'm not cuckoo," he said as he tore off towards the woods. He could feel and hear his heart beat in his eardrums. Tears began to burn and freeze on the corners of his eyes. He didn't know why but it suddenly felt like his father was behind him. Running and chasing him through the woods, whooping and crying out that he would catch him but never passing. Ray felt him running. Running for fun. Not out of fear or threat but because he was free. Because he was home. Because he was with his son. Because adventure awaits.

CHAPTER 33

Grigonis House – Pittstown, New Jersey, last year

"How's it running?" asked the man in the overalls.

Ava rolled the number 8 racer back and forth across the smooth linoleum floor. Each of the wheels touched the ground evenly and rotated in unison. The loud squeak vanished and was replaced by the sound of the soft clatter of finely working gears. She looked up at the man and smiled wide. Her grandfather would be thrilled. She zoomed the car in an arc around her to test the wheels under speed but stopped abruptly before hitting the thick white sneaker that suddenly appeared in front of it. Berta's deep accent brought everyone to attention.

"He's awake now," she ordered as she wiped her hands with a cloth and nodded knowingly to her mother. Her mother's arm, which held out a photograph, lowered to the table as she let out a long breath. She removed her glasses and gave Berta a tired smile of thanks as she pushed herself away from the scattered squares that sat in the box in front of her. The man sitting across from Ava looked anxiously at John Charles as if he suddenly didn't know how his legs worked. John

Charles kept his kind, calm expression as he stood up and waited for Ava's mother to lead them all out of the room.

The adults walked in single file through the first floor of the house on their way to Pop-pop's bedroom. Ava thought that every time her mother brought in one of her grandfather's visitors she sounded like her teacher before she brought the class to the snake exhibit at the zoo. Her voice low and measured telling them what they would see before they entered into the room, giving them a chance to leave if they thought they would get nightmares. The man who fixed the racer followed on John Charles's heels, taking two steps for every one of his long strides. Ava held the racer and darted past the grown-up legs to get into the room first. She didn't want to wait to show Pop-pop the fixed toy. It was his favorite. He would be thrilled. Ava had no time to listen to her mother fluff the pillows before she even entered the room.

"Pop-pop!" Ava shouted as she ran around his bed. Ava was getting used to the fact that Pop-pop's awake and asleep were not all that different. He hadn't moved or rolled over from this morning. He was still laying on his right side with his head stuck to his pillow, wearing a same pained expression. His eyes were watery and less open than his mouth. He let out a grunt of acknowledgment as she stood in front of him with the car. She held the racer up sideways so that he could look at it straight on. Her tiny hand touched his cheek. "Look, Pop-pop. It works. See? We can race again."

Her grandfather's hand shook as he lifted it off the bed. He then closed his eyes as if to take a breath. Afraid he would fall back asleep, Ava shook his shoulder.

"Pop-pop, get up," Ava whined. "I want to show you who fixed our car." Ava looked up at the men standing in the doorway. Berta squeezed past the group as she hustled over to the windows. She flung the curtain panels to the side to let sunlight tumble over the furniture and medical machines into the room. Ava looked at the man and waved him over. He slowly walked around the bed with hands still clenched inside his pockets. His face filled with concern as he studied her grandfather. John Charles followed but stayed back. He leaned against the dresser with his arms folded and smiled as if he just left the room for a moment and came back to continue the conversation.

"Ava," her mother said firmly. "Be gentle," she ordered as she sat across the bed behind her grandfather. Her mother petted his shoulder tenderly as she pushed her face close to his ear.

"Dad, there are some men here to see you. Some friends of yours," she said smiling. "We've been having a nice time reminiscing about some of your old friends."

Ava looked up at the man who fixed the racer. His eyes were firmly fixed on her grandfather when he did something Ava never saw men do when they came into the house. The man pulled the old tweed cap out of his back pocket and put it on his head. He then sat on the bed next to her grandfather and took his trembling hand into his own.

"Hey ya, Big Ray," said the man, his face lighting up as if someone just handed him a newborn.

Her grandfather's eyes drifted up to the man. They became larger and more alert than Ava had seen in weeks. Water pooled and rolled out of one of his eyes and into his pillowcase. Ava took a gauze pad from the nightstand and dabbed his temple.

"It's okay, Pop-pop. He made it work again."

Her grandfather's mouth began to open. Then with all the effort he could muster the loose pipes of his neck let him choke out three words. "He. Fixes. Everything."

None of them had heard her grandfather speak in weeks. Berta clapped her hands once in joy as she proudly looked down at her mother. "This is good. Yes?"

Ava kept patting down her grandfather's face before her mother shooed her away.

"Let's let them visit Pop-pop for a while, okay, sweetie?" she said as she waved her out of the room. Ava took the racer and begrudgingly walked past the men and out of the door to the racetrack of the living room rug.

Ava plopped down on the rug and turned the car around the groves of the braided rug, its wheels moving in perfect rotation, in sync and in grove with the width of the carpet. A smile crept on her face as the old metal midget racer with the chipped red 8 took a victory lap around the track, passing all crowds that sat at attention, each member of the crowd frozen in time in their frames. The racer passed by people she knew and some she did not. It passed Hal and Estelle on their wedding day. It passed Pop-pop and Aunt Olive during their high school graduation. It passed a worn ripped picture of her Pop-pop as a boy and his mom that he said used to be in his daddy's army helmet and it passed a picture of her grandfather's good friend in Germany who mailed it to him. It passed old pictures of Ava's mother in faded tones with thick white edging and new pictures of Ava in bright clear color. Finally, her car and attention stopped on one picture. It was a picture taken a long time ago of a little boy in a checkered coat and a man leaning over with one hand on the boy's shoulder and the other holding up a glove. A man with kind eyes and wearing only a white shirt during a snowy day. A man who seemed to be missing half his index finger and the top of his thumb. Ava picked up the frame and slowly walked back to her grandfather's room.

Ava stood in the doorway and looked up at John Charles, who was still leaning against the chest of drawers. He looked over at Ava peeking in and gave her a knowing wink as he touched the tip of his nose with his index finger. The other man remained on the bed next to Pop-pop. The two men seemed to be talking to her grandfather as if they were giving him directions to the corner store. Neither man looked like they would cry like every other person who came to visit. They were not embarrassed by the state of his body or the level of his illness. They were not bothered by the smell of him breaking down. Both of them were visiting an old friend. Nothing out of the ordinary. Nothing frightening. Nothing scary. Ava walked to her mother, who stood next to Berta and tugged at her shirt.

"Not now, sweetie," her mother said, her focus firmly on her father.

"But Mom, that man is here," she whispered, pointing to John Charles.

"What?"

"That man. He is here."

"What man?" her mother said, still concentrating on the conversation happening across the room.

"That man talking to Pop-pop. He's here," Ava said, poking her finger at the glass of the frame. "He's him."

Ava's mother began to reach for the frame until the loud chime of a cuckoo peeking out of the clock on the wall interrupted her thought.

"Must have had one left in it," she said. "We haven't pulled the weights on that clock in at least a year."

John Charles looked at the clock on the wall and then at her mother. "I guess that means it's time to go," said John Charles as he patted her grandfather's feet. "It was great seeing you, Raymond."

Ava watched the two men leave the room silently, say a few quiet words to her mother and then leave the house through the front door. Ava ran out of the room and looked out of the living room window at the men's departure. The man in the overalls turned back to get one last look at the house. He saw Ava in the window and waved. She stood amongst the billowing sheers and waved back as she watched the two turn and walk to the end of the long dirt driveway.

"Hum," said Berta as she roughly smoothed back the curtains in her grandfather's room. Ava saw both of Berta's profiles as she looked up and down the front yard. "I don't see them. They must have left out the back. They're gone."

"Really?" her mother said as she walked up to Berta. She too surveyed the land around the front of the house. "I bet you're right, Berta. They must have parked in the back. That's why we didn't see the car."

Ava cocked her head to the side. She turned and looked out of the window again. She saw a car. An old fashioned car. One that looked like the cars in her grandfather's pictures. It sat idling on at the end of the road. Next to the car stood a woman in a purple winter coat wearing a hat with a feather sticking off the top. She was busy smoothing the collar of a little girl with black hair, as if she were about to get her picture taken. Next to the little girl stood a boy as blond as snow hopping up and down in place with excitement. The men did not appear to talk as they marched side by side towards the group. The man in overalls walked with his hands still stuffed in his pockets. John Charles patted him on the back as if to let him know he did a good job. The sky grew pink as the sun began to cast splashes of color across the sky over the potato fields that extended on either side of the road. There was nothing out there but the group. Her grandfather's bedroom windows faced the same direction. Ava scratched her head. How could they not see these people standing in the middle of the road?

Then Ava heard her mother say a word she heard her say a thousand times. This time it sent a cold shiver into her ears and made her hold her breath.

"Dad?" Ava's mother called out. Her voice was quiet and high. "Dad?"

Berta's shuffling stopped. Ava looked across the room into her grandfather's doorway. Fear gripped her feet and planted them to the floor. Something happened. Something changed. Ava stared from across the room and watched Berta turn from the window and look in the direction of the bed, her face hard and jaw clenched. The beeps and clicking of the room seemed to quiet. All she could hear was her mother's voice softly call out. This time in tears.

"Dad?"

Ava watched Berta put her hand in her apron pocket and pull out a rosary. Her head dropped as she sat on the bed facing the direction of her grandfather. She put her hand up on her mother's back as she kissed the small cross on the line of beads.

"Dad?" a teary voice pleaded. "Dad?"

Ava's chest began to hurt. She was too scared to go to her mother but her mother needed someone. Someone who was not there. She wanted her mommy but she did not want to see Pop-pop on the bed not breathing. Ava felt her lower lip began to tremble as she pried her maryjane off of the floor. Then she heard the screen door slam shut.

"Dad!"

The word did not come from her mom. It came from a boy. Ava whirled around and whipped the sheers out of her way.

"Dad!" the boy cried out as he took off running from the house. Although Ava could only see the back of his head he appeared to be only a few years older than her. His Buster Brown shoes kicked up dust as his feet pounded the dirt driveway. He waved his arms in the air as he ran, making sure they wouldn't leave without him.

"Dad!"

Then the man in the cap stopped walking and turned around. His face burst in joy as he laughed and cuffed his hands to let out a hearty clap. His smile was so bright it even managed to lighten the gloom that had settled over her house. And with that smile, the man gave one big clap before he opened his arms. The boy cut across the end of the long driveway and up the road towards him, yelling and waving to the group as he ran.

The woman by the car stood with a large smile as she held the two excited children close to her. They all seemed to want to run to the boy, to greet him, but they appeared happy to wait their turn. It was clear whose arms the boy was running towards. It was the man whose arms stretched as wide as a net. The man who clapped like he was packing a snowball. The man who fixed everything.

The End

ACKNOWLEDGMENTS

With a full heart, I would like to thank the towns (and especially the public libraries) of Southold, New York, and Clinton, New Jersey, for being the best places in the world to live and grow. I would also like to thank my family, my father, and my friends, especially Marcia Hansen, who had to listen to me tell and retell this story for years in order to get it right. Thank you to Gretchen Young, Anthony Ziccardi, and Susan Raihofer for believing in me and my book. And most importantly, thank you to my writing group—Patty Smeltzer, Ingrid Pierson Massey, Jennifer Exley, and Kala Hill—for keeping me honest and writing Christmas stories in the blazing summer heat.

I heard it said that authors write the books they need. This was the case with my book. Many beloved members of my family passed too soon. Five in particular are Evan, Tim, John, Tom, and my mother, Marion. I hope that anyone who has a difficult time finding magic during the holidays finds some small comfort in this tale and in the hope that maybe, just maybe, we will get it all back.